Home *and* Away

Home and Away

Candice
Montgomery

PAGE STREET
PUBLISHING CO.

PAGE STREET
PUBLISHING CO.

Copyright © 2018 Candice Montgomery

First published in 2018 by
Page Street Publishing Co.
27 Congress Street, Suite 105
Salem, MA 01970
www.pagestreetpublishing.com

Distributed by Macmillan, sales in Canada by The Canadian Manda Group.

22   21   20   19   18   1   2   3   4   5

ISBN-13: 978-1-62414-595-7
ISBN-10: 1-62414-595-7

Library of Congress Control Number: 2017963798

Cover and book design by Laura Gallant for Page Street Publishing Co.
Cover illustration by Tashana McPherson
Author photo by McKaylyn Barth Photography

Printed and bound in the United States

For Natalie Layla who taught me what
it means to really, truly #staynorth.
Miss you, baby.

Chapter One

GAME 1 – WESTVIEW VS. SANTA MONICA VIKINGS

I take a major hit.

My midsection is screaming.

I forced the fumble, the ball flying out of the receiver's arms and landing sadly on the turf like a bird with a bad wing, but I failed to recover because Santa Monica's O-linemen are built like bison on steroids. They fall on the ball—and me— and I wonder if someone should just bury me here, now.

For two seconds, while I'm on the ground catching my breath, the static chatter of the crowd in the stands fades out. Immediately it comes back, acute. Sharp. Right along with a red blob. A red jersey. That is a body inside padding, all underneath a Westview jersey.

Josiah, my quarterback, holds his hand out to me. "Get up here, girl, we got a ball game to finish."

I shake off the rest of my haze, put my hand in his, and let him haul me up. The crowd cheers with a relieved sort of loudness when I make it to a full stand, and Coach signals Siah and me over.

"That hit was nasty, Tasia. You good?"

I nod.

"You good?" he says again. He likes us to vocalize when we take hits to the head. Answers to these questions don't have to make sense and they don't even have to not be bullshit. They just have to be loud enough to slow-stroke Coach's moral fiber.

"Yeah, Coach. I'm good," I say through my mouth guard.

I spy my mamma shoving her way up to Coach's side.

"Baby, are you—"

Glancing around fast and then looking straight back at Mamma, I nod at her. *I'm good, I'm fine. I'm okay.*

Even the water boy is laughing at me. It's the kind of situation I try to avoid, lest they think I'm just some little girl who can't take a hit. I can.

My shoulder is screaming and I'm a little panicked about going back out there after that. It happens every time I take a hit: The anxiety sets in. Then the whispered *What if it happens again? Worse.* I almost always swallow it down, but here, now . . . Mamma grabs me by the wrist before I hit the field again, pulling my lighter-skinned hand between both of her darker ones. She rubs them fast, the friction warming my fingers. Under her breath she says, "Jesus. Jesus, Jesus, Jesus." It's a chant, nearly a song.

We're not very religious. Not at all, actually. But this is a prayer. The same one I've gotten from her for every skinned knee and every hangnail.

Finally, she squeezes my hand and releases it. "You're okay. Yes?"

It's not even really a question. She is *telling me* that I am okay. The way I need her to. The way I *always* need her to.

I nod.

As I turn and run back out to the huddle on the field, Josiah high-fives me and then makes his way back to the sidelines.

"You didn't chip your nail polish or dislodge your tampon, did you, Taze?" That gift of a child is Los. Carlos, but Los. Number forty-four. He plays cornerback, like me. Or he tries to, anyway. Don't get me wrong—he's great at it, so I kind of respect him, but he's not so good at being a decent human, so the default for me is typically a little hate. Plus, he's no me, and there are rules about getting too friendly with your competition.

"Fuck off," I grumble. See? Hate.

I chuck my head at Los as the other team wraps up their huddle with a grunted, baritone-heavy "Break!"

"Pine is yours, Carlos," I say through my mouth guard, signaling that he should take a seat in his rightful place on the bench.

He shakes his head—and I know, I fricking *know*, he's about to argue with me—but then Coach whistles and we all look over.

"Tasia's in! Bring it in, Forty-Four."

Los gives me the finger before heading off to our sideline, and I fight a million internal battles with myself about retaliating. That'd only get me kicked off the field.

The other team's QB, an Asian kid, calls hike and then, in

seconds, the play is in motion. I sit low behind my linebacker, Israel, and then as soon as I see the play lining up, things slow down. I feel it. I know exactly where that ball's heading, so I break away and truck down the field and parallel myself right up on their wide receiver, who's setting himself up to catch his quarterback's long pass.

And I intercept it, using my quads to get high in the air. Their wide receiver doesn't like it, grabbing me clean out of the air in hopes that I'll miss the catch.

He's mistaken.

I won't. I haven't.

And when he full-on body slams me right to the turf in the end zone, I experience both a moment of elation and a second of *Christ on a pink bike, this will bruise tomorrow.*

I don't stay planked for long though, because the clock has run down, and then, beautifully, that's game.

I curtsy and mime-fluff my hair in the end zone for a couple seconds, skipping right alongside the other team's WR who tried to take me out, and then Josiah and Israel are there, grabbing me by the facemask, bashing their helmets against mine, giving me a few platonic swats on the ass.

Josiah's grinning like a fool as the rest of the team floods us on the field. "Atta-baby, Tasia! Way to be, Taze. Atta-girl!" We high-five as we line up off to the side of the field to greet the other team and congratulate them on a well-played game.

As we make our way down the single-file line, I take off my helmet and prepare myself for the other team's comments and quips.

"You let a *girl* play in this game?"

"That shouldn't be legal."

"She's hot—for a Black girl."

"I can't hit girls, but I can tackle this one? That's messed up."

"Dyke."

"I'd do her."

I look that particular spitwad right in the eye and say, "You'd try it, and I'd chop your dick off. Try me." And after a moment I smile and say, "But hey, good game."

Taze Quirk doesn't take anybody's shit. Not on my field.

When I finally find my mamma in the crowd, she pulls me in for the tightest hug. My mamma is the best hugger. Her hugs are solidifying and re-focusing.

"That's my baby! That's right. You played tough. How you feeling now, from that last hit?"

I shrug. "Little sore. I'm okay."

"You'll take an Epsom salt bath when we get home."

I pull away a little. "Okay, but . . . the guys and I sort of had plans? To go to Duke Ellie's to celebrate."

Her hands feel around my back, meeting only padding. "How's the new sports bra? Think we picked a good one this time? These are supposed to have better hold."

"Oh, God." I bat her hands away, twist my torso so she can't even think about trying to get her hands up underneath.

"Baby, don't get shy now. We need to be sure we're not risking any damage to your—"

She's not the kind of woman who uses some weirdo stand-in word for private parts, like *hoo-hoos* or *mosquito bites.*

My mamma's a professional. *Breasts.* That's more her style.

"Mom. They're fine. It's fine. But I really gotta get changed or the guys—they'll leave without me."

Mamma has this way about her chastisement. It's nonverbal. Involves only a lifted eyebrow and maybe pursed lips. "Tasia Lynn."

"I'll be home way before curfew."

She hesitates, but then says, "Not too late—"

"Yes, ma'am. No later than, like, eleven."

Mamma raises one of her perfect, thick eyebrows. She knows as well as I do, I'm not coming home anywhere near eleven p.m. Not with the win we just pulled off still singing in my veins.

"Thirty," I say. "I meant to say *eleven-thirty*. Probably." Maybe.

"Mm," she says, hugging me again. "Daddy wanted to be here. He got stuck at the office."

Solomon Quirk. Forever choosing work over his family. Or rather, me. It's really just me he's never been able to choose. Our relationship has always been just a little bit different. I nod at Mamma, and you know what? I don't even roll my eyes that hard. "I know. Where's Tristan?"

"Home." Mamma smiles gently. "He has that test. He's panicking."

What's the term for when your brother is a lamewad? "So he's studying."

"What you should be doi—"

"I did!" I didn't, actually. So I amend it: "I will. Tomorrow and all weekend, I'm staying in." I cross my fingers, kiss them, and spit on the ground.

Mamma cringes then gives this look as if there's Botox gone wrong in the bottom of her face.

"I'll text you where I am; the boys are waiting." I gesture over my shoulder.

As I start to jog toward the girls' locker room, where I'll be changing my pads out for a hoodie, Mamma calls, "I love you."

I glance back and grin hard, but don't say it back. I wave instead. Little moments like that, they creep up on you the way a spidering crack spreads. Later, you might wonder what else you were thinking about that was so important. So vital that you couldn't spare two seconds to call three words, eight letters, back.

I should have said them back.

Chapter Two

Stacy "Slim" Lim is my best friend in the entire world, which is the weirdest phenomenon, considering we aren't much alike. We've got similar features, big curly heads of hair falling down our backs—hers chocolatey, mine the queerest sort of bronze blond—full lips that neither of us know what to do with during Los Angeles's wannabe winters, skin somewhere between beige and brown, a tawny terra-cotta mix, hers just a shade or two lighter than my pale gold. We've been mistaken for twins on more than one occasion. More often than Trist and I have been asked whether or not we're siblings.

Tristan and I look nothing alike.

The main difference between Slim and me sits in the eyes. Mine are almond shaped, Slim's are sharper—her dad's Korean genetics.

As I run into the locker room amid all the changing cheerleaders, I find Slim shimmying out of her cheer skirt.

"How was that last hit?" she says.

"Grimy. Felt good after I got up, though."

She grunts. "Pain slut."

I kick off my cleats. "Come to Duke Ellie's," I say. Duke Ellie's is an all-night diner just north over the hill.

She hesitates, shirt hovering over her head. "Will Josiah be there?"

Will Josiah be there? Of course he frigging will. Josiah is QB1. She knows this. She also knows she's crazy about him and that he's very, very taken.

"Please come?" The rules of best friendship state, loosely, if you beg they must concede. "Slim."

She looks up at me as she wiggle-squirms into her jeans. I do the same, having pulled off my football pants, the nylon-spandex combo sticking to me where I'm still sweaty at the back of my thighs.

Neither of us can speak for at least seven seconds while we try to tuck our hips, suck it in, and do up the buttons.

"I won't leave your side," I say.

"You won't ditch me when all the boys start talking about football?"

"No. In fact, I'll go out of my way to change the subject."

She laughs, and that feels really good to me. "To what?"

"To . . ." Hell if I know, but it ceases to matter when, speak of the devil, Josiah's girlfriend, Kat, trots over.

"You guys comin' to Duke's? I just convinced my dad to let me go, even after he caught me and Josiah in my room last week." She laughs and it's dang cute. But don't tell Slim I think so.

Kat moved here from the Midwest. Toledo, to be exact. Her *a*'s stretch fat and flat and damn near ugly. This being-from-out-of-state thing, plus Kat's huge tits, make her infinitely cooler than I'll ever be. The accent loses her some Cool Points, but she's still pretty cool nonetheless.

But never, ever cooler than Slim—and best-friend law also dictates that I remind Slim of this, often.

Slim slaps on a good smile, a prettier-than-you-without-even-trying smile, and says, "We'll be there. You driving, Taze? Or am I?"

I'll never get used to the way Slim takes curves in her tiny Miata, so I tell her we can take my Jeep and hope to Christ she doesn't fight me on this, because I know my driving isn't her dig either.

As soon as we walk into Duke Ellie's, the table filled, like, twenty deep, a group of our friends lets off a round of cheers. Josiah stands and pulls up chairs for Slim and me. We don't plan it, but she definitely ends up in the seat next to him, and I in the seat next to her. So the seat order goes: Kat, Josiah, Slim, then me. But Josiah is a good boyfriend, and so he effectively angles his body so that the majority of his attention is focused on his girlfriend. I can't decide if Slim likes this trait or loathes it. Probably equal parts of both, which is pathetic and heartbreaking all in one fell swoop.

Slim and I share a plate of chocolate chip pancakes. We

double down on bacon and whipped cream, and I make multiple comments about having to run it all off later, as though I'm the only athlete at the table.

But despite all that, we have fun. We talk to the boys and, yes, we flirt with them. Only, I don't flirt with my teammates because that's like flirting with your pain-in-the-ass brother whose idea of fun is science puns.

Slim and I take selfies together and post them all over social media. Ones where I stare at the camera and Slim closes her eyes and kisses my cheek. Ones where Slim and I stare into each other's eyes and grin hard, showcasing our profiles. We both agree that this is the best pose, and I post mine to Instagram, with a filter that I don't think changes much about the photo but that I absolutely cannot post without, and caption it, "PROFILE GAME IMMACULATE w/ @SlimJimSandwich." Slim does the same: "My best friend > your best friend w/ @dontTazemebro."

After everyone's polished their plates and we've split the bill, I can tell Slim is a little bummed at being literally shoulder-to-shoulder with Josiah all night but having only been able to say two words to him ("Hi, Josiah"), and so I basically invite myself over to her house to help cheer her up and to pick all the marshmallows out of the Lucky Charms I know she has in her pantry. But before I can drop her off at her car back at school, I get a text from my dork brother Tristan.

come home STAT, something going on, mamma's about to call you

That worries me. Urgency isn't Tristan's standard mode of

operation. It's not Mamma's or Daddy's either. My family is *that family*—we do things at our own pace. People march to our beat, not the other way around.

And aside from that, I've always worried about my family a little. I worry about their safety. It's the way I was raised. I worry about how I sometimes see Mamma get weirdly manic when she's under a lot of work stress. I worry when I see Daddy get frustrated when he's trying to put something together—maybe some furniture, recently the ceiling fan in my room.

My parents worry about us, too. Mamma stays awake on the couch in the living room whenever Tristan or I are out late. I always know Daddy has checked on me at night when I fall asleep with my lights on and I wake up tucked in, lights off.

A minute later, I see my phone flash with *MAAAA* plus her photo. It's a great picture of her. I don't know why I think of this before I pick up the call. The picture is from maybe a month ago. Mamma at some CEO gala charity fundraiser dinner event her company put on to honor her. Her smile is big and bright, her skin is mahogany smooth, and her lifelong dreadlocks are in some complicated updo that probably took forever or cost hella cash money or both.

I swipe my thumb across the screen.

"Hello?" My stomach bottoms out before she ever says a word.

Chapter Three

"Hey, baby," Mamma says. "On your way home?"

I gesture a thumb over my shoulder, as if she can see me. "Um, I was gonna go to Slim's."

"Okay."

I pause. She sounds unsteady. It makes me feel unsteady. "Is everything all right?"

"Yeah, baby. Fine, fine. Everything's . . . everything is going to be just fine." She says it too loudly. "Baby, I've, um. I've got my hands full just now. You have fun at Josiah's."

She ends the call and all I can do is pull the warm phone away from my face and stare as it reverts back to my home screen a second before going dim again.

Something like butterflies sits in my stomach. Butterflies but worse. Butterflies on meth or something.

I fixate on two things before turning back to Slim.

1. She said to have fun at *Josiah's*. I know it's not a big deal. Slim's mom used to mix up our entire friend group for years,

and none of us look anything like each other. But Mamma, she's different. She's involved. If I say I'm headed to Slim's, she knows all the details before I do.

I wonder idly if she really did have a hundred things on her mind. Enough things she just couldn't take on one more—even if it is my whereabouts.

2. She said everything is *going to be* just fine. As in—it's not right now, but it will be. She sounded desperate. Like an addict telling himself he could totally have "just one."

It felt like a lie.

Slim steps closer to me, grabs my wrist. "Hey. Everything cool?"

I nod slowly even though it's a blatant lie. I don't know why I lie. "She wants me home right now. She needs to talk to me about something or tell me something, or, I don't know. But I think I really have to go."

Slim squeezes my wrist where she's got it gripped. It grounds me a little bit. It's why she's my best friend. She always knows the right move to make. "Did you do something? Think she knows we ditched Rawlerson's class again?"

I shake my head. "No, I just. I have to go."

"Yeah, it's fine. I can catch a ride with someone else," Slim says. "Go, go."

My stomach fills with this *hurry up* feeling, urgency sitting in the tops of my thighs and right up under the bridge of my nose. I both want to get home and don't. It's weird and uncomfortable in the same way as clothes that fit wrong.

Slim says some other stuff about texting her after I

know what I did, and I think I agree to do that, but I'm so preoccupied with having what I'm pretty sure is an anxiety attack that I can't be certain.

I don't even know how I get home. But I'm heading up the steps of this too-big-for-our-family-of-four McMansion and my Jeep is cooling down in our circular driveway.

Once I'm inside, I don't hear any voices. It's not totally abnormal, but typically at least Tammy, our live-in, is singing in the kitchen where she always just *has to* fold the laundry.

I drop my keys in the crystal dish on the table like I have every other night this week. That's normal.

I realize I forgot my gym bag and my football pads in my car. That's not.

I don't know where my phone is. Nor is that.

Once, I read in *Teen Vogue* that in the event of an anxiety attack you should play a game with yourself called "Threes." You find, focus on, and name three things you can feel, taste, smell, see, or hear.

I do that now as I walk upstairs.

And honestly, it helps.

Smell. The cinnamon Glade plug-ins that Tammy loves. The remnants of detergent in my shirt that my sweat didn't do away with. Mamma's too-heavy perfume in the air, indicating she's recently been down this hallway.

Hear. The ticking of the foyer's grandfather clock. The neighbor's dog barking at nothing, as usual. The washing machine running its fast cycle.

It helps so much that I'm nearly breathing right by the time

I make it up all the stairs and walk on sure feet into Mamma's room, where I can hear someone wrestling with papers.

Taste. The calm. The clarity. The feeling that I am probably overreacting.

No one's inside the room as I walk in. The bed's made and Mamma's purse is on top of it along with her keys and some brown postal wrapping paper.

It's got our address on it in big blocky letters.

It's got my name on it too; only, whoever's written that portion took their time. Curved the "T" into its "A" and "S-I-A" with care.

It's the sound of someone sniffing that draws me into Mamma's walk-in closet.

I pause just inside the doorway as she rifles through a dingy shoebox.

It's the hard consonant that falls out of her mouth as she swears that shocks me into movement.

"Are you okay, Mamma?"

Everything—and I mean *everything*—falls in that moment. Mamma, the high shelf she's reaching up to, the box she's trying to shove onto it.

We both yell, "Oh, God!" But it's Mamma that springs into action.

"Tasia!"

I can't move.

"You're home."

The box. The papers have spilled everywhere.

Mamma's talking almost as fast as her hands are reaching

for the box's spilled contents. "I thought you were going . . . somewhere."

Photos, clippings from the local newspaper with my name on them, a copy of my birth certificate?

"To Josiah's or Slim's or . . . where? Where did you say?"

I lean down and grab the crumpled photo of me as a kid out of her hands.

I can tell it was taken from afar and then zoomed in on. The most immediate details are clearest, and me? I am the hazy outline of a child that wants to blur into the background.

I look happy, though. That much is clear. Unaware. Carefree. Gap-toothed—probably because I'd had, like, three of my bottom teeth extracted—and mid-run at the local playground. I was six, maybe seven years old?

"Angel," Mamma says.

I'm breathing heavy and I know they say you should definitely not do that when you're in the middle of an anxiety attack, but, like, *who can help it?* Who ever has control over this type of thing? No one, I bet!

"What is all this?"

There's this super-old Polaroid of a smiling Mamma clutched up tight to some white guy, very nearly pressed into a kiss. They're smiling into each other. They're happy. They're everything I'm not right now.

"Let's go downstairs, angel."

My mind works double time, a computer on the verge of overheating, as it puts things together.

"This was in that brown paper?"

"Tasia, hold on, honey."

"Did someone send this stuff? Poppa and Gram, or . . . ?"

Mamma stands. There's another paper in her hand. It's the photocopy of my birth certificate.

It takes me the space of two seconds to note there's no one listed on the line designated *Paternal.*

I take it from her and hold it up close to my face as if that'll help me make sense of this. It's like when you turn down the music on the car radio when you're lost and trying to follow your map's driving directions.

My eyes glance up from the paper and find hers.

"What is this?" I step backwards, right onto a newspaper clipping about the time Slim and I tied for thirteenth place in the city's annual 5K NH Lymphoma run. We were thirteen at the time. They thought it was comedic.

"Tasia—"

"Who sent this stuff, Mom!"

She hugs me tight. So tight I feel like she's trying to break me instead of hold me together. I wonder how I might solder steel into my spine. It's working, this break-you-apart hug. Of course it's working. It's Mamma. And I am a quickly deteriorating cliff's edge.

I hear Mamma saying something. It's like she's a radio that is losing its signal. She fades in and fades back.

"Angel," she says. "I don't know how to tell you . . ."

Fades in and fades back.

"Didn't know how to tell you . . ."

Fades in. Fades back.

"I'm so sorry—what I'm trying to say is . . ."

Fades in.

"You had a right to know who you are. You *have* a right to know . . . ."

Finally, I push her away from me. She's crying.

"Tell me what this is."

She nods. She's caught. Slowly, she bends down to pick up what I originally thought was a shoebox. It is, instead, a memento box. There are flowers, patterns of plants and herbs, covering its top. "I think . . ." she begins. "No." She's choked up again, and I just need her to come out with it. Patience has never been my strong suit.

"Mamma!"

"I'm sorry! I'm so sorry I lied. To you."

The fading is back. I catch more bits and pieces. But it's enough.

" . . . about who your father is."

"Daddy wasn't there . . ."

" . . . love you so much and—"

"He never knew . . ."

" . . . been watching you."

My legs, already Jell-O from the game, give out beneath me.

I shake my head. But something in me is just trying to rearrange all the puzzle pieces it already has. Has probably always had. The puzzle piece that says my skin is lighter than Mamma's and Trist's and Daddy's. That says I don't share quite as many features with them as I should.

I chalked up my coloring and my hair to Mamma's Creole background. There's a huge discourse within the Black community about the varying skin tones within immediate family. It's not uncommon to have a family of six where both parents have tawny skin and two out of the four kids are an umber sort of brown. It's not a happy discourse. It's a result of slavery. It's the reason light-skinned girls with "good hair" get asked what we're mixed with. And because it's common to see this skintone diversity within Black families, I never had any reason to question why I look so much lighter than both Mamma and Daddy. And Mamma and Daddy—they just let me assume it, let me hold it as gospel.

Once when I was nine, I swallowed an ice cube out of a cup of soda my Auntie Sandra gave me. Tristan and I were never allowed to have soda, but Auntie Sandra had given us one to share, so I guzzled it as fast as I could. Until that ice cube. Swallowing it hurt. I panicked in the few seconds it took to half melt and then slide down my throat fully, thinking it would get lodged there or freeze my insides. I didn't know how to call for help. What could anyone else do, except tell me to calm down and that it would melt *eventually*? It would pass. The skin above my upper-lip began to sweat, my underarms started to prickle, and I was a few seconds away from tears when Tristan grabbed my hand and said, "Use the straw next time. It'll melt but it kinda hurts, huh?"

All I could do was nod and swallow repeatedly like a gasping fish out of water. Trist kissed my cheek, took the cup of soda from my hand, and threw it into the nearest garbage can. I think he knew I was done with soda after that.

Fuck *a straw*. All I could think was *good riddance*. I never drank soda again. Neither with nor without ice cubes.

And that's always been my relationship with Tristan. He's been my protector in so many ways, despite being the younger of the two of us by two years.

That ice-cube-in-the-throat thing kind of reminds me of this feeling.

"But Tristan . . . ?"

Through tears and a sob, Mamma whispers, "Your half brother."

"Did he send that to me? My . . . this other man? Did he send that box to me?"

She's quiet a moment before she says, "I don't know."

I turn, running back into the room where the brown postal paper with my name and address on it lies.

"There's no return address," she says from behind me. "I checked."

I turn to her. Crumple the paper. Throw it at her.

And I run. I run as fast as my legs will take me down the hall, down the stairs, through the foyer, to the crystal dish with my keys in it and out the door.

In the distance, I think I hear Mamma alternating her sobs with her shouts of my name.

As I drive away, I think I maybe even hear her scream, "I'm sorry!"

Chapter Four

I don't end up driving far before Mamma texts me and my home training kicks in.

PLS LET ME KNOW WHERE YOU'RE GOING.

slim's is all I send in reply.

WHEN WILL YOU BE HOME

I don't answer that one because I really don't know. I can't think straight.

And then I'm pulling up at Slim's place. It's as much of a monstrosity as my house. Honestly, it could be an exact replica. No one in this city has any originality, so naturally, all the McMansions look the same and sell the same, and make you feel the same—dead and rich and unoriginal—and that's just that.

Slim's housekeeper, formerly known as her nanny, lets me in. Gracie speaks like four languages—that I know of—and whichever she greets you with at the door is typically an indicator of her mood. She's been chasing us since we were in diapers and spends a good amount of time chasing us around these days too.

"You've eaten?" Gracie says.

I nod.

She *tsks* and pinches the skin at my ribs. "Go upstairs. I'll bring you something in a minute."

Gracie says this every time she sees me. "Go upstairs. I'll feed you in a minute." I don't understand how she can look at me now and think I'd want food. As if food is the great fixer of all things.

Well, it's not. People go through breakups and girls eat their body weight in Ben & Jerry's. Know what it does for them? It increases their pant sizes and reduces the amount of room they have in their freezer.

When I let myself into Slim's bedroom, she's on her balcony taking selfies with the starless blue-black sky behind her.

"Oh, hey!" she says, and then pulls me into a picture with her that catches us from the lips down, skyline behind us. She captions it #north and then posts it to Snapchat even though my grimace just screams *she wasn't ready*. "Did you get in trouble?"

"North?" I ask her.

"Yeah, like *north of Sunset*. It could be, like, A Thing you and me do. Hashtag-north-vibes. Hashtag-north-bitch." I get it. Because we grew up and live north of Sunset Boulevard.

I nod. "And when we go over the hill—hashtag-south-as-fuck."

"Yes! And our parents could be, like, the hashtag-OG-norths."

I start to laugh thinking about how Mamma would take that sort of thing and run with it. She doesn't use social media aside from Facebook, but she'd make it work there, too.

It strikes me hard and hot to remember why I'm even here, and I run into Slim's bathroom and throw up until my body heaves repeatedly off the floor, empty.

"Whoa. What in the heck was that about?" Slim says from the doorway. "What a waste of pancakes." She pulls a tiny bottle of water from the mini-fridge in her bedroom and then moves behind me, quickly undoes my braids, and ties my 3C mess back with one of her thick scrunchies.

I swig some water, spit it into the sink, and swish her cinnamon toothpaste around my mouth.

I meet her eyes in the mirror. "I think my dad's white."

Slim doesn't laugh or gasp or anything like that. She just says, "Oh, yeah?" Like it's a joke. Like I make jokes about this type of thing all the time. I don't.

"Slim."

She pulls her bundles of curls into a messy topknot, assesses herself in the mirror.

"*Slim*," I say again as she turns up the song on the radio. Some rap song where the guy repeats *pipe it up* over and over again. I think the song is about anal sex.

"Stacy, Jesus Christ, will you listen to me? I'm having a meltdown because my parents are liars and I think my biological father is blond Christian Bale and I lost half a brother and my only living grandparents aren't my actual grandparents." I choke on the breath I'm trying to pull in. "Oh my God."

No, no, please don't hyperventilate again because hyperventilating sucks and is really uncomfortable. Poppa and Gram aren't my actual grandparents. Do I even have grandparents? Mamma's parents died when she was thirteen. Her sisters raised her. Daddy's parents are all I have. Had.

Had?

And then I'm in Slim's arms and I think it's supposed to be comforting, but really, it's just getting harder to breathe. I hold completely still, like that time my front tooth came loose after Trist hit me in the face with Mamma's car door. The thing was going to come out either way, but I was convinced staying absolutely still would protect me from having it fall out prematurely.

Gracie comes in quiet like a breeze, delivers not food but Kleenex. It's like they want me to be crying, but tears aren't really my dig. At least, they weren't before now.

"If she's light-headed, she needs to put her head between her knees," Gracie says.

"I thought that was for vertigo?"

"That's for vom," I say. And they both nod like I'm an authority on vomiting or vertigo or having your head between your knees.

But the vomiting's over, so I'm not really sure what's supposed to help me now. I pull away from Slim after the feeling of suffocation starts to bleed its way across my face and cloud my vision.

"There was a box."

Slim picks lint off my shirt. "What?"

"There was this box of, like, stuff. Pictures of me as a kid and a copy of my birth certificate and clippings of that time Mamma and I got featured in the paper for the tree planting stuff and, like, some articles from the local paper about my football awards—"

"Maybe it was old stuff your mom just had?"

"No," I say sharply. "No. She was trying to *hide* it from me. Like, up at the top of her closet. I caught her trying to hide it. And there was this old pic of my mom, like, all hugged up on some white dude from back in the day."

I feel like I should be stumbling over these words but I don't. They come out smooth and raspy the same as all my other words. And Slim, bless her heart, she doesn't bat an eyelash.

"You ever met him before?"

"Who, white dude? No."

"So where'd this box come from then?"

"I don't know! That's the problem. Like, maybe he sent it? Or maybe he didn't . . ." I pause for one long beat. "Slim, do you think . . . do you think maybe he doesn't know?"

"About you?"

"Yeah."

"But then who the hell sent you that lurker box?"

Exactly what I'd like to know. I mean, Mamma clearly wasn't worried about whoever sent this thing. So it doesn't necessarily make me feel unsafe.

I can still trust her at least that much.

"So white Christian Bale, huh?" Slim says.

I nod. "White Christian Bale."

Slim sits on her floor and pushes into one of her bendy-girl cheer stretches. "What're you thinking?"

I shake my head. "I can't believe she'd *lie* about something like this."

"Does your dad know? Solomon, I mean."

Oh, Jesus, the differentiation kills me a little bit. "I think so? I ran out of there before I got any real answers and I kinda, like, tuned out a lot of what she was saying."

"Tuned out?"

"Yeah, I just . . . snapped a little. I wasn't tracking."

She laughs. "Okay, Tyler Durden, what does that even mean?"

"Remember that time we shared that brownie from the Venice beach boardwalk?"

"Yeah." And then understanding dawns. "Ohh . . . okay, yeah. If your focus was anything like that time, I totally get it."

She would. That was the time Slim admitted the ghost dog, Zero, from *The Nightmare Before Christmas* freaked her out as we sat watching the clock on my car's dashboard move even though it felt like nothing else in the world was. All we'd wanted were some Jack-in-the-Crack curly fries.

It was the longest anyone had ever sat in a 24-hour drive-thru, I'd wager. My hearing went out twice, I'm pretty sure, and it felt like my tongue had gotten so cottony and swollen, it flooded my mouth.

Naturally, ordering "three large curly fries and DON'T FORGET THE RANCH!" was basically impossible.

Now, I shrug. "Might've been worse."

"Eckh," she says.

"Yeah."

"What are you gonna do?"

I laugh and fall back on the floor next to Slim in her spread-eagled position. "I have no fricking clue."

"Well . . . " I know it's coming. Something I'm probably not going to want to hear from her just now. "You *could* just do nothing."

I give her a look. A better "exasperated side-eye" than the emoji version could ever pull.

I hate that she's acting as if this only rates about as high as a broken fingernail on the scale of Life's Biggest Problems.

Why isn't she more upset about this?

It's unreasonable. I know, I know, I know it is. But I need her to feel exactly what I'm feeling. I need *someone* to feel that with me right now. The anger and the hurt and the confusion and the helplessness. I can't keep feeling all of it alone like this.

She picks the polish off one of her nails. "So. What do we want to do then, huh?"

I love that she says "we," like this involves her.

"I just want answers." I can't tell her what I really need: that I need her to be as angry as I am. Slim's not built for anger anyway, so I don't even know why I'm expecting that from her.

I just feel really, incredibly, ridiculously alone. And that's new and strange for Slim and me—the disconnect. An emotional wound that can't quite be shared.

She shakes her head, stands, pulls her pants off, and climbs under her covers. I do the same and climb in on the other side of her bed. I guess it's a given that I'm staying over. I power my phone down at the same time as she turns the light off in her room.

"You could've probably had a few of those answers had you not run out of there like some chick running from the Maury Povich cameras."

What does that even mean? "Yeah, well. I'll get them in the morning."

Slim yawns. "Yeah."

I yawn. "Think Tristan knows?"

"Nah. He'd have told you."

True. I turn my phone back on and text him.

up?

waiting for you to come home

I'm not. I'm at slims

k. you ok?

no. I wonder for a second if he knows.

Then he texts, *want me to come there?* And I know instantly that he does.

no. Then, *did you know all along?*

I don't even know what's going on. mamma's been crying for like an hour and Dad's had them shut in his office for about as long. no one's telling me anything.

I promise I'll tell you everything in the am. sorry. I know that sucks. love you.

you too.

see you in the am

yeah

Chapter Five

Purpose comes in the morning. I wake up imbued with it. Like someone's injected it, golden and dancing, underneath my skin.

I wriggle out from under Slim, aka the world's wildest, most cuddly sleeper, and pull my jeans back on. Slim mumbles that she loves me and I try to tiptoe past her father, who is already awake and seated at the breakfast table, as I leave. Instead, Mr. Lim asks me if I want coffee, if I need breakfast, if I'm okay.

No, thank you, long sigh.

Yes, probably, but I'm okay, long sigh.

I don't know, I don't know, I don't know, long sigh.

I am made up entirely of long sighs, until I get home and sneak my way into the pool house, where Tristan sometimes falls asleep.

Getting him awake is the stuff of miracles, but I manage it. It's what happens next that worries me.

Tristan pulls me into a hug. He stands and stretches long and hugs me so tight, and it is so exactly the thing that I need, so sure and full and perfect. Trist and I aren't huggers, and I wonder if maybe it's because they'd all be like this. Shattering and restorative at once.

None of my family does the hugging thing. We reserve *I love you*'s and physical affection for bank holidays and birthdays. Mamma's more free with it than any of the rest of us, but that's just Mamma. She was raised Southern, so I think she couldn't help it even if she wanted to.

Tristan is shaking a little bit and when he says, "I'm mad at her, too, T," I know why. He means Mamma. And I think, for a moment, maybe someone *is* feeling this with me? Maybe Trist can be my person. The one who gets it.

I pull away a little. "Did she talk to you?"

"No," he says, looking down at me. Tristan hit puberty, like, right out of the womb pretty much. He grew six feet and his voice started to crack around age ten or so and then began its deep descent around age twelve. He's got this honeyed bass tone thing going on in the pipes, and all my friends talk about it like I'm supposed to care. "I only know what I listened in on. You need honesty. Mamma's gotta give you that."

"Did you get caught? Listening in," I clarify.

"Nah. I'm stealthy as hell."

With an eye roll, I deadpan, "You're goofy as hell, is what you are, but sure. Let's call that 'stealth' if it makes you feel better."

He shoves me. I shove him back. He smiles, but it dies when I ask, "So then, you know I'm not really your sister?"

"Pretty sure half siblings still means you're my sister, unfortunately for me."

"Oh, wow. How nice for you that you've grown a sense of humor much faster than you've been able to grow facial hair."

"Ha-ha. Yes, I know Mamma lied. That your dad is, like . . ."

"White. You can say it. It's not a swear." I've always said that to white people *about* Black people. *You can say that I'm Black, you know. I am. It's not a swear.*

"Yeah," Tristan says. "Well. Anyway, I know that she, like, lowkey tried to hide that shit from you."

"Tristan, don't say *shit*." I hate it when he swears. I know I do all the time, but it just feels like my little brother shouldn't. My little half brother. My half little brother? Whatever. "What else?"

"I know 'bout the box. Kinda. Not, like, details about what's in it though. Oh, and that you freakin' reamed her out." Tristan laughs.

Nail-biting is not a thing I've ever really made a habit of. But since last night, I've bitten my already-short-for-football nails down to the quick. "If I'd 'reamed' Mamma out, do you think I'd be standing here right now?"

"Fair," he says.

"What else?"

"Eh. That's really it."

That's really all there is, I guess.

I plop down heavy on his bed. The pool house is on two levels. All glass walls and open floor plans. "I don't even know what questions to ask." I pause for a second. "Can we make a list?"

Tristan's so good at this. List-making. He makes lists for everything. For things he needs and things he doesn't. He makes lists for fun and for school and for other people, even when they don't know it. Last year, our Poppa—Daddy's father—complained about having a stressful week coming up. Poppa is pushing ninety years old, so when Trist made him a to-do list for the week, a healthy meals list, and a list of financially-preferable alternatives to his daily meds, I thought it was meant to help. But when I asked Poppa if the lists were helping at all, he claimed he didn't know what I was talking about. Because Trist never gave them to him. I glance over to the wall at my left where a Post-it list of different red fruits sits. A list on his bedside table is, to my best guess, things that begin with the letter X?

Tristan's already got a list started, it turns out. There are only three questions on it, but it's not a bad starting point.

Does Tasia's real dad know?

Who sent the box?

Why did you lie.

That last one isn't even posed as a question.

"You wanna add anything else?"

I shake my head.

"Want me to stick around for the inquisition?"

I nod.

Look at me, acting my shoe size and not my age.

Trist walks out of the pool house and in the back door of the main house, and this is the easy part. All I have to do is follow, and so I do.

It's like I'm the prodigal daughter returned. The back door slams and Mamma and Daddy fast-walk into the room to greet us.

"I'm so glad you're home safe," Mamma says, even though I was only at Slim's and my staying there is a thing that happens more often than not.

And it's not that I don't believe her relief, but I keep getting this feeling like she's making it about her. Her crying makes her the victim. Her compassion makes her the accustomed; it means she's had time to get used to this that I haven't had. It feels unfair.

"I have questions."

Daddy nods. "And we'll answer them. Let's go into the den."

"Tristan," Mamma says. "Baby, maybe you should give us a moment to—"

"She wants me to stay."

And at the same time I say, "He stays."

Daddy says, "All right." And then we're all sitting in the stiff-ass antique chairs in our den.

"I have questions," I say again.

"Yeah, honey," Mamma says. "Anything you want to know."

With Tristan's list in hand, I say, "The man in the photo is my real dad?"

Mamma gives a jerky nod of her head and she's *already* crying. Again.

"God, can you please stop crying long enough to answer even one of my questions?"

Daddy's eyes cut toward me. "Tasia Lynn. Don't think

this situation means you can just talk to your mother any way you please. That's not how this works."

I roll my eyes and find it lucky that I get away with that gesture. My parents have never been the ones to tolerate eye-rolling.

"I'm sorry," Mamma says. "I have . . . omitted the truth for a long time. And that truth is that . . . I was young. I needed to tell people something when I got pregnant with you. I was nineteen and I didn't know what I was doing, so I just tried to smooth things over as much as I could—"

That's sort of what Mamma does. She smooths things over, just as they happen, in that moment. She's a fixer in the boardroom and she's a fixer at home. Like a trauma surgeon—her only goal is to patch things up with immediacy.

I can feel my heart swelling in my throat.

She continues, "I . . . It was a rough time for me. I was young. Too young. I wasn't married, I was only nineteen."

Wait. Nineteen. "But you said you were with Daddy since seventeen."

Mamma hangs her head. Pauses. Something important happens. "I was. We were together in high school, had planned to be together while we each attended separate colleges. Merrick was my . . . He taught at my university."

"Merrick? That's his name? Merrick?"

She nods. "Merrick d'Aquin"

Tristan nods along like he's taking all this in. Like it's helping him make sense of things again. Like these answers are sufficient.

It's incredibly selfish of me, but I don't like how comfortable he's getting with her excuses. So I dig, even though I know he won't get why I'm doing it.

"He was your professor?"

"Yes. Well, a student-teacher, technically," she says. Like the distinction matters.

In that photo, Merrick didn't look that much older than Mamma and Daddy.

"Were you raped?"

She doesn't even flinch. I wonder if she's been asked that question before. "No."

"Did he force you or coerce you . . . for a grade or something?"

"No."

"Did you love him?"

She's silent again. I know she probably hasn't ever been asked this, because the answer tears out of her like an animal getting free of its cage. "I thought I did."

"Do you still?" No one would have asked her this. In our family—in Mamma's *and* in Daddy's—when you make a mistake, the emotions behind it, they're not important. Not enough to talk about. The focus is typically one of two things in a Black family: *How could you embarrass me like this?* and/or *How could you be so stupid?*

Love? No. No one would have asked her if her heart played a role.

"No," she says. "I don't know him anymore, he doesn't know me."

"You cheated on Daddy with Merrick. With your teacher."

"Yes." It's like hearing a gavel rap against wood. The verdict is very final.

I turn toward Daddy, not wanting to ask the question on my tongue. There's really no choice because he's still as stone. Daddy's normal mode of silence tends to run a little warmer. Comforting, like sheets from the dryer. But this silence—it's quiet, like fog rolling in. "You knew about the pregnancy all along? You were there when I was born."

I've seen the photos of him holding me. He looked so happy that day. I don't understand how that much happiness was even possible for a kid that's not even biologically yours.

"Why did you even agree to raise me?"

The weight of his words must be incredibly heavy for all that his shoulders fall. "It seemed like the right thing to do."

I nod. Ouch. Well. Always a good day to find out you were nothing more than a *moral obligation*.

I take a deep breath before my next thing. "Who sent that box?"

Mamma shakes her head. "I really don't know. I'm sorry, I don't have any idea who sent it or why."

"Does he know about me? Merrick?"

Another head shake. I'm getting a little sick of nonverbal responses but I understand she's just trying not to cry. She's holding back the tears for me. "I never told Merrick I was pregnant. I left school as soon as I started to show. Broke things off with him. Came home and did some community college while I lived at your Auntie Sandra's."

"So then, he couldn't have sent the box, right?"

Daddy steps in. "Well, we don't know, Tasia. Just because Mom didn't tell him at the time doesn't mean he couldn't have found out." The tension around his mouth doesn't even loosen when he speaks.

"No," Mamma says. "No. That's not Merrick. If he found out, he wouldn't do this . . . cryptic watch-from-afar thing. Passive aggression was never the way Merrick operated."

Daddy's arms lift and then his palms slap his thighs loudly as they come back down. He's not given to big gestures, but if ever there was a time for them, I think it's now. "Sloane, give me a break. You said it yourself—you *don't* know this man anymore. We can't say whether or not he'd have done this. It's been almost nineteen years. People can change."

"He could not have been the one to send this," Mamma says. She seems certain in a way that she hasn't since yesterday.

"How are you so sure?" I eye her carefully.

"I just . . . know, in my gut, that it's not who he was. Can't be who he is now. Trust me," she says.

"Ha! This family is a fricking joke."

Daddy cuts a sharp eye at me.

"So," I continue, "You don't know where this guy is or if he's even alive or in jail or anything? We don't know anything about him now?"

Everyone's silent. And I guess Mamma doesn't feel inclined to answer my question, because she doesn't even look at me.

I glance at Tristan. He seems . . . angry. More angry than I've seen him. Tristan is not a person who fidgets. He lists and that's the extent of it. No fidget spinner for him. Except, now he's sitting in a chair in the far corner, one knee moving a mile a minute. At a glance, I catch the index and middle fingers of his left hand picking at the skin of his thumb.

"Trist?" I whisper.

He doesn't look at me. Refuses, only shaking his head in answer.

It's such a small thing. So inconsequential in the grander scheme of things. Trist will always be my dork brother. Half, full—it's all just semantics. He was right earlier. Trist is Trist. He gets me. That doesn't change just because our labels have changed on a technicality.

But he is mad at me right now. Obviously he's mad at me. He probably expected me to uncover some of this. Maybe just gently peel back the Band-Aid a bit. Not rip it off and shove a rusty fork in the wound. I'm digging for me, though. I have to. It's got nothing to do with him, and that—the fact that I'm asking the hard questions and not letting Mamma's tears and "trust me" pleas fly—that's Mamma's fault.

Just one more thing Mamma and this box and its sender have taken from me. And it makes me pissed at her all over again.

All I want is to reassure Tristan that I'm still here. One hundred percent.

He needs time, though. That much is clear.

I look at Daddy. "Are you Tristan's dad? Like, biologically?"

I need that distinction to be clear before he says he's my dad too.

"I am."

"But not mine."

"Tasia, I am always going to be your—"

"Don't give me the answer you read in a parenting magazine—you're not actually my dad, just say it." I say it so calmly. I think it actually hurts him. God, I feel like such a monster. Trying to land all my blows with as much force as I can, taking care not to pull any of my punches.

"No," he says. "No, I'm not."

I dig my fingers into my hair and pull. By the time the dust settles, I'll have no fingernails and no hair and probably very little sanity left. "Why did you have to lie to me?"

I glance at each of them for just a moment and no more. Mamma, then Tristan, then Daddy.

There are no more answers to be found here. And for all that I've been kept in the dark about this thing that affects literally only me, so has Tristan.

I expected him to fight them with me. To dig with me. I thought that's what the list was. Yet he seems . . . placated. He seems okay with what's happened during this entire conversation tonight. I needed him to be the one to get it with me, but I watched him nod along with Mamma and Daddy as though her tearful monologue was just the balm he needed.

And now that leaves me. Me and this guy. Merrick. Unless he's the one who sent the box.

It dawns on me how badly I don't want that to be the case. If he knew and sent the box, but didn't try to reach out or see me or . . . anything, that would be screwed up on so many levels.

But also, what if he *isn't* the one who sent the box?

What if he's still in the dark about this too? What if . . .

I look up, finally breaking the room's murky silence. "I think . . . I want to talk to Merrick."

Daddy clears his throat.

Mamma sobs.

It is the loudest I've ever heard her cry and I don't care. I can't. I don't have the energy for this anymore. I cross my fingers, tap them against my thigh. It's hard to care about anything except myself right now.

Mamma speaks with a hand pressed against her lips. "Angel," she says, "we don't even know where he is or how to locate him or how to find him or if he'd even be willing to—"

"No. You're not *listening* to me. I need to find him. Because if he and I were the only ones lied to about this, then I can imagine how he might feel finding out after all this time. And if he didn't send that stupid box, then I want to know who did. I am not comfortable not knowing things about myself. And I am not trusting you two to tell me the truth."

Daddy adjusts his stance, removing his watch and rolling his sleeves up. "Tasia, listen—"

But I don't let him get a word in. I'm on a roll and I can't be stopped. "Not anymore. You had *eighteen years* to come clean with me. So no, I won't listen to what you have to say. Because, apparently, I can't trust it." I glance at Mamma. "That ship sailed yesterday when you tried to hide that box from me. He needs to know."

I mean, personally, *I'd* want to know if I had a whole-ass

kid out there somewhere.

Tristan's head cuts to me. "Why?"

"What?" I say.

"Why do you need him to know *so bad?*"

I shake my head, confused. What's he even asking? He's looking me right in the eye, holding my stare for what feels like days, weeks, months, before he finally turns and leaves.

Before I do the same, I exhale, face Mamma, and say, "I want that box."

"Angel—"

"No *angel,* Mom. I need that box. I'm going to find him. And you're not going to hold me back, because this is a decision I'm making for myself. Independent of you. Which is how you raised me to be."

Mamma, shaky and tearstained, leaves and returns with the box less than a minute later, during which time Daddy and I don't speak.

He doesn't even look at me. I know, because I can't look away from him.

I can't believe I didn't see it all this time. How not alike we are.

Mamma sets the box down in front of me on the squat coffee table she and I, once upon a time, found at Goodwill.

I don't say thank you before I pull the box slowly into my arms, cradling it like it is my anchor to this reality, and make my way upstairs to my room.

The door shuts with a definitive click, and I twist the knob's lock before sliding the box under my bed.

When I'm ready—when I can breathe again—I'm going to find him.

I'm going to find this guy, find out if he's the one who sent this box. If he's the one who took a lit match and kerosene to my entire world.

Chapter Six

My family doesn't do meals together unless we're obligated by some outside party, like Mamma's colleagues or Daddy's partners at the firm or, I don't know, whatever morality comes with holiday cheer.

None of that changes by the evening. But I still come downstairs, planning to eat my body weight in the apple-and-cinnamon granola bars that Tammy makes from scratch in lieu of the carb-heavy dinner that's on the stove. Trist, seated at the table, eats a bowl of pasta fit for someone three times his size. Usually he does this with a copy of some digest mag or even the newspaper—which I don't actually believe he reads.

Mamma's not around. Probably putting out some corporate fire at the office. She won't be home anytime soon. It's late now, about eight p.m.

Daddy, I know, is prepping for a big court case Monday morning.

I grab three of the frosted squares and pile them onto a plate.

"Hey," I say. I pull out a chair at the table and sit next to Tristan. He glances up from the folded-over book he's reading.

"Hi?"

I smile at him and it feels much creepier than I hope it appears.

"Stop forcing it," he says. Tristan is nothing if not direct.

Fighting hard not to dissect the granola bar before I eat it, I ask, "Am I? Forcing it? Does this feel forced?"

"Yes."

"How?"

He sets his book down. He's agitated. I can see it in the set of his shoulders, the loosening of his jaw. "When's the last time you ate at this table?"

Thanksgiving. Two years ago. "I don't know. How would I know that?"

"Aha. And you just sat here. Next to me. And you said 'hey,' like we needed to make conversation."

My head falls back. "I don't see how switching things up is so awful, Trist."

"Right. Switching things up. Just relax. Stop forcing it. If you need to talk, call Slim."

"I can't talk to Slim." I can't tell Slim about this until I'm ready to talk the subject into the ground. Slim is a fixer too. And in order to fix, she needs to ask questions. Which would be fine, if I had any actual answers. She doesn't understand that sometimes you just need to sit with your turmoil and let it stew.

Trist shovels food into his mouth like it's going to run off his fork. "Why not." Not a question. Tone dry. He doesn't care.

"Because she wouldn't get it."

"Fine. You think you need a professional to get it—tell Mamma to call Dr. Viseri."

Dr. Viseri is the family shrink Mamma made us see when our Uncle Lawrence died last year. Some police brutality dispute that she swore was going to affect us. So we all saw Dr. Viseri once a week for about a month straight, because she was right. It did affect us.

Tristan thinks I need a shrink. I don't.

"I don't need a shrink, Trist."

"Then, chill, Tasia. Jesus. I'm trying to read, so can you, like, go?"

I stand. The two bites of granola I've taken are like tar crumbles in my mouth now.

I make it far enough to dump my granola bars back onto their tray before Trist says, "Hey." So I turn to him. "You're my sister, okay? You're my sister no matter what. I don't see why anything has to change. Why we can't just pretend like this never happened."

Pretend like this never happened. Pretend like I'm not different than who I always thought I was. Pretend like I'm not broken down into racial fractions now, instead of a whole part of this family.

It strikes me that he totally and completely does not get it.

"I don't think . . ." I start, unsure about how I should navigate this. I hate feeling unprepared. "I don't think you understand what this means for me."

"What's there to get, Tasia? Why does it have to mean anything? Who cares about that guy."

I don't. But I might. Or I could.

"What if I could be better, though?" A better person for knowing him.

"Better how? Teez. If this box had never showed up, you'd have been entirely the same. Your life would have continued to be as full as it's always been. Why does that have to change?"

I shrug. It makes sense, I guess. "I don't know. It doesn't, but . . . ." But he doesn't get it.

I turn around and walk upstairs to my room before any more words make it out of my mouth.

As I pace circles around my room, I'm unable to settle on one thing. Netflix requires too much quiet, too much sitting still. Reading isn't a thing I ever really do by choice. Homework . . . well, obviously I'm not going there. I start to fold the clean laundry in my basket but then stop because I realize I'm too tired to do that.

Thoughts are coming too fast. Every time I decide I want to do one thing, I get distracted by another thought.

Predominantly, thoughts about the box under my bed.

I wanted to wait to look through it. I don't know why. It just feels like I should. It feels like I should give myself more time. But what will time do? All the waiting in the world could never have prepared me for any of this.

In the work of a moment, I'm diving to reach under the bed, pulling the box out, and glancing over my shoulder toward my open bedroom door as though I'm about to start my very first Google search for porn.

That was years ago, and anyway, it didn't make me feel nearly as suspect as all this.

Still, I slide across my wooden floor and kick the door shut with a sock-covered foot.

The box, I hadn't noticed before, is actually very pretty. Vintage in the way of things that is almost signature to Europe. The flowers on it are curling and arching and delicate.

I set the top aside and rifle through the box's contents. At one point, they might have seen some semblance of order. Now, pages are crumpled, bent, and even ripped in some places. There's evidence of Mamma's struggle with this thing.

I'm looking at a copy of my third grade class photo, smiling at all that wild hair and the gaps in my teeth, when I see the Polaroid. Mamma and him. Merrick.

It's not hard to have his name come up. It's actually just a little bit too easy.

"Merrick," I whisper to myself.

There's an envelope inside filled with more pictures. Most of them are clippings from the local paper, overviews and short stops in time, from fundraisers Mamma has organized or launch parties or dinners with Daddy's law firm partners.

When your family comes into money as fast as mine did— when they are not white, blond-haired, and blue-eyed—and achieving things no one ever thought they would, people sit up and take notice.

They mark that kind of success down in concrete ways.

I'm skimming through the manila envelope's contents

when I start to notice how most of the clippings are cut, and a few of them have a section of the image ripped off. Like, torn by hand. The piece that's missing?

Me.

There's one photo of all of us. Tristan, Daddy, Mamma, and I distinctly remember me, right there on the edge.

Except now I'm not there. I'm missing from at least four of these torn photos.

On a whim, I reach up to my desk and drag my laptop off of it. It's the work of moments to boot it up, load up Safari, and hit Google.

I type in his first name slowly, making sure I've spelled it right and, even though it's definitely not necessary, capitalized everything correctly.

The results for him are stunning. His web page is one of the first things that come up in my search. I know it's him because his face has changed very little from the Polaroids.

MerrickdAuquin.com

He's a musician. Or, like, a composer, I think?

I don't hesitate even a second. I click the link and follow it through, browsing his gallery first, which has a scant number of photos of him. He's aged, sure. But that same boyish face is still there. One of the eight available photos is of him in a music studio, and there's one where he's standing on what looks like a concert hall stage, one of him at a piano, smiling.

I have his smile, the way it leans to one side sans permission.

In the uppermost right-hand corner of the page is his contact link. It leads me to a page where I can fill in my name, email address, and enter a brief message.

It's not the doing that halts me. I have no problem sending him this message right now.

It's *what* I send him that gets to me.

I lie. I create the fake email. Say I'm interested in buying a piece he's composed for a film I'm producing. I don't use "Tasia Quirk" for the name portion. Instead, I use "Lynn Strange."

It's corny as hell, but that's what I settle on.

I count backwards from three, and then hit submit.

My hands immediately start to sweat in that gross way where your palms start to smell like warm pennies. I decide then and there that I can't go back to the box today.

I've done enough, pushed myself far enough.

Placing the lid back on the box is almost an act of aggression, I slam it on so hard. It's almost as though it's done something to offend me.

Other than tear my family apart.

Chapter Seven

I used to wish I was adopted. In fourth grade, Anna Takahashi joined us—the new girl in class—and told us how her foster parents of two years had officially adopted her the week prior.

She talked nonstop about how her mom was a surgeon and her dad stayed at home and how, as an adoption present, they'd gotten her a dog and how she'd named the dog Rebecca, which, to me, seemed really stupid and unfair to the dog.

Anyway, kids at school loved her. She was *adopted*. So that weekend, after my Saturday morning kids' soccer game, I went home with Slim and badgered her parents about maybe adopting me.

Tasia Lim didn't sound nearly as good as Tasia Quirk, but I'd get used to it.

Her dad humored me. Drew up a contract on a brown paper napkin. Told me to have my parents sign it and bring it back.

They did.

That Monday, I went to school and told everyone I was adopted. I was Slim Lim's sister now.

It was great, until I realized that Slim's mother had never been very kind—not just to me, but to anyone, including Slim—and I remembered how Mamma had mentioned us going on the Disney cruise over the upcoming spring break. It was meant to be a family trip. I remembered how great my bed was in comparison to Slim's, which had always been just a smidge too high for me to climb up on gracefully. I remembered the big family reunion we'd had back in NOLA. It was probably the most fun trip I had ever or would ever take.

Being a Lim meant I wouldn't get to be part of any of those things. Didn't it? Being a Lim meant I wouldn't get to be a Quirk.

Needless to say, I went home after school that day and begged Mamma to undo the adoption.

She did.

I learned a lesson. And eventually, I'd come to understand that isn't how adoption works. There are definitely no brown Taco Bell napkins involved.

And so, even now, lying in bed, listening to Mamma and Daddy have the world's most stilted conversation, I still wouldn't wish for a different family. I don't think I would trade them, even after they've lied to me and changed everything.

Would I?

It takes a very slow minute for me to wonder . . . What if I'm better equipped to handle a new family now?

What if the Lims weren't a good fit for me, but the d'Auquins are? What if there is more than one d'Auquin? What if Merrick is married and has other kids. What if he has two dozen older siblings. What if he's gay!

I hear the stairs creak as Mamma and Daddy make their way upstairs. Normally I sleep with my door closed, but I've been hearing them gripe at each other all night. It's all been about me. I need to know what they're saying. Or what they're not saying, as the case may be.

". . . court Monday morning?" Mamma says.

Daddy grunts.

They never discuss each other's schedules. But they're at a halt now, so they've got to come up with other things to fill the silence in this too-large house that's becoming less of a home by the minute.

The conversation they're having now… It's like discussing the weather with a complete stranger. Just admit you both don't care and go about your day.

The door to their bedroom opens. The squeaking hinge on their door is different from mine, which is different from Trist's, which is different from Tammy's.

I hear Daddy exhale long and slow. I imagine him sitting on their bed, the gold comforter dipping beneath his weight as he bends over to unlace a shiny black wingtip. I imagine Mamma dragging her feet into her bathroom, avoiding the mirror as she often does when she wants to deny her age for a while.

They're at a cease-fire in the middle of a war neither of them ever wanted to fight. This is the moment I realize they're trying to move on like nothing's changed and I'm the obstacle that won't let them.

We're not a religious family. But sometimes, on Sundays like this one, Daddy goes into work, his own place of worship, and spends the day buried in his religious text—which changes depending on whatever case he's fighting at the time.

And occasionally, on those Sundays, I go with him.

I sit in the window seat and watch football tape on my iPad or pretend to do homework while I instead watch Daddy make calls or comb through a book with tiny lettering, not unlike the Bible.

Today feels like a Sunday when I really need to go with him. I just . . . need.

Need to be there with him. I can't help thinking maybe there's a chance he'll talk to me about this. About why he kept it in all this time. Why he never told me, or if he's ever had a conversation with Mamma about coming clean to me.

I need to go with him today, more than ever.

My alarm goes off at 7:30 a.m. sharp and I make my way downstairs, but not before I check my email for a response from Merrick.

There is nothing.

Daddy usually leaves around eight, or a little after that. But when I make it to the bottom of the stairs, I find him with the door open, briefcase packed and ready to go.

"You're leaving already?"

He turns quickly. "Ah, yes. I have a lot of work to do today and needed to get a head start. Good morning."

Apparently he really needs that twenty-five minutes.

"Can you wait about ten or so? I just need to find my jeans and a hoodie and—"

"Not today, Tasia, I really need to get going."

"Okay," I say. What might be—definitely is—happening here dawns on me. "Well, maybe I can Uber and meet you in like an hour?"

Daddy sets his briefcase down, closes the door. "It's probably better if you . . . if I just go in and handle what needs handling."

I nod.

As he picks up his briefcase to leave again, I ask the thing that's been aching to jump off my tongue. "Are you afraid of me?"

He shakes his head, smiles that confused smile he sometimes gets when I talk about football or pop culture too long. That solidifies it for me. I don't even need him to answer anymore. I mean, are we not built to fear the things we don't understand?

But he does. He *does* answer. Haltingly, adjusting his stance, foot to foot. But it's an answer nonetheless. "I know that everything that's happened hasn't been easy for you. It hasn't been easy for any of us. But I need you to know it's okay to take your time with it."

Take my time?

"To process it. To take some 'you time.'"

Me . . . time.

Awesome. Now I'm the one who's confused.

He walks toward me, pulls the brown leather wallet out of his back pocket, and hands me a fifty. "Spend the day with yourself, just live like it never happened," he says. "Could be good for you. Get out of your room, away from what's in that box. For now you could do nothing and that would be okay. Might help you untangle some of whatever it is you're feeling if you just slow down."

I know that the box is enemy number one for both Mamma *and* Daddy. I know this. *Whatever it is you're feeling.* It's this part that really gets me. He doesn't know what I'm feeling and he's not interested in trying to figure it out, either. This is the equivalent of "Get lost and figure it out yourself."

I stare at the crisp bill still in his outstretched hand, half disgusted by the offer.

Like it never happened. Untangle whatever you're feeling.

I expected . . . more. More than "pretend and do nothing" as some form of advice.

I shake my head. "Parents aren't supposed to run away from their problems, but I guess you aren't really *my* parent, so the same rules don't apply anymore."

Then I turn and go back upstairs.

I wish I'd taken the money beforehand. I wish I had looked him in the eye when I said it.

That night I hear my parents arguing again. I sit in bed under cool sheets listening to the leaves scuttle across the ground outside my window. The yelling is still about me, but mostly about how neither of them really knows what to do. How to control me or "rein that girl in," which gets thrown around a few times, along with the fact that I am, apparently, not mature enough to deal with this in healthy ways.

I pull my phone out. I have a text from Slim, I ignore it while I scroll through some pictures of Mamma and I. There are at least a dozen more of us on my Instagram, and I go through those, too. Still, looking at them isn't helping me forgive her, love her, the way I hoped it would. Doesn't help me get the words out of my mouth that I'll need to speak to her again. It only hurts a little more, a little deeper.

Finally, I pull the cold sheets off my bed and carry them to the guest bedroom downstairs, away from their accusations and the shouts.

I pull up the Gmail app on my phone, pull the page down to refresh it.

Nothing. I knew there would be nothing, but that didn't stop the hope from spreading across my chest like watercolor paint.

In Mrs. Hitotose's twelfth grade English class, we're reading *The Scarlet Letter* when it happens. Kevin Prideux, the school's resident basketball beefcake, raises his hand to wax poetic about Hester Prynne.

"I mean, Hawthorne does kinda show us that Hester is, like, sort of a badass."

Hitotose clucks her tongue and mutters "Language, Kevin," even though we all know she doesn't really care.

"Sorry," he says and continues, "but, so, it's like . . . she's strong, but also her strength is shown to us through her loneliness. She lives a lonely life and it's basically, like, Hester versus society at one point."

"Good," Hitotose says, making a circuit around the room, her heels clacking on the shitty decades-old wood floors.

I stare off into space. My book's open but I'm pretty sure I'm not on the right page. I checked out pretty much the second Kevin decided he knew anything about women. Even fictional ones.

I roll my eyes. "Give me a break."

"Something to add, Miss Quirk?"

I pull myself up a little straighter in my desk. "Uh. No?"

"Obviously there's something—otherwise that outburst wouldn't have happened."

"I just think it's kind of dumb to be like, 'Yeah, she's so strong and that's what's important' when this woman was ostracized from everyone and everything she'd ever known."

"She had Pearl," Hitotose says.

"The kid was a burden and that's it. In chapter five or something, Hester's, like, killing herself trying to figure out how she's gonna feed them both. That's not family, that's obligation. Hester is alone and that's what's important here. Her strength doesn't negate her struggle."

The entire class goes silent.

"Good," Hitotose says, pleased.

And it hits me, much like this in-class debate, that I can't just let things go. I can't walk away from the box and what it means and its sender. I have to find out who else knows about me.

I don't want to be solitary in this issue anymore.

Congratulations, Tasia Quirk. You are lonely Hester Prynne.

Slim catches up with me after class. She is the least organized person I know. Makeup is half falling out of every pocket in her shoulder bag.

"Hey. What was that about?" she says, following me to my locker. People work overtime to get out of her way, her long legs eating up the hallway floor.

"What was what about?"

"Uh. You never speak in Hitotose's class. Like, ever."

"Yeah," I say. "But I couldn't exactly get out of being called on."

Slim side-eyes me hard. I pretend I don't notice it.

"Is this about your Daddy Issues?"

"Ew, Slim. Don't say 'Daddy Issues.'"

"Why? You haven't brought it up in days. I'm just saying, you're being weird, so…"

I laugh. "It's nothing."

"Aha."

"Stacy. I'm serious. It's nothing."

We both stop at my locker as I swap out my English books for my gargantuan APUSH textbook. My copy of *The Scarlett Letter* gets chucked into the back of my locker harder than it deserves.

"Wow, Taze. Tell me how you really feel."

"I hate that book. It puts me to sleep," I concede.

"Right."

"Tell me about Josiah."

She stops, moves her arm in front of my locker to block me from physically abusing any more of my books. "You never want to talk about him. So why now?"

I shrug. "We haven't in a while."

"Okay, except it's only been a couple days?"

"That's a while for you, Slim. Who are you kidding?"

"Fair point. Still, something's up with you. You're just acting so much weirder than you usually do. And you didn't even text me back last night."

"I went to sleep early."

"You didn't tell me you were doing that."

She's right. I didn't. And usually that is a thing we do. We text for so much of the day that "good night," or more accurately, "I'm about to start drooling on my APUSH textbook so I'm gonna KTFO" just happens to be part of that.

"Whatever." She moves her arm, rolls her eyes, then looks me square in mine. "Swear to me that you're okay. Like, I get super anxious when you're worked up over something like this. So just . . . swear you're not gonna have a psychotic break in the cafeteria tomorrow while clutching that lurker box to your chest or something." She makes it seem like all this is taking a bigger toll on her than it is on me. Like she absolutely needs me to be solid—or else. If I know anything at all right now, it's that this is definitely not going to result in a solid Taze.

"If I was, I don't think I could promise you anything in advance—"

"Tasia."

It would be so great if she weren't making this about how she feels. No way can I be responsible for her emotional needs right now. So I tell her what she wants to hear, the thing that'll get her off my back.

I stare at the smooth space between her eyes—and I lie. "I'm fine. Nothing's wrong."

The lie eats me up inside.

The bell rings in what is probably the most well-timed excuse for an exit I've ever experienced.

I slam my locker shut.

Chapter Eight

GAME 2 — WESTVIEW VS. MALIBU SHARKS

The game the following Friday night is a real ass-kicking. It's one of those where you swear every other player on the team has never even seen a football before.

We play *that bad.*

To make matters worse, the other team's spectators are heckling me so bad, it seriously messes with my focus. I get sloppy on a second down and end up colliding with one of our own safeties, like a fricking idiot who doesn't know up from down.

We hit so hard my helmet goes flying off. Head, meet turf. The back of my skull vibrates for long minutes and my eyes start to feel cold.

That, much to my dismay, is a pretty clear sign that I'm concussed.

It takes me probably a minute to get up. One more to make it to the sidelines, and maybe another couple to find the bench.

The other team has their medic take a look at me. Some aggressively blond guy everyone calls "Jimbo," which seems real unfortunate for him.

Mamma comes from the far end of the field where all spectators sit, reaching me just as Jimbo begins his examination.

"Looks like it might be a concussion, but I can't say for sure. Definitely would say take her to the ER just to—"

"No!" I say.

"—be sure."

"No," I say again, more firm this time. Jesus, my head's starting to throb. "I have to be in there for—"

"Definitely no more football tonight."

Mamma's hand meets my shoulder. "I'm her mother," she says to Jimbo. "I got it, I'll take her."

No one argues. Obviously. Except me. I do my damnedest to stay in the game, or at least ride the bench for the rest of it. But even Siah won't look at me long enough to see the way I'm begging with my eyes. Probably good anyway. It's more threat than actual pleading, TBH.

In the car, I'm quiet as the "you'll never be allowed to play football again" panic sets in. When Mamma tries to "Jesus" me, I tell her that my head hurts too much for noise even though I maybe do need what comfort she's offering. I need the reassurance, but I don't want it from her. Not her or Daddy or Trist or Slim. Not anymore.

Who's left?

Still, I can hear Mamma whispering it under her breath.

I want to scream. Irrationally, her voice is making me want to scream.

But it's the most she's spoken to me in days, and vice versa.

At the local Kaiser ER, we get checked in fairly quickly.

A nurse in hot pink scrubs calls, "Tasia Quirk?" Only she says it like "Tasha."

As I stand, Mamma stands with me.

"It's fine," I say to her. "I can go by myself. I don't need your help."

She looks shocked, her face pulling long, eyes rounded and wide.

The nurse smiles and puts her arm around my shoulder like she's protecting me from Mamma. "You can have a seat here, ma'am. We'll update you momentarily."

An hour later, after I get one IV bag of fluids and receive my concussion diagnosis, I'm released with strict orders.

No more football for the next seven to ten days. No practice, no scrimmages, no drills, no gym workouts.

Our game next week is pretty early—on a frickin' Wednesday, of all days (super rare)—because the big shot school landed us broadcasting rights for the local CBS station or something. I ask if there's any way I'll be ready. His answer: a very unbothered, "Definitely not. You'll likely be out for the week. We'll get you a note to excuse you."

This game—I can't miss it. It's a big one. We're playing the Buccaneers. My team and our cheerleaders are missing the second half of the day's classes just to travel to the other school up in Palm Springs. As long as I've been on the team, we've been in this out-and-out rivalry with them. The Bucks vs. the Westview Wildcats has been the game I've been killing myself on the field over *for weeks.*

When I exit the ER back in the waiting room, Mamma tries to pull me into a hug, but I hold my papers out at her instead.

She skims them fast. Exhales. "Okay, this isn't too bad. A concussion just like we thought." She reads under her breath as we walk back to the car. "No football for the week."

Halfway home, the car silent save for the soft swoosh of us passing other drivers on the freeway, I say, "I'm going to miss the Bucks game on Wednesday."

"Oh, angel . . ."

"It's fine."

"You can still *go* to the game. You'll just have to watch instead."

"If I can't play, I don't want to go."

"Baby—"

"I super don't want to talk about it, so."

"Okay," she says. It's new territory for her. The *not*-talking-about-it thing. It's new for us both, because Mamma and I—we talk about everything.

We used to be able to talk about everything.

Except then she failed to talk about the *biggest thing* with me and now that's all shot to hell.

I run a mental list, imagine scratching names off a white sheet of paper one by one: Mamma. Trist. Daddy. Slim.

"Okay," Mamma says again.

I use my fingernail to scratch three words into my football-pants-clad thigh: Who is left?

No one knows me like the walls in my mamma's home.

We've lived in this house since I was five and it's never felt as foreign to me as it has this week. I've walked through every single room—making excuse after excuse to avoid friends and, as far as I've been able to, family—but I've felt like a stranger in all of them.

I end up in the big study upstairs, going through Mamma's phone to find out if Merrick has contacted her recently. Because it's Sunday, Mamma usually adheres to the Sunday Sabbath rest thing, not taking any work calls or answering emails. I don't know why. We haven't been to church in ages. It works out well for me, though, because she's MIA from her preferred workspace.

But there's nothing there. No trace of him whatsoever, and I still haven't gotten anything in my own email inbox. I check his webpage multiple times a day to make sure it's still up and running and not swallowed by the Internet Babadook.

Spoiler: It's still there.

That box is really all I have and it's like he doesn't exist outside of it.

I spend long minutes standing there, wondering if it was all made up, Mamma's confession about him. I wonder if it was all a dream.

"What are you doing?"

I turn and find Mamma behind me. "Just looking for . . . a report folder. I finished my APUSH report and need to keep it in something bound."

She walks over to the cabinet beneath her shelf and pulls out a box of them, handing one to me.

"Thank you."

She nods. "What else were you doing?"

"Nothing!"

Her head tilts. She knows. That outburst was uncalled for. It was a red reaction instead of the casual blue or purple it should have been.

And also, contrary to popular belief—parents *aren't* idiots.

Mamma opens her mouth and then pauses. Finally: "I want you to know I'm here for whatever you need."

I nod. "Okay."

I start to hope this is the moment we fix things, and all these plans spring up in my head about Mamma helping me look for Merrick and finding out more about the box and getting to know him . . . getting to know me.

We're silent once more, and then she says, "Do you think you can ever forgive me?"

That right there—that's her shooting down every reunited-and-it-feels-so-good delusion I just created, and God, this doesn't feel like my life anymore.

I glance at her and don't even know if the answer to her question is yes. It doesn't feel fair that she's asking me for *anything* right now. How is it fair that she should get to make requests like this when I haven't even had a chance to figure anything out?

She hasn't even tried to help me figure it out.

She keeps talking and, somehow, I know she's explaining herself to me again but I've managed to zone out. I've managed to find a space that feels safe.

It's the same space I occupy when I'm on the field. When I'm at a home game and things just feel better, and the turf is familiar under my cleats, and it's third and long and our O needs the ball back, and so I have to run. I have to focus on what I need to do and how best to get it done. These are the types of situations where you don't think. You can't. There's no time for that. As a cornerback, you just trust your instincts and you trust your lineman to put some heat on the quarterback, and that—oh my God, *that*—is where I go mentally right now.

I turn and walk away from Mamma while she's midsentence. Walking away from my parents seems to be a theme this week. But all of them, from Daddy to Tristan to Mamma to Slim—all of them have been directing me, pushing me— to feel a certain way about my life. Sometimes without even knowing it. They've all been leading me by the hand in the wrong direction or just washing their own hands of it, not helping me at all.

None of them has answers other than *leave the box alone* and *please forgive me.* None of them can give me the comfort or solace or calm that I've found on the field. They did once. But not anymore.

I'm solely responsible for obtaining that now. It's all on me.

As I make my way out of her study, my phone pings in my back pocket. I pull it out as I ascend the stairs to my room, hoping this isn't Siah forgetting to loop me out of this week's practice emails.

I hold my thumb against the home button to unlock it and it opens up right to my Gmail app—the last app I used.

It's from him. Merrick.

He finally emailed me back.

Chapter Nine

M.DAQUIN: *Lynn, thanks for reaching out to me about a piece of music for your film. I'm happy to chat with you more in order to find out if something I already have in my catalog would suffice or if I can create something new for you.*

L.STRANGE: *Mr. D'Aquin. I do believe I would like to commission something new from you…*

L.STRANGE: *Are you, by chance, a Los Angeles local? I prefer to meet with artists in person to assess for myself whether or not their style is right for my projects.*

M.DAQUIN: *Understandable. I am local. It's not something I normally do—meet with my clients before they're officially my clients—but if you're fairly local to the San Fernando Valley, we can meet to discuss prospects.*

L.STRANGE: *That would be ideal.*

L.STRANGE: *I am local. How soon can you meet?*

M.DAQUIN: *How's tomorrow afternoon, around 1 p.m.?*

L.STRANGE: *15045 Ventura Blvd., Sherman Oaks, CA 91403*

L.STRANGE: *I'll see you at the address above at 1 p.m..*

L.STRANGE HAS LEFT THE CONVERSATION.

Game. Set. Match.

Chapter Ten

Blu Jam Café is packed when I arrive, box tucked under my arm like a football. A secret football.

Someone bumps me just as I enter the swinging door. Even though it's a weekday afternoon, there are moms meeting for coffee, having arranged a "play date" where their bad-ass kids can yell about having to poop as they pick apart their gluten-free banana nut muffins.

That's essentially Blu Jam's weekday aesthetic. It's partially why I chose it to meet him.

Kids my age who use the Internet aren't dumb about it. Not like our parents think we are. We don't meet strangers in their homes—even if there's a good chance for some kind of parental lineage there—and we don't give out personal information to adults or whatever.

The point is, I go into this meeting carefully. Full-on knowing Mamma and Daddy would tan my hide if they knew I'd left the house to do this when, in actuality, I'm supposed to be home, resting, recovering from a concussion.

But I had to. And I had to do it alone.

And Merrick . . . if he's not the one who sent the box, why should he continue to be kept in the dark about this? How is that fair?

Admittedly, my curiosity is a much larger force for why I want to find him than anything else. I don't do much of anything altruistically.

It takes me all of thirty seconds to spot him, sitting at a relatively small table for two, manspreading as he reads the paper.

He's got shoulder-length hair, much shorter than what it looked to be in the Polaroid. Half of it's up, the other half down. He's wearing a jacket-style flannel, dingy-looking, paint-splattered jeans, and a lazy brow.

He is still very much the same as the guy in that photo. I'm not sure how that makes me feel, but as I walk over to him, I crack my chest open and let all feelings go.

I stand in front of him for just a moment too long before he glances up from the paper and says, "What—you need this space for the outlet or something?"

Holy crap, he didn't send the box. He'd have recognized me from the photos if he had. He didn't send this box.

Oh, God.

I hadn't realized before now that I was hanging on to him being the one to have sent it. I mean, it was the only logical conclusion. I had hoped it wasn't his doing, but it would have given me answers. It would've also meant Merrick was a manipulative jerk, but I want some understanding right now. That feels more necessary than whatever I'd get from his having nothing to do with any of this.

But I'm spinning and I don't know which way is up anymore.

Jesus, here come the nerves—a sort of vibrating, tickling sensation settling into my skin.

"N-no, I . . . uh. I'm Lynn. Kinda." I clear my throat, heft my backpack higher up on my shoulder.

He pauses. I can see the confusion spreading across his face. The brows soften just a little, enough to creep up his forehead. Both his nearly nonexistent lips and eyes stretch thinly. He tucks his chin down just as he asks, "*You're* Lynn?"

I nod. Shrug.

"Lynn Strange?"

I nod again. "Listen," I say, pulling the empty chair out and sitting. I lean in toward him. "I am Lynn insofar as I am the one who sent you that message about buying your music or whatever."

He nods like I do. Slow. Measured. "So you . . . do or do not want to discuss working with me?"

"Uh, no. Sorry. I probably can't afford you and also I am not a director."

"You lied."

"I lied."

He reclines in his chair further, his legs stretching into my space. "What is this, kid?"

I exhale. Just say it, Tasia. Just get it out. I set the box on the table. He glances down at it. "I have good reason to believe I'm your kid and also maybe you know who sent me this box and, like, if you don't know, then maybe you'd be down to help me figure out who did?"

He laughs.

He laughs in my face.

"Is this a joke? My sister put you up to this?" He lifts the lid of the box, barely glances inside, and then drops it. He doesn't even close the lid properly. "Halfway across the globe, and she's pulling childish pranks on me?"

"No," I say firmly. "No. My mother is Sloane Newark. Or, was. She's married now. Sloane Quirk. B-but her maiden name is—"

"Sloane is your mom?" His eyes search my face, like there's some understanding to be found. Too bad, buddy. No answers here. Trust me.

The look on his face is, like, equal parts confusion and… elation? He takes a slow, deep breath in and doesn't release it.

"Yeah. That's what I'm trying to *tell* you. And I think I'm your kid and I didn't even know, and that weird 'I ate something bad' look on your face seems to indicate you didn't know either, and here's this pic of you two"—I pull the Polaroid from the box—"and somebody sent me this box in the mail a few days ago, and I had hoped it was you because clearly someone's been watching me all these years, which should probably creep me out more than it does and—"

"Christ, please, stop talking," he says. He's got his eyes shut tight and I hold my breath, waiting for him to open them again. "How old are you?" he says.

"Eighteen."

"Jesus. Are you supposed to be in school right now?"

"Wow, that is such a dad thing to say—"

"Please." He holds up a hand.

"Sorry. Yes, I'm supposed to be in school. I mean, I would be if I weren't home for the week with a medical-grade concussion."

"I—What?"

"I got a concussion after I—"

He holds up a hand like he just can't *bear* to hear any more. "Please. Stop. So this means your mom doesn't know you're here."

"No."

"And your . . . dad? He doesn't know either? You said your mom's married."

"Yeah. He doesn't know."

"Okay." He stands. Then sits. Then stands again before glancing at me and sitting down. "Okay. Sloane knows about the box?"

"She tried to hide it from me."

It sounds accusatory. It is, a little bit. I don't intend it that way—to sound like I'm tattling on her. But it comes out and I guess I'm expecting him to be on my side. To look me in the eye and agree that yeah, she messed up.

When did this thing even morph into sides?

Merrick shakes his head. I wish he'd give me more than that. I need to know he's taking me seriously. To know that maybe he'll help me the way Mamma and Daddy so far haven't.

"She thinks I'm your dad too? Why wouldn't she have told me? What's your name?"

I pull a corner of his newspaper toward me, begin to fold the edge. Give my hands some busywork. "That was a lot of questions. She knows. Maybe you wanna talk to her? My name's Tasia. Tasia Lynn Quirk."

He nods. "Tasia."

"Yeah."

"You're my kid."

I nod. "Think so."

"I have a daughter."

I nod. "Think so."

The laugh—a cackle, really—that he lets loose is loud enough to cover the entirety of this ridiculously crowded café.

Chapter Eleven

He sobers.

And the look on his face quickly morphs from mild intrigue to complete elation. Like a kid finding a shiny quarter on the ground, and then going all Dr. Jekyll, cackling over a new experiment. I am his new experiment. It's basically the most insulting kind of amusement possible.

I think that's going to be the worst of it until he laughs in my face. Again.

Loud, raucous laughter that comes from deep in his belly and basically climbs out of his mouth.

It's less easy to see him not taking me seriously than I thought it'd be. The reaction I almost expected was a little bit of anger. For him to be on my side. But this? This is different. This makes the skin under my arms prickle. This feeling is a hot comb too close to the scalp.

He sobers, suddenly. "My daughter," he says. And I brighten. Okay! Yes! We can work with this.

"Yep," I say.

"I don't know how much of this I'm buying."

Okay, wait, wait. No.

No.

There is this need to move welling up in the balls of my feet. To walk or run or, I don't know, do lunges or drugs or something. Coach'd be so proud. About the lunges. Not the drugs.

"I know, I know," I say, holding my hands up in front of me. "I just really think—"

"I mean, what were you thinking was going to happen?" His voice is sharp and hard. It's alive. I want him go back to laughing at me. He explodes out of his chair. I'm actually pretty amazed it doesn't fall over or melt into the ground. "You're Sloane's kid?"

I nod. I don't know exactly how we went from "my daughter" to "Sloane's kid" before I could blink twice, but I nod again anyway.

"Call her," he says. "Call her right now."

"This isn't some elaborate joke."

He's drawing the attention of fellow coffee drinkers now. Generally, whenever an adult is screaming at a teen girl in public, it's cause for concern.

So it probably doesn't help that Merrick is white.

My phone has been pulled out even though I have no intention of calling my mamma. She'd be furious. More than furious. She'd lock me in the basement for the rest of my life.

And we don't even have a basement.

Problem is, my other options aren't much better. They're

significantly worse, depending on how you look at it. Call Slim. Call Trist. Call Daddy.

Jesus.

So, of course, I make it worse. "You could follow me to my house? Talking in person would be better."

He seems to be mulling it over, mouth scrunched up tight, lips jumping from side to side. I can almost hear him thinking through every possible scenario in which this might be a sick prank.

Finally, with much more ease than I imagine, he says, "You drive?"

I nod.

"What do you drive?"

"A 'ninety-six Jeep."

He whistles. "And you're sure this is smart?"

No. "Oh, yeah."

"The responsible thing would be to schedule a time to discuss this with your parents."

"Uhh, or," I say, "or, you could follow me to my house, and we could get this all out of the way sooner rather than later."

Merrick rubs his hand along his stubbly jaw. I wonder, ridiculously, how often he shaves. "What's the rush?" he says.

The box. This stupid box and whoever sent it is the rush. "Look, maybe I just want some answers. Maybe I just want someone to tell me the fu—fricking truth for once. So what if I'm eager to know more about you? More about *me*. I'd think you might feel the same."

I see it reflected in his face, the moment my words land. His resolve. He's throwing a couple bills on the table and heading out the door ahead of me a moment later, without a word.

I have to run to catch up. "Wait! I'm parked, like, a million blocks from here!"

His Benz pulls up behind my Jeep, headlights flashing up the white and red-bricked drive and Mamma's heritage rose garden.

Merrick whistles as he gets out of the car, rounding the front of his beat-to-shit Mercedes to stand next to me. My own eyes follow his gaze as it takes in the monstrosity. The McMansion I call home.

"Yeah, I know." There's really nothing more to say about it. To me, it's just . . . home. It's the place where I brush my teeth before bed at night and where Tammy and I binge-watch episodes of *Toddlers & Tiaras*. It's the place where Tristan's lists can be found in every secret nook and cranny. It's the place where Daddy spends his entire Sunday if he can't seem to drag himself into the office, reading what is presumably the same section of the *LA Times*. It's the place where Mamma loves us all best.

Merrick knocks on the door once we've made our way up the drive and across the porch. I look at him like he's nuts. "You don't have to knock. I live here—"

Mamma swings the door open. I'm a little shocked she's home this early; it's three in the afternoon. And all that is rendered irrelevant anyway when she takes one scathing, blistering look at Merrick, snatches my arm to pull me into the house, and points at him with the other.

A ripe "fuck you" leaves her lips.

She kicks the door shut with whatever appendages she hasn't used to tell my birth father how unwelcome he is here.

Before I can say anything she beats me there. "No."

"Mamma—"

"No, Tasia. I cannot believe you would do something like this. How did you even *find* him?" She's walking away from me, and the farther she gets, the louder her voice echoes against the walls of the foyer.

I follow, knowing very well that she doesn't want an answer to her question, but that I should be right behind her regardless, if only so I don't do anything else this dumb. Like letting Merrick into the house.

"Mamma, please."

She rounds on me so fast, I almost miss it. "'Mamma, please'?" she says. "'Mamma, please' what? This wasn't some mystery game with a riddle you needed to solve. What would possess you, Tasia Lynn Quirk."

"d'Aquin," I say, arms folded now. The point is to emphasize how done I am with all this. But mostly the arms I've got so tightly folded up against my chest are just to hold my lungs and heart in place, to prevent my ribs from falling onto the floor, right in front of Mamma's Jimmy Choos.

"What?"

"Technically, it's d'Aquin, isn't it?"

"Tasia—"

I back up a few steps, like Simone Biles making space for her running start. I feel infinitely less badass, but distance from Mamma . . . it helps some.

"I need this. You *owe me* this, at the very least. Some answers. Some truth. Mamma, why won't you give me this?"

She's quiet for a beat, and then opens her mouth to speak again right as I notice Daddy standing in the entryway, a few feet from her. I don't know at what point he walked in. It doesn't seem relevant until he says, "I'm going to let him inside, Sloane."

Mamma turns to him, stumbling backwards a single step. Seems I wasn't the only one who didn't realize we'd become a party of three.

"Solomon, I…" but she doesn't say anything beyond that. And I don't think she will.

Daddy walks past us both and the whiff of his cologne I get is so strong, so much more pronounced, I wonder how it took me until now to notice all the rose and amber, all the peach nectar and patchouli.

I look at Mamma while Daddy's and Merrick's voices hum in the background, seeming much more quaint and warm than this situation probably warrants.

Suddenly, I feel very small. Like this decision was too big for me to have made myself. My heart beats a little faster in my chest, fast enough that I can feel it pulsing in my neck as I struggle to swallow.

I messed up. I shouldn't have done this. Why did I do this?

I'm caught up in the whirl of my decision when it hits me that *I know* why I did this. Answers are why I did this.

And then we're all at the edge of the foyer, very nearly into the den when Daddy says, "Let's all sit down. Talk."

And no one else moves.

Not until I do.

Chapter Twelve

He opens with the worst possible line. "You look fuckin' great, Slo."

"Language," Mamma says. And I already know how most of this talk is about to go. Trash. It's going to go in the trash.

"It's not like I haven't heard you and Daddy say the word 'fuck' before," I add helpfully.

"Tasia Lynn."

I hold my hands up. There's not much room for me to push right now. "Sorry."

Still, though I shouldn't push much verbally—not where I don't have to—I can't help liking the fact that Merrick is… misplaced in our den, with his tattered shoes on Mamma's probably antique rug. I want him to track mud everywhere, because I'm awful. Want traces of who he is to stain this space so no one forgets who he is. Why he's here. Who I am. I want his presence to pull on this place like marionette strings, long after this puppet show is over.

Daddy and Merrick have the same bizzaro habit going, as no one looks at anyone else. They each, simultaneously, use one fine-boned middle finger to rub the same area of their respective faces—the space just below the left corner of their mouths, chin held in hand.

It's weird. They could be opposite sides of the same coin in Mamma's wallet. Daddy, dark and clean shaven. Merrick, light with a beard and a bit of its shadow.

Mamma gestures toward the couches, but not until both Daddy and Merrick clear their throats at the same time.

Once we're seated, Mamma's the first to really speak. "This situation is . . . messy, I know. But, Merrick, you can't just come here—"

He looks at me. Dammit.

"I, um. I asked him to come." I hurry on while I still have the floor. "I looked for him. I found him. I asked him to come here."

"How?"

"Google."

"Tasia—"

"It's just that there's all this information coming at me and he's the biggest missing piece, and so I figured, if I just found him—"

"Without speaking to us first?" Daddy adds.

"—then a lot of what I'm worried about could be eighty-sixed. Like this box thing? Mamma, he *isn't* the one who sent it. He's just as much in the dark as we are. As I am," I correct. Because Mamma and Daddy—they aren't in the dark about who I am. They know very well. Have always known and decided not to let me in on the secret.

"So, I think having him here is worth it. Even if you guys don't. Even if—and I'm sorry—it makes either of you uncomfortable to have him, to have the truth, in your face again."

Mamma looks at me, but only for a moment. Then she looks at Merrick. "You didn't send the box?"

"No," he says quickly. "You didn't tell me I had a . . . a daught—a kid."

Mamma almost shrugs. Almost. It's probably meant to be a shrug. She wants to appear more unbothered than she really is.

"Yeah, well. You can barely get the word 'daughter' out of your mouth, Merr. How do you suppose the rest of fatherhood would have gone for you?"

"That's not fair."

He's right. It's not.

"No," Mamma says. "You're right. It's not. But there's no plan for any of this. No step-by-step guide that tells us how to handle this. I haven't had time to think about you as part of her life, and so—"

"What a coincidence!" Merrick shouts, hands thrown aggressive octopus style into the air. Like he's joking and jovial, conversing with an old friend. Guess technically, he is. "Neither have I," he continues, and then deadpans, "But whose fault is that?"

With palms pressed together, Mamma brings her vertical hands to her lips, tapping them against her lips as she builds her case. "Fair. That's totally fair. I still don't like the way this all unfolded."

Merrick reclines in his stiff-ass antique chair and crosses his legs, one knee over the other. "Do you guys really not know who sent that box? Seemed like a lot of stuff in there."

"Mm. *Stuff* you'd have to be basically her parent to get. So if you didn't send the box, and it certainly doesn't belong to Solomon or I, then who did?"

"He said he has a sister," I say.

"*He* is sitting right here."

I glance at Merrick. "Okay, so, my . . . aunt, I guess?"

"I mean, yeah. My sister would be your aunt."

Right, yes, I understand how family lines work. He's definitely looking at me like I don't. "So, like. What if *she* sent it? What if she knows about me and—"

"Let me stop you right there, Carmen San Diego. That's not my sister's dig, okay. Emily is . . . unconcerned and unbothered and just generally ungoverned by anything that isn't hair bleach or red wine."

"Okay. But how do you know this isn't some big thing she's hiding?"

"Well," he says, the picture of logic and calm. Asshole. "I guess I don't. But it's probably not her."

"We can't rule it out on a probability. I need this to be definitive."

"Tasia, angel," Mamma says, but again, I'm on a roll, Miley Cyrus–style. I can't be freakin' tamed.

"I need to know the truth. Facts and not *probably*s or

*maybe*s. I need . . . to do this for me."

"Angel," Mamma says, shaking her head at me.

"I need this. That box means something. It means truth. It was sent *to me*. Someone meant for me to find this. Someone . . . cared enough to let me know."

I just can't help thinking maybe there's more to it. Whoever sent the box must know more than my parents.

When Tristan was maybe, I don't know, five-ish, he used to cry to Mamma about needing help with any number of things. Tying his shoe, or finding the TV remote, or putting his new one-million-piece LEGO set together—because that's Tristan. And Mamma, being Mamma, would oblige him. Hold his hand and basically *give him* what he needed.

And then Trist would tell her that wasn't right and attempt to solve his problems his own way. In the end, he always wound up following Mamma's instructions. But the point is, we were never sure we didn't know more than our parents. Tristan and I, we've never been the type to take the first answer. The easy route.

It's not who we were as kids and it's not who we've grown up to be.

So this thought—the thought that strikes me like a linebacker on a mission—comes on so suddenly, it must be followed.

Merrick is the first step to finding out who sent this small piece of me.

Merrick, who is sitting in our living room looking as shaken and off-balance as it's possible for any middle-aged white dude to look, I presume.

Merrick, who is still my best hope for getting any immediate answers.

Mamma will give me a solution that won't feel like a solution. And while it may end up being one . . . I can't trust her anymore. Who can I trust but myself right now?

Mamma's talking over Merrick, who's talking over Daddy, and they're all saying basically the same thing.

"Angel, you know we care about you. Daddy and I, we love you and—"

"We can take our time with this. There doesn't have to be any rush all because he's suddenly shown up here. If we take this through legal means—"

"I care. I wouldn't be here if I didn't care. I mean, we could maybe not involve my sister, if that's at all possible—"

Hope to possibility. A gamble. I have to figure this thing out. Because to keep going on like this . . . trash, honestly. I'm not for it. I wouldn't go entirely out of my mind because of it, but there wouldn't be any way for me to live in my skin anymore if I didn't try to figure this thing out. Not comfortably.

A roll of the dice. "I think I want to move in with Merrick," I mumble.

But they don't hear me. Of course they don't hear me. None of them are even looking at me. Which is hilarious if you consider that they're all talking about me.

A little louder. "I want to move in with Merrick!"

Finally, I have their attention. Which, honestly, is a lot. Having the full weight of a set of Black parents' attention on you is . . . yeah, yikes. But then to toss in the added weight of Merrick's disbelief—well. It's an interesting trifecta. He's like a real-life version of the white-guy-blinking GIF.

Mamma does the Black Woman Head Swivel, right in my direction. You know the one—starts in the neck, travels on a wave, lands with a crash as smooth and dangerous as any ocean could manage. "Excuse me?"

In for a freakin' penny. "I'm moving in with Merrick."

Merrick clears his throat. "Kid, I don't think your parents—"

"Are you not my parent?"

"Biologically, maybe. But there's a very fine and nuanced difference between . . . that and being a parent."

That's the thing, I think. That's the thing that gets Mamma to green light this ridiculous plan I've cooked up in her kitchen. He knows and understands what this means—not for me, but for Mamma and Daddy.

"Angel, we don't know what his living situation is like. We don't know *where* he lives."

Except I do know what his living situation is like and I do know where he lives, because I'm really handy with the Internet, and curiosity and cat killing, etcetera.

I turn to Merrick. "Please?"

One callused, tattooed hand comes up to rub his neck and then runs through the back of his hair. "Kid . . . I don't know."

"It's not like you live in a different state or like you're getting married anytime soon—"

"How would you know—"

"You gotta adjust your privacy settings on Facebook."

"Jesus."

"I'm honestly super low maintenance and I really need this, okay? I need to know what I'm missing." I can tell my argument isn't swaying him, so I push on, voice lower now. It's just he and I in this. "Put yourself in my shoes. I've been lied to for my entire life. *You've* been lied to for my entire life. And there's someone out there who's connected to us both and has known the truth. Don't you want to know who that person is? Don't you *need* to know who that person is? I gotta know." I pause. Take a breath. I keep forgetting that my breathing shouldn't be these short, shallow bumps of air escaping.

"I need to know for me," I say.

He's nodding with me now. Probably doesn't even know he's doing it. Almost got him.

"I need this. I'm asking you for this. Please."

He exhales through his mouth. Seems I'm not the only one having to control their breathing. "All right, kid. Let's do it."

"Yes!"

"But!" he says. "But, you gotta give me a couple days to put some sh—stuff in order."

Ugh, no. What. "But if—"

"Three days. That's all I'm asking. Not a lot."

"Merrick," Mamma says, finally reminding me she's still here. But Merrick holds up a hand. Not a "be silent, woman" hand but an "I've got this" hand. The former would've gotten him snatched.

"Three days," he says again.

I nod, the fight drains out of me. "I'll see you Thursday."

The sun is setting now, Merrick having left almost immediately after he agreed to shake his life up for me. Mamma and Daddy sat in the den for hours afterward. But still, they seemed to be as MIA mentally as Merrick is now physically.

I hate the way the light hits my bedroom windows during the warmest part of the day. There is no way to keep it out. Not blinds or curtains or freakin' plywood or anything. Right now, it's just one more thing for me to be mad at. The intensity of an LA sun—unlike any other.

I pull a duffel from my closet. It's old as dirt and, though it's empty, it contains the most memories. That's part of the reason I grabbed it.

Summer of ninth grade, Slim and I bought these matching canvas duffels and decorated them with spray paint, glitter glue, and markers. They are entirely ugly. Like, aggressively hideous. And it's not like I don't have other luggage. I do. But this is the one I need now, and I throw an assortment of clothes into it. My Thrasher tee, a pair of jeans I bought two sizes too big from the men's department of Macy's, some workout clothes because I live in them, a green dress that I can't fathom wearing but had to own anyway. Somehow it too makes it in there.

I'm packed much more quickly than I figured I would be.

It's not as if my life can be reduced down to one bag. My room actually looks pretty much the same.

My stomach growls and I wonder again where the day went and what percentage of it I've spent angry.

Mamma's voice is nothing more than an echo from downstairs as she speaks to Merrick on the phone, his name changing from two syllables to four as it leaves her lips and hits the walls. My head feels completely submerged under water.

I remind myself again—I asked for this. I need this. The alternative is staying here. And I can't do that. Not anymore.

Now, Daddy is nowhere to be found as Merrick and Mamma talk, and I wonder if that was his choice, if Daddy opted to be left out of this decision to let me leave.

Chapter Thirteen

GAME 3—WESTVIEW VS. MISSION BAY BUCCANEERS

The night before I'm set to leave comes sooner than I expect. Wednesday's game against the Bucks goes differently than I expect. I watch from behind the home team's bleachers, doing my best to remain unseen. The sun rummages through my skin and anxiety sits on the very top of my scalp. I should be out there.

We win. *They* win. Without me.

During it all, avoiding Slim like the plague is easier said than done; texts go unanswered, calls and her casual drive-bys are ignored. I remind myself that she loves me unconditionally. That our friendship has persevered through worse. (Like that time we ended up wearing the exact same dress to the eighth grade dance.)

The same happens with my team. I essentially go off the grid. There was already the understanding that I'd be spending the week recovering at home, but for the span of those two days, I really wash my hands of everyone.

It's easier than talking about answers I don't have, about how this box has basically claimed me and split me open.

Mamma and Daddy skip speaking to each other until they can't anymore. Until the night before.

Reaching for my phone on its charger, I press the side lock and see the time: 9:37 p.m.

Mamma and Daddy are arguing. He hasn't said a single word to me in the two days since the Big Talk.

With half of my heart beating in my throat while the other runs wild in my chest, I slip out of bed and press my head against the floor so I can hear their voices from under the doorjamb.

"Are you out of your mind? She's not leaving this house." Daddy has never been very good at arguing quietly. He does everything else at the lowest possible volume—talk, sing, whistle, walk. But it's like his passion is too big for his body. I always thought I got that from him.

"What choice do I have, Solomon? She wants to go!"

"She doesn't just get to have everything she wants. She doesn't even know what she wants. And giving in—that's not what parenting is."

"Who's giving in?"

"You are! Without discussing it with me at all."

"Don't you tell me how to raise my daughter, I know damn well—"

Daddy laughs. "Oh. She's *your* daughter now?"

"I—Solomon. N-no, I just . . . "

I exhale and imagine she's done the same. "I didn't mean it like that. I just . . . What choice do I have?"

"Tell her she can't go."

"And make her hate me even more? I can't do that."

"This isn't about whether or not she hates us. This is about pushing through this mess with as minimal damage as possible."

"I know that!"

I hate that she doesn't correct him. Nowhere in any of that is my best interest considered.

"So do your job, Sloane! Tell her she can't go! Why in the world do you think you can trust this guy to protect and raise our daughter?"

"I can't have her hate me for this one, Solomon. What about that don't you get? I know this isn't the best option or the best decision, and I don't trust Merrick d'Aquin even an iota, but this is me putting a Band-Aid on it. I am not just letting my kid pack a bag and leave."

"Yes, you are," I say. But no one is listening to me. I'm not even here.

Mamma says quietly, so quiet I almost don't hear it, "I'm at the end of my rope here. I don't know what to do." A pause. Then: "I don't know what I'm doing anymore."

I shouldn't have listened in. I knew I shouldn't have and I did. I grab a towel from the hamper in my closet and stuff it under the door, pull all my blankets from my bed, drag them as far from my door as possible. I end up underneath my computer desk, a blanket beneath me, a sheet on top, no pillow. The noise is muted. It's tiny blips of inconsequential sound, like the voice of the Peanuts teacher.

I swipe up and hit play on my phone. Daniel Caesar's voice breathes, "Let me know, do I still got time to grow? "

I fall asleep wondering the same.

Chapter Fourteen

Thursday: Merrick doesn't arrive until the streetlights come on.

He seems oblivious to the tension practically stacked on Mamma's shoulders, cracking jokes and talking about the architecture of Beverly Hills suburbs as though anyone has the capacity to give a shit currently. Daddy retreated to his study earlier this afternoon and hasn't returned. Normally, he's still at work this time on a Thursday, so there's absolutely nothing abnormal about him not being here, save for the fact I'm leaving and he's only steps away.

"Ready, Tasia?" Merrick says.

I look to Mamma. "No Tristan?"

"I called him. He's in the library. You know how he gets—phone's off, unreachable. But you'll see him, angel."

"Yeah," I say, hefting my bag up on my shoulder. Merrick takes it from me before I get it situated and hands me his keys. "So I guess I'm ready."

"Wanna get the car running and pull it around front? Wait—do you drive stick?" He turns to Mamma. "Can she drive stick?"

Mamma says, "She drives stick" just as I echo, "I can drive a fricking stick shift."

Merrick nods. He's uncomfortable. He's smiling too big and it only makes him look like a lost dog that's thrilled to be out of its gate.

"Let me talk to your mom for a sec?" he says. "Meet you in the car."

Mamma smiles at me, expectant, when I glance at her.

I turn away and head outside but not before I hear Merrick say to her, "Am I out of my depth here? Anything I should know about teen girls?"

With my duffle settled in the tiny backseat, I wonder why Tristen isn't here. Why he hasn't said goodbye to me.

I'm glad I don't hear the rest their conversation. I remind myself again that this is the getaway I asked for. The fresh start I need. I remind myself that they don't get it. That the box is tucked inside my canvas duffle and waiting for me to pick it apart. To find the truth.

Merrick drives like he just mainlined eight grams of cocaine in as many minutes.

He texts while he drives. I'm pretty sure he's supposed to lecture me about not doing that exact thing. He catches me staring and smiles, holds up his phone. "Had to cancel some plans."

This news makes me feel weird. Like chewing a spoonful of sugar. Unexpectedly unenjoyable. "Okay," I say. Thought that's what he had two days for.

It explodes out of my mouth when I ask, "How old are you?"

"Forty-three," he says, and grins big. According to that grin, forty-three is the new twenty-one, but I'm having trouble buying that, and he can tell, I think. "What? What's that face?"

"What face?"

"I don't know, like you just watched me blend up raw hamburger meat and drink it like a smoothie."

When he says this, my face doesn't change, so I know he's right. I shake my head.

"All right. You like this song?" Merrick says. He turns it up as the streetlights appear and then disappear, appear and then disappear in the car's dark interior.

I don't even know this song, but Merrick says, "The B-52s, man."

I want to laugh a little; he just called me "man." Like we're friends. I do laugh, because why shouldn't I? Then Merrick looks at me like we're in on the same Ponzi scheme and laughs a little too. I know he feels good about the fact that he made me laugh.

"You eat yet?"

No, and I'm so hungry, I'm about to start chewing on his leather seats. "Yes."

He hesitates. "Well, I gotta see a guy about some tacos. Think you'd be interested in that?"

"I like tacos."

"We have confirmation. Apparently you are my kid."

We don't actually hit up a taco place. I mean, this is Los Angeles and there are a ton of them. Open at all times of night and day. It would be relatively simple to find one and eat our body weight in carne asada tacos. Instead, we head down the hill, into the Valley. Merrick stops at a Whole Foods and loads up a cart with taco-making goods. A brick of cheese, carrots, which is weird, chicken, steak ("You eat meat, T?"—to which I nod), cilantro, an onion, some sort of bottled sauce, sour cream, avocado, and an orange—also weird.

He grabs a beer—some IPA Blasted Pointer or something—and then asks me if I want one.

I look at him like he's nuts.

He is.

And he laughs hysterically, just to prove it—so loud that other shoppers stare at us—before telling me to grab whatever non-alcoholic thing that I want, so I grab a jug of aloe water.

Merrick's apartment is weirdly homey. Nothing like a bachelor's apartment ought to be. It smells a little sweet, like laundry washed in too much detergent, and I like it.

He holds everything—my bags, the groceries—depositing our uncooked food on the counter before leading me to the back of the apartment, down a long hallway. He navigates the space in the dark and when I walk—*thud*—into a wall, he laughs and flips a switch on the wall to illuminate the space.

Merrick's guest room is a storage space, pretty much. There are boxes and gym equipment and easels—most of them are broken down—and the metal legs and wheels that go under a bed and, just so much stuff, including six guitars, a saxophone, and a cello. It's overwhelming.

"I really wasn't expecting you" is all he says.

I don't mention that he had two days. I suspect he was drinking himself silly and trying to grasp this new reality.

"It's okay." I don't beg him not to send me back, but I want to. Even though we're so not #north anymore. We're more west, actually. Northwest, technically, in the least Kimye way possible.

Even though Merrick is a stranger, I want to stay with him. He's my key to figuring out the unexplained parts of myself. He calls me "man" and offers me tacos and listens to cool music. He's musically inclined and he smells like the Citrus Spice fragrance of Downy and he makes me laugh and I just want to get to the part where I trust him already or have some more answers or know who sent me this package that flipped my life on its 3C head.

"Let's leave your stuff here. We'll make up the sofa bed in the living room for you until I can clear out this space. I have a bed in storage you can use. I'll move it in tomorrow while you're at school."

"I've a week of excused absence. Can't go back till Monday."

He's quiet. "Oh."

"I'm concussed."

"Oh," he says again. "That's right, your mom mentioned.

Okay, then maybe you can pull your weight and do the heavy lifting?"

And just like that he's made me laugh again. And I hug him because I feel like I can do that even though, probably, we're not there yet. But I wonder if this is step one on the trust scale. Like, maybe if there were a manual, this inter-action would be listed first.

He hugs me back immediately. He hugs me back tightly. And then he pushes me away from him and says, "Let's make you some street tacos."

With his arm draped around my shoulders, we walk back into the kitchen, pinging against the hallway walls like we're inside a pinball machine.

My hypothesizing about how he spent his two days is basically confirmed when I glance over at his trash can and next to it is a fruit box filled to the brim with empty beer bottles.

At least he recycles.

But we do make the best damn gentrified street tacos I've ever had.

When Merrick pulls out the mystery bottle, I see it's peanut sauce and I stop him before he opens it. "I'm, like, deathly allergic to peanuts. Like, you would actually kill me if you opened that."

I can see the confusion happening for him.

I try very hard not to think about the fact that I left my EpiPen in my haste to come here. It's the kind of worry I wouldn't have an issue telling Mamma or Daddy about. But I can't open my mouth to say anything to Merrick about needing it.

But maybe that's unnecessary now, because in under a second, the bottle is tossed—closed—into the garbage. "Close call," Merrick says. "Sometimes you can do a bit of a fusion thing, with chicken and the carrots and peanut sauce. Sort of a bastardized bahn mi taco."

I shrug.

"No problem," he says, and he cooks up everything with sesame oil instead, and we don't talk about my family life or my allergy or Mamma or any of that while we eat.

Instead, we talk football. "Cornerback? No shit?"

I shake my head, no, none.

"The kid plays cornerback!"

I want to ask him who he's yelling this to. I don't think he even knows what a cornerback does.

"I love that. How hard was it to get them to let you play?"

"Hard. I had to do all this research on past cases, look up the laws and stuff. It helps that Daddy is a lawyer becau—" I stop.

Merrick smiles. "It's okay, T. It's all right. He's still your dad, okay? Solomon is still your father. So, what's the worst battle wound you've gotten from playing?"

I peel my knee-high sock down to show him the sick green-blue-purple-yellow bruise on my shin.

"Gnarly."

"Yep. It's not the worst, but it's the worst I've had in a while. You paint?"

"I do paint, yeah. Or I'm trying to. They say it's a good stress reliever."

"Are you stressed?"

"Isn't everyone?"

I shrug. Did I do it? Is it my fault? Does my existence stress him out? "Is that your job—painting?"

"It is not my job."

"What is? You still teach? Or is the music thing, like, it."

He shakes his head but says, "I compose film scores. So, yeah. The music thing is it."

"Mm. Music for movies."

"Film scores, yeah. Mostly for movies, but . . . you've seen the website."

Awkward. Yeah, I have, haven't I.

Still, it's weirdly impressive. He's so right-brained, whereas both my parents are left-brained.

"What're you working on now?" I pile the leftover onions and cilantro on my plate with my index, middle, and thumb fingers.

Merrick smiles into his plate. "I'm not actually—"

He's interrupted by a knock at the front door. And before I even have enough time to wonder if it's Mamma come to bring me back or Tristan come to verbalize all his disappointment with me, Merrick taps my wrist twice with his fingers.

Without waiting to be let in, a boy enters. Or, he's that awkward cross between a boy and a man in the same way that I am the uncomfortable cross between a girl and a woman. He's not terribly tall, though at five-foot-four myself he's easily five or six inches taller than I am. The perfect candidate for any *My acne was so embarrassing* commercial, his face is curiously clear of it. Dark brown hair, though it's shaved close to his scalp and mostly covered by a cap, and skin the color of whiskey diluted with tepid milk.

It's not until he comes fully into the room that I notice what a frickin' weirdo he is.

His eyes are two different colors, like they couldn't pick just one before the womb spit him out, the right one blue and heavy, the left, broken and hazel. He's got four different earrings in each ear, gauges at the lobes, and a hand-rolled cigarette tucked behind the right side. A backwards pink cap on his head, a fur-lined vest over his tie-dye tee, and a blue bandana around his neck.

I'm painting a picture here that even I couldn't dream up. At least the black jeans and boots are kinda normal.

He pops the hand-rolled into his mouth. "Who's the broad?"

I hate that his voice is so *yes* when, with every word, I'm a little more annoyed. And, like, when he speaks and that little vein pops out in the side of his neck, I want to salute him and say, "Keep up the great work, sir."

I don't, though. Because attractive boys think they get to have everything and say whatever they want, and that's just not the way I'm operating.

Merrick stands and takes our plates to the kitchen. "Call my daughter a broad again, Kai. I'll kick your ass down that flight of stairs you just walked up."

"Since when do you have a fucking kid?" The boy laughs. "Merrick. Merrick," he says, following Merrick around the kitchen island. "I have to tell you something."

Merrick's undivided attention is a little intimidating, but the boy takes it head-on. "Yeah."

"Your daughter is Black."

"Get out."

"What?" he yells. "C'mon. I was joking. I mean, not about her being Black—she is seriously, actually that."

"Get the hell out, El Khoury."

"El Khoury?" I say.

"Kai El Khoury. That's my name. And, listen, I'm just here to see a man about some tacos. I was only kidding. Mulatta." The boy turns to me. "Tell your sperm donor I was only joking."

I laugh. Easy on the eyes, yet annoying and politically incorrect. Add to that, entirely ridiculous. He's his own person, that's for sure. Dancing to the beat of his own timpani and all that.

What the hell kind of drugs does he do?

"I'm clean. I don't touch drugs ever. Crack is whack, yikes no pipes, and my Adderall is prescribed."

Damn. Did I say that out loud?

"Yeah," Merrick says. "You talk to yourself often, T?"

"No, I don't."

"T like Tease? Like, coc—"

"Go home, Kai!" Merrick shouts.

"After tacos." And the boy, Kai or whoever, walks into the kitchen and makes himself a plate of like fifty tacos.

"What's your name, mulatta?"

"If I tell you, will you stop calling me mulatta? That's a slave reference."

"Not in my country it's not."

I scoff. "Where's your country?"

"What's your name?" he volleys back.

Merrick returns to the table, pulls the hand-rolled out of Kai's mouth, and rips it in half. "He doesn't have a country. Asshole's adopted. Doesn't know where he's from or why he's so goddamn ethnic."

The way these two talk to and about each other. Jesus.

"The reports strongly suggest my origins are Turkish."

"Strongly suggest," Merrick mouths at me.

"You can call me Uncle Kai."

"Uncle?"

"That's not funny, Kai. My parents adopted him," Merrick adds helpfully.

"I . . . have grandparents." I shake my head. It's so weird to think about having this whole other set when I've so recently lost a set. Figuratively.

"You do. Mémé and Pépé. It's French for *grandmother* and *grandfather*."

"I figured." Then, "Think they knew about me? Do they know about me now?"

"Not a chance they knew. And, uh, no, not yet. Haven't been able to sit them down and . . . you know," Merrick says.

"I was born there, you know."

He's no good at changing the subject in subtle ways. "In France?"

"Yeah. We lived there awhile before my parents decided to move here."

I raise an eyebrow and twist my curls up into a topknot. Kai's eyes follow the movement.

"Really?" I say.

"Ouí," Kai says. "But they're severely French. Kinda. I mean, considering how long they've lived in America. So, your name, infime?"

I glance at Merrick to be sure Kai's not calling me a soul-sucking bitchcunt or something.

Merrick clarifies: "Tiny."

I nod. "Taze."

"Who?" Kai says.

"No. I'm not asking you to Taze anyone. That's my name. Tasia, but Taze."

"Well, that's dope," Kai says with a mouthful of taco.

Damn right it is.

Chapter Fifteen

At night, I fall asleep to a recording Merrick's put together for a new film coming out later next year. His biggest job yet, he says. But when he tells me the name of the film, I don't know it. Apparently, most of the music he's composing either goes unused or gets paired with an underwhelming film or some witching hour infomercial. "That's showbiz, but money is money," he laughs.

"Fall asleep" is probably a reach. I toss and turn for long hours and only *think* about the box. I can't bring myself to get up, walk into the other room, and get it. Not yet.

I'm frozen by how close I might be to figuring things out. Can't decide if it's good or not, even after spending the past few days thinking all I needed was answers. And now that I'm this close, I'm not sure if that's all I'll need.

Maybe answers are just the catalyst.

Maybe I should be reaching for more.

Am I even allowed to ask for more at this point?

The springs in his couch poke into my ribs, but despite that, I do fall asleep eventually.

Salt to a paper cut, I have weird dreams that speak to my abandonment issues in spades. In one of the dreams, me, Trist, Mamma, and Daddy go to the park for a picnic. Mamma unloads the basket and hands a drink to everyone except me.

She tells me she forgot. Forgot to bring my drink.

I wake up crying and nothing about it feels like a release.

Merrick is a light sleeper, so he wakes up with me. He hugs me awkwardly and I sit stiffly in his arms until my muscles begin to ache and I fall asleep again.

In the morning, Merrick makes what he calls "eggs in a basket." A slice of toast with a hole cut in the middle. Then you coat a skillet in butter and crack an egg in the middle of the bread until it's fried enough to flip.

It's amazing: the sweetness of the butter, the just-enough salt and cracked black pepper Merrick adds—it doesn't need anything else. Mamma would love it, and I wonder for a few minutes if she's ever had Merrick's eggs in a basket.

I shove in a too-big-to-really-call-it-polite bite and hollow out my mouth to cool it. "So I was thinking maybe we could have coffee or something with your sister."

Merrick drops an egg just as Kai walks in again. He left so suddenly last night, right after he wolfed down his second plate of bahn mi tacos, offering nothing more than a solid "See ya later, Taser."

"Well, good morning, fam," Kai says. He's got on a baby

blue hoodie today with a graphic of an anime toast girl, and brown corduroys.

"Is that OMOCAT?"

Kai glances up from the fidget spinner in his hands. "Yeah! You know their stuff?"

"I love their stuff."

He nods, a smile ticking up the right side of his too-wide mouth.

Go away, blush. Go! Get outta here. God, he's cute.

"You want eggs in a basket, Kai?"

He sits on the barstool next to me. "Yes, please. But can we discuss a name change for it? 'Eggs in a basket' is so—"

"Juvenile," I say, just as Kai says, "Suggestive."

Huh. Opposite sides of the coin.

Much like Kai and me. I kinda like that about people. It's why I love Slim so much. We're so different. She's everything I'm not.

I wonder if Kai could be that too.

I wonder if Slim will burn all the clothes she's ever borrowed from me when she learns I'm thinking things like this. When she learns I'm keeping things from her. The guilt sits in my stomach like a gas station burrito.

My brain needs a redirect. "So, Merrick? Coffee? With dear old sis?"

Kai nearly falls off his stool with laughter.

"What the hell is wrong with him?" I say.

He can't contain himself. He might be having a heart attack induced by laughter. The feeling that sets up shop in my chest isn't anger per se. It's, like, mild embarrassment mixed with some amusement? I think?

"Sorry, sorry," he says, then turns to Merrick. "But, please, do not give her to Emily!" He grabs his head as if Emily's in there attacking his brain meat with a pick-ax.

"Give her to—What?" Merrick's definitely burning some eggs by now. Or the basket. Or both? Whatever. "What's wrong with Emily? I mean, I know *what's wrong* with Emily. But what's wrong with Emily?"

"Yeah," I say. "What's wrong with Emily?"

Kai stands, places his hands on his thin hips. "Oh, you know. Nothing. Except that she's a loud drunk and she's awful."

Okay, so the answer is everything. *Everything* is wrong with Emily. Aunt Emily.

But I wonder if that's just proof positive. That she maybe sent the box. Or that she knows who did. My heart starts to beat overtime in my throat, and the physical sensation of what I can only call anxiety sits in my stomach and flops around like a fumbled football.

I have to talk to her.

"Merrick, will you set it up?"

He glances at me, then slides a stacked plate in front of Kai. "Why are you so intent on this?"

"Please?"

He exhales. "You're really gonna fight me on this, huh?"

"I just . . . yeah. So, will you please?"

"All right, all right. I'll call her. See when she's free."

My stomach plunges again, if that is even possible at this point.

"So what's your deal?" Kai says, mouth full of food.

I point. "You got a little something. There on your chin."

He doesn't even look up at me. Just smiles into his plate as he uses his fork to chop another massive slice off his basket of eggs or whatever. "I know. This for now, that for later. So?"

"I don't know. I don't have a deal."

"Aha. But you're hashtag out here trying to have coffee with Satan's favorite Barbie doll."

She sounds kinda cool. "She's my family."

"Mm," he grunts, mouth full. Then he pulls a pen out of his pocket and grabs my arm. He writes ten digits on it in the world's most delicate penmanship. "If I'm not around when you meet her, text me. Before, during, after, I don't care."

"Why? So you can say I told you so?"

"No," he says. "So I can come over and we can shit-talk her. Shit-talking someone is always more fun when all parties are on the same page."

I mean, yeah, I guess so, but . . . "That really the only reason you want me to text you?"

Finished with his meal, he finally lifts his head, comes up for air. "What other reasons would there be?"

I flick his shoulder. Walk away. "I'm going for a run."

Saturday, Kai's MIA and Merrick is napping, which seems weird for someone his age, and it's honestly the first time in a while I can say I'm bored, which is how I find myself as I'm sitting upside down on the couch with my head hanging off the end, wondering if stars feel things.

Slim's name lights up my phone and I stare at it overly long before actually answering it this time. Mostly out of guilt, but I'd be lying if I said that boredom didn't play a role.

"Wow, well hello, stranger. Nice to know you haven't bitten the steel end of a—"

"Stacy, please be more dramatic."

"What! This isn't Dramatic Slim, Tasia. This is Pissed-Off Slim. I am angry at you and I'm even more angry that you think you can condescend to me about it. And if the roles were reversed, *you* would be just as peeved, so stop trying to make me feel like I'm overreacting."

I pause. She's right. "I'm sorry," I say.

"My feelings are valid," she continues. "And you'd know that if you—wait, what? What'd you say?"

"I said, I'm sorry. I'm sorry I made fun of your feelings and I'm sorry I've been shutting you out."

"Say you're sorry for being a shit friend."

"Slim . . . "

"Say it, Tasia."

"I am sorry for being a shit friend, Stacy."

"Good. What else."

What else? "I sweater God—"

She laughs. "Okay, fine, fine! I feel like I don't even know you anymore. How are you? How's everything with your fam?"

"Uh. Okay. Just . . . if I tell you this thing, will you promise not to be upset with me?"

"I don't make promises I don't know that I can keep."

"You need to promise me right now or I won't tell you." I will. But she doesn't know that. Or probably she does. Slim is my best friend for a reason.

"I hate you. Scout's honor, or whatever."

"Good. Okay. Cool. So, uh. I sorta moved in. With Merrick. My birth dad."

She's quiet. And the music I heard playing in the background goes suddenly silent.

"Slim?" She says nothing. "Stace? Stacy."

"*You moved in with a stranger!*"

I flip off the couch and fast-walk into the other room. "Oh my God, he's not a stranger, he's my dad."

"Your dad that you don't know. Your dad who is *a stranger.*"

"Stop. Saying that."

"Does your mom know you're there?" She gasps, then, all in one breath: "Ohmigod. Did you *run away? Are you a runaway?*"

"What kind of afterschool special . . . Slim. No. I didn't run away. My mom knows I'm here. I found him. And then he came over and we all . . . uh, you know. *Talked.*"

"Talked?"

"Aha."

I hit the speaker button on my phone and fall into a backbend, as I spend the next few minutes explaining to Slim what happened.

When I'm done, she says, "I just want you to know, I am *so mad at you*. I'm still just incredibly pissed that you kept all this from me."

"I didn't want to talk about it. I didn't want you to ask me a million questions."

"Why?"

"Slim. You see? Don't ask questions. Just . . . leave it. I don't know anything yet. I don't have answers. I just needed someone to get it. And I don't think anyone really can. So I left."

Here's why Slim is my best friend though. She says, "Wanna see a movie with me and some girls from the team?"

Laughing, I fall out of the backbend. "Who?"

"Jessa and Kelan."

I agree, jumping on the chance to get out of this apartment. All I want now is to hug my best friend. That's all I want.

After I hang up, I head into the bathroom to change, but Merrick stops me.

"Who are you going with?"

I stop. I guess he overheard.

He's asking me who I'm going to hang out with, and honestly, it's weird. Mamma and Daddy never ask. Not because they're bad parents, but definitely because they know I'm always with one of three people—Slim, Josiah, or Tristan.

"Slim. My best friend. And two other cheerleaders."

"You play football but hang out with cheerleaders?"

"This isn't the nineties, Merrick. I hang out with the Drama Club and the band and the stoners, too." What a lot of people—parents—don't know is that in most high schools, you take friends anywhere you can get them, so long as their interests speak to yours on some level. And eventually, you become a cheerleader who plays clarinet and blazes, too.

Merrick nods like this is news to him. "And Slim is . . . female?"

"Yeah. Stacy Lim, so, Slim."

"Ah. Clever. Got it. She got a weight problem?"

"Merrick."

"All right." He holds up his hands.

"So, I'm going," I gesture to the bathroom but say it like that's my way out. It kind of is. This conversation, it's not an interrogation per se. But it's not the "have fun, be safe" send-off Mamma usually gives either.

"Yeah, yeah. Of course."

Once I'm changed, Merrick gives me the address here so Slim can pick me up. He offers to give me twenty bones cash, but I decline. I've had a debit card for as long as I can remember and Daddy has always given us—Tristan and I—an allowance based on our grades. I can't go out and buy several hundred dollars' worth of cocaine or anything, but I can do dinner and a movie with my friends anytime the thought strikes me.

I know I'm privileged. That thought doesn't ever escape me. I have it good. But it is obvious Merrick lives paycheck to paycheck with small bouts of frivolous spending and lavishness sprinkled in.

I thank Merrick for the offer even though I've never thanked Daddy.

As I slide into Slim's front seat, she leans over to look out my window. "That him?"

"Hello, Stacy. Who?" I glance over. Merrick's standing in the doorway glancing down at us from the top of the stairway. "Oh. Merrick? Yeah."

"He is sexy."

I turn on her like she just ripped a chunk of curls out of the back of my head. "Eww, what?"

"Not, like, *sexy* . . . I meant, like, *dad sexy*."

"Eww, what?"

"What?" She makes a left turn.

"Can you not."

Slim lifts her hands off the wheel, steers with her knee. "Okay."

I explain everything—about Merrick and his basket of eggs or whatever, about Kai El Khoury, except I try to keep that part brief, lest she think I'm more invested in him than I'm ready to admit so soon.

I change the subject before she can ask any questions in her very Slim-like way. "So remind me, who's coming to the movie?"

As we pull into the parking lot and Slim parks her Miata, she gives me the rundown. And I'm shocked. It's mostly football guys, plus the two cheerleaders she mentioned. Which would be fine if that were Slim's bread and butter. The football guys are not her preferred company. I am Slim's preferred company. And Slim is my best friend because we have almost no personal interests in common. What we do have is where we come from, what we look like, and where we go to school. And maybe that's enough.

I think one of the things that makes us closest is that we're just more comfortable around girls than guys. That isn't any less true because I play football and she cheers. Two sides, same coin.

At eighteen, I don't think either of us has it entirely figured out. We still laugh too loudly and for far too long at things. We also know what it takes to get a boy and keep a boy—and neither of us is new to that, but who wants to operate like that all the time anyway? Constantly on. Constantly fighting whatever it takes not to eat your lunch too fast, or to ask the members of your lunch table to clarify something that might make you look dumb.

But it's nice. After the movie, the other cheerleaders leave and Slim and I are the only girls, and that's weird, but we still enjoy ourselves. We all pile into a booth at Duke's, and it's only then that I realize Josiah and Slim are talking to each other more than either of them is talking to me.

Slim touches his arm, and he flicks one of her tight little barrel curls.

Josiah picks a stray eyelash off her cheek, and she shoves him a little every time he makes her—*specifically her*—laugh.

All in all, it's a nice distraction before I ask Slim to take me North, to my house, so I can pack a few more things and get my Jeep.

Luckily my parents aren't home.

Luckily Tristan is, because I'm hoping he'll help me carry some of the heavier things out to my car.

Tristan does not help me carry a single stitch out to my car.

"Have you even thought about this?" he says as he follows me outside, a spectator. No Good Samaritaning for this Quirk child.

Jerk.

"Trist, don't talk to me like I'm five. It's already happened. This place, Mamma and Daddy, they make me uncomfortable. If you were in my place you'd—"

"Get it," he finishes. "Yeah. I know."

"Okay, so just . . . stop acting like I'm leaving the country." It's so far beyond what I'm used to from Trist, this reaction. I would never wish this on someone else. Ever. But I do wish he really could understand.

"Whatever. See you at school." And that's all he says before he walks back into the house and I continue to load my life into my nineties-era monstrosity on wheels.

When I get back to Merrick's after nearly an hour and a half of sitting in bumper-to-bumper traffic on the 405 North, he's asleep on "my" couch, wearing the paint jeans and a white T-shirt with a tear around the collar.

I wheel my suitcases into the back bedroom and find the bed Merrick promised is there. There are sheets, pillows, and blankets on it.

Instead of storage, the space is now my new bedroom. And it's great. I love the way the ceiling is too high to reach and how there's a skylight. How there's a reading nook right next to the window. But even given all that, I still don't feel good about calling this place "home."

There's a Post-it stuck loosely to my pillow.

Dinner with Emily tomorrow at nine. Been in OZ 2 months and now she's back, you're welcome. Let me know if you want to cancel. I would be happy to do exactly that. (I mean, there's nothing wrong with her that you should WORRY about, but. Just.) Anyway, you're welcome. —Merr

I close the door and lock it. Take my clothes off and sprawl, naked, as exposed as I can possibly get, on the floor for long minutes.

Chapter Sixteen

"How do you like your new space, kiddo?"

My first thought the next morning is whether Merrick will make me breakfast every day from now on. Because he's at it again, but this time it looks like French toast.

I don't miss the fact that a woman wanders out of his room. She doesn't speak to me or acknowledge me in any way. She's pretty. Got dark skin, like Mamma. But where Mamma has dreads she's been nurturing for years, this girl has hair like mine. A lion's mane of tightly spiraled curls, hers inky where mine are copper and gold.

She lifts an arm in the air and calls out, "See you later, Merry. Thanks!" as she leaves.

My second thought—curiously enough—isn't about her or who she is or her awful taste in nicknames, even though maybe it should be. No, my second thought is if Merrick really thinks it's okay to call me "kiddo."

"My space is good. I can just eat cereal, you know. Or a granola bar."

"Bah. Cereal? Really, kid? Cereal? Cereal isn't real food."

I shrug. "Umm. Hey. Was that your . . . girlfriend? Or . . . ."

He laughs? He *laughs*. "No, not my girlfriend. She's my friend."

"Your super-comfortable sex-friend?" It'll be, honestly, just really fricking annoying if Merrick is That Guy.

He chokes on his sip of coffee. It's better than laughter. "Jesus Christ, Tasia."

"I'm eighteen. I know what an FWB is."

"I don't!"

I lift a finger as I explain each one. "Friend. With. Benefits. She's your fuck-friend." I shrug.

"I don't think your mother would like that you just swore. Now, back to breakfast?"

"Are you telling me not to?"

"Swear?"

I nod.

"No, it happens."

Okay. "There won't be time for French toast and eggs in a basket on school days."

Merrick stops abruptly. "School days."

"Yeah. The mornings before school. Six a.m. wake-ups. Although, now probably five a.m., since commuting will take an hour and a half with traffic instead of fifteen minutes."

"Commuting?"

"Merrick. The travel time relative to distance between places? You know what a commute is."

He waves that away. "No, no, no. I know that. It's just . . . I honestly didn't think you'd last the weekend. Which is—well, that's on me, but, I should have taken you seriously. Should have planned better and considered the reality of all this."

The feeling that comes over me is like when you turn a ceiling fan off and it slowly comes to a stop. "I—Oh. You didn't mean for me to . . . ? But the bed?"

"Yeah. For when you visit. I thought you'd visit from time to time. Maybe a couple weekends, or a week here and there over summer, or—Kid, I just didn't know you were serious about being here, and—"

Here they are. The outpouring of words, building inside me that I've got no control over.

"Oh, no. See . . . Taze . . . er—Tasia. I just—"

Aaaaaand here's the levee. The dam. The fissure, the crack. Broken. Drowning in this heavy tornado of emotional sludge.

"I can't live with her," I say, as though he's suggested something so outrageously disgusting, something so laughably ridiculous. "They don't get it. They don't get it at all." Oh God. "Dammit," I whisper. "They lied to me."

"Tasia—"

"They lied to me. They lied to me. They lied to me and nothing will change that. And you know what, I still don't even know why they lied, because none of them will help me understand. Because none of them *can* help me understand." By the end of it, I'm screaming. Shouting at him.

And he's holding me together and he's whispering that I can stay, that he'll talk to them and make it right, that he's glad

I trust him. And that just makes the tornado swirl faster in the cavity of my chest, because I don't. I don't trust him. I want to, but I don't yet. But I'd rather stay with a near stranger than these people who have lied to me my whole life. Merrick's just the lesser of two evils. Merrick is the new start that I wanted, that getaway I asked for. Merrick is my skeleton key to that rusted lock of a box. Merrick is a means to an end.

Soon he's on the phone with Mamma.

I get a text from Tristan that seems to come only minutes after Merrick gets off the phone with her.

he's pulling you out of westview?? seriously? he's about to pull you out of school?

I shrug as I text him back. I don't have words. *I dont wanna go back there*

to wv?

to that house, tristan

He doesn't text back.

It's after-hours on a Sunday, but I hear Merrick on the phone, the speaker blaring at full volume, the tinny voicemail cracking like it's pushing through puberty, as Merrick leaves a message for who I assume to be the administrative team at El Camino Real High School. After Merrick hangs up, he asks me to log on to my Westview web portal and print my unofficial transcripts. And that's when the realization starts to really settle in my bones, in my chest, in my heart and lungs, if this anxiety is anything to go by.

ECR. My new school. It's north, but not my kind of #north. This is *Valley north*. Too north. So north, it's rank.

I start tomorrow and it might almost be a good thing because I'm pretty sure I heard Merrick mention Kai goes there, except then there's all the things I don't think about.

Not until they're right up in my face.

Chapter Seventeen

So, Emily is batshit crazy.

She's a mess of frizzy blond hair a la Taylor Swift circa 2006. It's a little daunting, all that frizz. It could almost be sentient, I'm pretty sure. But she handles it well, which makes sense since she's a hair stylist, according to Merrick.

Her blond, though. It looks like mine. Or, I guess technically mine looks like hers.

"Look at you!" she says. She comes at me like I'm a rescue dog she's about to save from the pound. "Oh, my God, I'm in love with your hair. It's so . . . *bushy.*"

She did not just . . .

At first I think this might be the thing that makes it easier to interrogate her.

I'm wrong.

She piles on hard, that woman. So hard, it's difficult to get a word or a thought or a blink in edgewise.

The thing about Kai thinking she's awful is that now I think she's awful and I can't see any way around her awfulness.

But if I hadn't known how Kai felt, it would have been solidified after this first meeting. Because now I have my own proof. Tristan once told me that it only takes seven seconds to form an impression of someone upon first meeting them.

Within those seven seconds, three things happen in quick succession.

She stains my face with wine by kissing me on the cheek.

She compliments me by complimenting herself. "Oh, she's gorgeous, Merr. She's got our eyes"—then to me—"You've got eyes like mine."

And, third, her hands go to my hair. "You know. I could do a thing or two with this. Fix you up a little. Bone-straighten it out. You'd have so much length, beautiful."

Merrick tries to divert by offering to cook, but Emily says she has "*bags and bags*" of organic foodstuffs in her car. I don't know what she's planning to make, but Kai has already said he has no plans to eat it.

"Girl, I ain't eating whatever you got in those bags." He's been vocal. Loudly. Multiple times from the couch across the living room.

And though he "ain't touching that mess," he does still somehow see fit to volunteer us both to retrieve the groceries. Emily pulls a bottle of red out of her purse and asks Merrick where the corkscrew is.

Oh, thank God she managed to bring the wine in.

"Don't leave," I say to Kai once we're downstairs and unlocking Emily's car. I wonder if he'll at least stick around long enough for me to question Emily.

"I can't stay here. I'll strangle Emily before she even makes it to the bottom of the bottle—and that's going to happen very fast, Taze. Very fast."

I groan and we carry the bags back up to the garage apartment.

We're in there five seconds before Kai decides to be a traitor and says he's leaving. I trail him to the door, he hugs me and presses his lips to my ear, whispers, "Don't let her touch your hair," before he's gone.

I shiver from the remnants of his whisper, and then again at the thought of being alone with Merrick and Emily together. That second trail of goose bumps is entirely different and unwelcome near the first.

But it's the peripheral sight of the box in the corner that gives me purpose. The little kick of *can't stop, won't stop* that I need.

Dinner is mostly bread and cheese and a mixed medley of sautéed vegetables, which Emily says is "a Frenchman's way." I don't know what this means, but I thank Merrick repeatedly for stepping in and taking over most of dinner. I wind up having to remind him about my peanut allergy two separate times as he cooks.

We're having after-dinner drinks—I'm having water— when I finally build up the courage to say something to Emily.

There's a running loop in my head about balancing grace and politeness with curiosity, and then there's an even wider loop around that first loop that's basically screaming, GET YOUR QUESTIONS ANSWERED AND SEND YT FEMINISM BARBIE ON HER PINOT NOIR WAY. It's an effort not to gulp my water but to sip it slowly. "So how long have you been living in the city, Emily?"

Okay. That definitely feels casual. Right?

Jesus.

"Well, after finishing college—"

"Dropping out," Merrick coughs out.

"Whatever! After *dropping out* of college, I moved back here and stayed with Merr awhile."

Interesting.

"So you two are pretty close, then?" Close enough that you'd know he had a secret daughter.

She laughs. "God, no. We're not close. Merrick is just too nice to tell me no."

"I see."

Merrick, who is studiously ignoring us, grunts.

"What were you studying in college?"

"I wasn't studying, really, but it definitely says biology on my transcript." Emily laughs too loud as she takes in a mouthful of wine.

"Biology?"

"I wanted to be a doctor. Can you believe that? Me. A doctor." More laughter. More wine. And more wine again.

"Oh, wow," I say. I am very clearly the picture of innocent and interested. "I've got a friend doing an internship at Cedars-Sinai. Ever been there?"

"Tasia," Merrick warns.

But Emily bulldozes forward. "Nah, I hate hospitals. Probably the only reason I haven't gotten plastic surgery yet." She turns to Merrick. "Think Mom and Dad are pretty pleased about that one."

Mom and Dad. Grandparents. "I see."

Emily giggles.

"What?"

"Nothing, just . . . when you say 'I see' like that, I can totally see how you're Merrick's kid."

"And that wasn't apparent before?"

"Not like that, but, I mean. Merrick owns one pair of jeans and they're covered in paint."

"I own more than one pair of jeans, Emily."

"Mm-hmm. I just can't really see him being somebody's *dad*. When he told me about you, I laughed, like, totally just laughed in his face." She turns to him. "Still totally sorry about that, Merr. I'm an asshole. Anyway, he got all serious and then I had to get serious back and finally I believed him when he said you wanted to meet me."

She makes it seem like I was begging to meet her. Like she's that important to me.

Her answers? Those are important—or, they were. Not anymore.

It's obvious she had nothing to do with the box. I even left it out on top of the bookshelf and she hasn't glanced at it once. I don't even feel that sad about it. I think I kinda knew it wasn't her dig. If I'd taken my time and sat down and really thought about it, I'd have realized that. Just based on what Merrick has said about Emily.

Also, I mean, okay: Emily hasn't even been *in the country* the past two months.

Plus, like, Emily is one sandwich short of a picnic basket. There's no way she schemed all this and sent me that box. There's no way in hell or heaven.

And I'm not, like, the queen of reading people or anything, but this doesn't seem like an elaborate lie or a cover-up. She seems more invested in her split ends or how her wineglass suddenly somehow got empty again.

"Yeah, yeah, I was real stoked to meet you. And my grandparents."

Merrick, who is mostly not paying attention to us, speaks up again. Another warning. "Tasia Lynn."

He almost sounds like a dad. Huh. Interesting.

"Oh, Mom and Dad will love your stupid guts, I promise." Emily tucks a strand of hair behind her ear, and then, after pondering the risk, she does the same to mine.

I flinch away but not quick enough.

"So, my grandparents. How lovely, what are they like, when can we meet?" All of this I say louder than is necessary. I enunciate every syllable and make sure to death stare at Merrick for the last part so he knows the ball is, ultimately, in his court.

"Soon, Tasia. Soon. Just give me some time. We have time, let's take it."

I recline, bang the back of my head against the rocking chair I'm sitting in. And then I do it again, because I can and because it makes Merrick uncomfortable to see me simmering with a little bit of anger.

Mamma would have snapped her fingers and given me A Look. Would've cleared that up right away.

Daddy would have kissed my forehead and walked away from me without another word or acknowledgment.

"Fine, fine. Ix-nay on the meeting the and-gray-arents-pay."

"Well, I mean. I'm sure you'll get to soon," Emily says. She stands, searches the floor for her other very ugly strappy sandal heel, and ultimately finds it under the couch. "Anyway, Mom and Dad will probably flip once they find out."

"You haven't told them about me yet, Merrick?"

It's as though he's been caught in the middle of some playful mischief. He is a boy, chastened.

Tristan and I used to watch *The Andy Griffith Show* with our Poppa. His reaction reminds me of it. All big exaggerated gestures and forced nonchalance. It's just not the kind of response you expect from an adult man meant to be your dad, TBH.

I don't exactly have any reason to doubt his word, so when he says, "Not yet. But I will. Patience, young Padawan," I accept the fact that he just changed the subject.

Head cocked to one side, I say, "Is that a rapper?"

"Oh, my God."

Emily laughs behind her hand. "You'd call them Mémé and Pépé. That's what Kai calls them. That's what all the neighborhood kids call them. I mean," she rushes to add, "you don't have to call them that. They're your grandparents.

You call them whatever the hell you want."

"I see. So, where do they live?"

"Porter Ranch," Emily says.

So not far from Merrick's side of the Valley. It wouldn't be difficult to get to their place for dinner or coffee or a quick HERE'S YOUR LONG-LOST GRANDDAUGHTER drop-in.

Just before Emily leaves, she stretches, promises Merrick she's "good to drive," and then whispers, "Welcome to the family," in my ear as she hugs me goodbye.

And just when I think she's not so bad, she turns around and yells from her car, "I always wanted a little sister!"

Jesus Christ.

Kai definitely owes me reparations for this.

Chapter Eighteen

That night, after exactly three minutes in the shower before the water goes cold thanks to Merrick's marathon shower prior, I sit on my bed and text Josiah about what happened. Tell him I'm leaving Westview, that I am no longer on the team.

That part, the part where I'm going to lose what I think are all the best pieces of me, is the thing I hate most. I'm giving up so much to escape all this hurt my parents have practically covered me in, and it's finally occurring to me that escape comes at a cost. That there is a fee for answers. For untangling the headphone cord of lies Mamma and Daddy have let me live.

My phone starts to blare in my hand. It's Siah on FaceTime, so I answer quickly.

I hold the phone in front of me. "Hey—"

"Is this a joke?" he says. "Tell me you're kidding."

"Kidding about which part?" I didn't tell him about my parents, but I'm sure he'll find out.

"All of it, Taze. Obviously. You pulling out of school and not being on the team? What are we supposed to do in the middle of the season!"

"Would you *please* stop yelling like this isn't also a thing that affects me?"

He's sitting in the massive computer chair I know is meant to accompany the desk in his room but somehow always ends up *not* near that desk. He pushes off against the wall and goes rolling across the room. "I know. Sorry."

His phone beeps and he pulls it down to look at the notification.

My hair is starting to air-dry. I should really pineapple and wrap it before that happens. "Who's that?"

"Nobody," he says. Then, "Kat." But it's a lie. I know it is, because Kat got grounded last week for failing that Trig test and her parents took away her car and her phone. Savages. He continues, "Wanna Skype the guys? I know they wanna talk to you about this too."

"I guess." I readjust so that I'm hanging upside down on my bed.

"You guess?"

"Jeez, Siah. Yeah. I guess. I just don't need any more people yelling at me for something that isn't my fault."

He rolls his eyes. I almost don't catch it because he spins himself in a circle again.

We end our FaceTime call just before his spinning makes me dizzy enough to vom, and switch to Skype.

I hate this. I hate this, I hate this, I hate—

"Yo! Teez, is this for real?" Israel says. From where his camera's positioned, I can tell his bedroom is a mess. It always is. "You're really leaving Westview?"

I shrug. "I'm sorry."

"Jesus, don't apologize, T. Just . . . what's going on? You're leaving *right at the brink of senior year.* That sounds sus to me."

"I know."

"So, not gonna tell us what's going on, then?"

"Is it money?" Josiah says.

Westview is a pricey school, but no. Even if my parents went bankrupt today, they'd still have enough in assets and property to milk for a while.

Merrick could never afford Westview.

"No," I say. "Jesus. I just. I moved in with some other family in the Valley and they're too far for me to commute all the way to Westview."

Is scratches the back of his neck before saying, "The Jeep would never survive that trek daily."

"'Zactly," I say.

"All right. So why'd you move in with this family, then, if it's gonna upset your whole dig? Senior year, football. Friends who actually put up with you."

"Bite me, Josiah, you love me like the little sister your impotent dad will never give you, so take *that* to the bank."

Siah grumbles, "My dad's not impotent."

Israel laughs. "There is literally no other group of dudes on the planet who would get that kind of joke from you, Tasia. You're making a huge mistake by trading us in."

"I know I am."

I make some dumb excuse about having to end the call because Merrick wants me to take the trash out. It's a flimsy cop-out and I don't even care very much. There's just not really room in our friendship for me to unload something like this on them.

Girls are only accepted as "one of the guys" in a group of dudes so long as said girls swear never to feel emotions out loud around said dudes.

But I feel so bad about lying to them that after we end the Skype call, I actually do take the trash out. Once I make it down the stairs of the garage apartment, around the side, I swing the bag up and into the big blue dumpster.

On the way back, I find Tristan standing in front of the stairs that lead to Merrick's.

"How'd you get here?" is the first thing I say to him.

He doesn't answer.

"How'd you get Merrick's address?"

Still nothing.

I cross my arms over my chest. "Great, just. Why are you here, Trist, if you're just going to ignore every question I'm asking?"

He shakes his head, and I can feel it—literally feel the anger and the frustration. Can see the disappointment coating his entire self.

I abandoned him. That's why he's here. He said nothing had to change and I went and voluntarily changed everything.

"Trist. I'm sorry, 'kay? C'mon." I reach for him but he steps back.

And then, without saying a single thing, he turns around and walks down the street.

I know exactly what this was. I abandoned him first, and so he needed to have the final word. He needed to be the one to abandon me.

And this feeling, I hate that I did it to him first. That I maybe made him feel like his name sat in my stomach, left there to rot.

I'm on the phone with Slim as I park my car in the ECR High parking lot. I shouldn't be, because this school is huge and it'll be like I'm a lost little friendless freshman all over again; I need to focus so I don't end up walking into a classroom thinking it's a bathroom, or get trapped in a custodial closet, which is an actual thing that happened to Tristan once.

"I don't understand why you can't just drive here. Westview High isn't that far."

Yeah, it is. "Merrick doesn't want me to have to commute for that amount of time just to get to school every day." The Jeep definitely couldn't handle too many months of that. It's two freeways and I'd be driving during peak rush-hour times. Early morning and right after football practice, around five p.m.

Football. Jesus. That reminds me, I gotta talk to the coach or the athletics director or whoever.

"The guys here are way better-looking." Here they seem

to understand girls don't appreciate the hair-like-2010-Justin Bieber look.

" . . . Really? Like, better-looking how?"

"Yeah. Like, I don't know. They all have that heroin-chic redness under the eyes. That's probably it." I lock my car and then look around for signage or a map or something to tell me where I'm going. First stop, admin office for my class schedule.

"Totally your type," she says.

I've never really had "a type." In the past, I've been able to appreciate aesthetic here and there, but never enough of one kind to label A Type. My thoughts stray to Kai's fractured, two-toned eyes and wonder for the span of a second if my type is just . . . Kai.

My shoulder bag is pretty much empty, but I heft it as high on my shoulder as it'll go. "My type? Dudes who don't sleep a lot?"

"No. Drug addicts."

"Fuck off. I have to find the office. I'll call you at lunch as I eat my sandwich from a lonely bathroom stall."

"Oh. I see Josiah. 'Kay, I gotta go." She hangs up so fast, I get whiplash.

I text Tristan even though, knowing him, he's already turned his phone off for the duration of the school day.

good luck today

What I really mean is good luck without me. I know *I'll* probably need it.

When I walk into the office there are three orange plastic chairs pushed against a wall, and a girl with her head shaved lying prone across them all.

She looks uncomfortable.

A blond woman stands behind the long desk counter, gesturing me forward. "Don't mind her, honey. How can I help you?"

"Umm, is she okay?"

"That's Dahlia. She's fine. Strange and truant, but fine."

"Yeah. Umm, my name's Taze—er, Tasia Quirk. It's my first day. I'm just here to get my schedule."

"Let me check the new student bin." She rifles through a lonely-looking orange bin. It's only got three files in it. One of which must be mine, because she pulls it and says, "Okay, here you go. Tasia L. Quirk. Senior." She says it like TAH-see-yuh.

I raise my right hand like I'm already in class, about to ask the teacher for a hall pass. "Actually, it's Tasia, like Asia with a T."

Linda (per her used-to-be-white-but-is-now-yellowish nametag) cocks her head at an angle. "I see."

I feel someone at my right and find Dahlia there.

"What kinda name's Tasia?"

My face screws itself up. "It's Greek."

"Aha."

Linda comes back over with my printed schedule. "Just want to confirm a few details. Allergies?"

"Uh, peanuts?" I say, glancing at Dahlia.

The woman checks off a box then says, "What level would you say this allergy rates?"

"Severe."

"Airborne?"

I nod. "Yeah."

"Okay, honey. All set. Have each of your teachers sign this slip at the end of class and then bring it back here at the end of the day. If you'd like to have an EpiPen stored here in the office, you'll need a note from your primary care physician, also signed by your parents."

"Linda, when do I get to go?" Dahlia says.

"When you learn to stay present for the entire school day. Sit."

Dahlia rolls her eyes and whispers, "If I boned the principal I might feel like I could talk to students any old way too."

I laugh. She smiles. It feels like a victory for us both.

"I like your hair," she says, but doesn't touch the way most people do. My hair is a halo around my head, and typically I don't react well to people touching it. But this girl with her massive eyes and olive skin . . . I'm okay with her.

"I don't know how to tell you that I like your hair too, but I do."

"Who says that?"

"Who shaves their head?"

"It's a long story." She holds out her hand. "I'm Dahlia Locke."

"Taze . . . Quirk."

"Dope name, girl. Own it." Dahlia slings her arm around my shoulders. "Linda, if I promise to go to all my classes and keep Taze as my buddy during lunch and free period, can I go?"

Linda looks like she wants to say no, but Dahlia says, "Please! Please please please, Linda."

"Please?" I say.

When it's clear we've won, Dahlia and I scoot out of the office and giggle our way down the hall. She kisses my cheek. "Yes! You pulled that out for me."

The shrug I give says, *I guess.*

"What you got first?" She snatches my schedule. "Trig, eww. The hell? Why?"

I shrug. That one says, *I have no idea.*

"I'll show you where it is."

Dahlia makes it through the entire day at school. We eat lunch together and have three classes together, aside from homeroom.

After school, Dahlia's there again. I catch her walking across the quad, after I spot Kai—and light up inside, unexpectedly—but right before she walks up to him and places her lips on his.

It ruins me.

Chapter Nineteen

I'm already backing away when my phone vibrates in my pocket. It says LOCKE in all caps and flashes a picture of Dahlia, grinning, teeth white as the back of our shitty-ass president's knees, complexion clear as the 101 freeway on a Tuesday at two a.m.

"H-hey," I say, wondering when the hell I was away from my phone long enough for her to have added and personalized her contact information.

"Taze, we're going to hang in someone's basement. Where are—oh, I see you. C'mere!" She goes up on her toes a little to wave me over.

Kai's head swivels in my direction. He gives me a nod. Not, like, The Nod. But, like, a good one. Or maybe I just think it's a good one because it's Kai. Because last night, I spent at least eighteen minutes thinking about how I'd fit pressed right up against him, or trying to imagine how it'd feel to wrap my arms around his thin middle and feel his chin meet the top of my head. Because maybe I also imagined him lifting me up against him by the back of my thighs and—

"Merr forced you into this shitbox, huh?" And Jesus God, he's right in front of me now.

I nod.

Dahlia rummages through her bag as she says, "Oh, cool. You know Kai already?"

He side-eyes me like I'm about to maybe pickpocket him. "Tasia is Merrick's daughter."

"Merrick has a daughter?"

He turns to Dahlia and says, "He has a daughter now."

"But Merrick is—"

"White, yeah."

"We know. So what about a basement?" I ask.

"Scott's," she says, pointing to a guy with floppy brown hair. "Scott Medina's. We're going," Dahlia says.

"Um, I gotta talk to the football coach."

Dahlia looks grossed out. Kai pulls out a pen and moves behind me. I feel it roll across the skin of my exposed shoulder. He's drawing on me and it feels amazing. He could be writing MIXIE SLUT-BAG BASTARD CHILD and I still wouldn't make him stop. Probably.

"You don't need to do that if you wanna go to the games," Dahlia says. "You can just . . . you know . . . go."

"Taze plays football," Kai says. His face is so close to my skin, I can feel the warmth of his breath. "Like, on the team."

I pull away from Kai after the fiftieth time that my eyes roll into the back of my head, the pen sliding across my skin like a train running off the track. God, that feels good.

"Where can I find the coach's office?"

He moves closer to Dahlia, takes her arm, starts to draw on it. The fastest forming lotus ever. I'm watching him so closely that I don't realize I'm also being watched. By Dahlia, a fox's sly grin sliding across her mouth, her brow lifting. I'm stuck solidly inside it until—

"I'll take you," Kai says. "Coming, D?"

"Uh, no," she says. And the moment's over, Kai's pen tucked away somewhere secret. "But come to the basement thing at Scott's when you're done, yeah?" She only looks at me when she says it. Then she kisses Kai on the lips again, which would have made me feel awful except then she kisses me on the lips too, then twirls away toward a crowd of people. She hops on some guy's back and they take off down the hill toward the parking lot.

Kai walks ahead of me and I don't even try to hold back. "She's weird as hell."

He nods. Pops a hand-rolled into his mouth. "So am I."

"You're not wrong."

"So are you."

I laugh. "No."

"Yeah."

"If I'm weird, it's not on the same level as you and Dahlia."

"Fair enough."

We take two lefts and a right and then we're walking out of a gate and across the football field. It's huge. It gives me chills. Westview's field is standard, but this one seems bigger

157

than a regulation-size field. The bleachers circle the field, and from where I'm standing I can spot at least three couples underneath them, lips locked, teeth checking.

The coach's office is through the men's locker room. The same way it always is. So I bolster my resolve and push my way through. Kai doesn't follow me.

I panic for just a small moment, whisper a prayer under my breath that this will be easy. I asked for this, I remind myself. I needed this.

Lucky for me, I don't catch any free-ballers or waving dicks as I walk through. And there's not a big fuss when I make my way down the hall and past the showers, either. Some of the boys gape at me as they change into their cleats, jerseys, and basketball shorts, but that's it. And then I'm knocking as I turn the knob on the coach's door. Across the front it says, COACH J. RASS.

It makes me sweat a little that I don't know his first name.

When I walk in, I cringe. The coach is reaming some tall blond kid.

"I don't care, daggone it! You cheated on this test, Jay. You know how I feel about cheating. Cheat on your test, you'll cheat on your wife. I don't allow cheaters on my team."

"Coach—"

"Unacceptable. Turn in your jerseys and get to detention."

I freeze in the doorway. This guy is nuts. I mean, I'm not a fan of cheaters either, but Jesus Christ.

The cheater, Jay, shoves by me as he storms out of the office.

"Who the hell's in my doorway? Get in here, girl."

Coach J. Rass is a Scandinavian-looking overlord. He looks like he's pushing fifty. Maybe older.

"What?" he barks.

I jump.

"The dean send you? You the new office girl?"

"No, sir."

"Why you lurking in my locker room, then? You some kind of pervert?"

"What? No, I-I just . . . I'm Taze Quirk. I'm new. I want to try out for your team, sir."

"I coach football. The volleyball coach's office is through the ladies'."

I nod. "Yes, sir. I'm aware. But I'm here to try out for the football team, sir."

Everything gets quiet. The walls, the clocks, Coach Rass. I know the guys in the locker room have either vacated to the field or they're all listening in on what's going on.

"You played football before?"

"Yes, sir."

"For an official team?"

I nod. "Sir."

"Touch?"

"Tackle."

"With boys?"

"Yes, sir. Only ever with boys." It's true. I've never played tackle with another girl before. I'm in the middle of teaching Slim to throw a football. It's not going well, but only because she doesn't care about the fact that the football needs to reach my hands when she throws it.

He nods. "What position you play?"

Hot damn, he's considering it? "CB, sir."

"Roster's deep at corner."

"I know, sir. I played for Westview. I was one of their starters. I'd be willing to challenge for playing time."

He laughs. At me. In case that wasn't clear. I'm getting sick of white men laughing at me because I'm female, because I'm Black. Because I'm a Black female.

"That's precious. I don't allow girls on my field. Ever. I don't even know what kind of regulations that would violate. And God forbid you"—Dear God, not a tampon joke—"need to take a personal day for PMS pains during the season."

"Oh my God."

"Mine too, little girl. Now please get on out of my locker room. My guys got practice soon and this conversation has taken up too much of my time already."

"But it's perfectly legal for me to play on your team. At Westview—All you have to do is—I can try out, and if—"

"I don't give two bitches in a flying cooch about what your mom told you regarding your talent and your dreams and your girl power. Now, I'm sorry, and I know it's rough being the new kid. But there's no spot for you on this team. Not this season, and probably not next either, but you're free to try me again next year."

Shit. The dam. I feel it spidering, fracturing, cracking, release release release.

I run.

Chapter Twenty

Okay. That didn't go well, did it? My face is still leaking when I push my way out of the locker room and straight into Kai.

He grabs me by the arms. "Whoa. Hang on."

I don't know why I finally realize what he's wearing. Nikes, rust-red track pants with black leather patches at the knees, fitted. A long, oversize gray knit sweater that reaches past his hips. A purple, backwards cap on his head, the handwriting on which just says *Thot Topic* all over it. If it's a joke, I'm not sure I get it.

Kai laughs. "Merrick says the same thing. It is a joke though."

"Goddammit."

"It's okay, Talky. Tell me what happened—wait. Are you crying?" He looks horrified, like he's just been told he'll be locked in a room alone with Emily for an hour.

Female tears? Shit! Run!

Denial comes out so fast, like, "I'mnotcrying."

"Yes, you are. Stop it," Kai says. He uses his entire hand—palm and all—to wipe the very obvious tears off my face. "Stop it. Stop crying."

"You're crying." I try to move away from him, but he uses his sleeve to wipe snot from my nose while using his other hand at the back of my neck to keep me still.

"*Stop,*" he says again.

"*You stop.*"

He growls and stops his cleanup, then walks back toward the locker room.

"N-no. Wait. Kai. Wait!"

"I'm just going to ask him—"

"He said I can't play. Can't be on the team. I just want to play football and have parents who love me and don't lie to me, people who get it, and I want to be enough of one thing to satisfy people, but apparently that's not happening for me."

And Kai is so silent for a second that I worry he's going to tell me to suck it up and get the hell over it. He doesn't. He wraps his arm around my shoulder and puts his ugly purple hat on my head.

I feel his lips press into my head. It's not a kiss. It's something different. More solid. And I'm so done with holding things back today that I literally just can't anymore, so I say, "Kai, is Dahlia your girlfriend?" There. It's out and running around like a wild thing. The giant green jealousy monster inside me rears up at the thought of them being A

Thing on even the most minor level. And I'd swear earlier Dahlia was shoving it right in my face.

"Mm," Kai says. "Nah, I don't think so."

And even though I don't know what "I don't think so" means, I take it and run with it.

I run, again.

Kai and I get in my Jeep to head to Scott's, but before we get on the 101, he has me detour to a place called Bounce Boba Loft, where we stop and get HK bubble tea with honey boba.

"Your dad's a lawyer, right?" Kai says as he uses his fat straw to chase a tapioca ball.

"Yeah. So?"

He shrugs. "So if you want to play football, maybe he should step in."

"You have a point, but I'm not speaking to him." And I give Kai a basic rundown of why exactly not. Why forgiveness is just an eleven-letter word right now. "I mean, they both lied to me, so."

"Well. You just don't want to need him. Your dad or your mom."

"Well, I *tried* to need them both, and they dropped the frickin' ball. They don't know what the hell they're doing. I need people who know what they're doing. Who want to give me answers." Who want to help me figure out who sent that stupid detonator of a box.

"None of us knows what we're doing. All you got, really, is people who are willing to figure it out."

My head cuts sharply in his direction, which wouldn't be a problem if I weren't driving. Kai yells, "Jesus, can you drive, please!"

And so I turn back to the road, and I drive. But that's the thing—Mamma and Daddy *aren't* willing to figure it out.

"Look," I say. "Even if I was that desperate—"

"Aren't you?"

The Jeep is not a quiet vehicle. It's old and creaky and clunky and made entirely of metal, probably. So, while I may be having a quiet moment, the Jeep and everything else around me is not.

"No," I say finally. "Or, kinda. Not really."

Kai slurps. Grabs my bubble tea out of my cup holder and sips a little. "You are."

"*You* are."

He laughs. "Yeah, okay. But listen. If you got your lawyer dad involved, the coach would have to let you at least try out. He only said no to you because you're a girl."

"That's sexist."

"Hey, don't yell at me. *I* know it's sexist. I'm just telling you that it's also a fact. Turn here."

I make the left-hand turn, chewing on a tapioca ball as well as his words.

"You don't even really have to be the one to ask for help."

I glance at him briefly. "Where am I going?"

"Turn left on Platt. You could probably get Merrick to ask

him to step in."

Tristan would call that the coward's way. Kai, the exact opposite, obviously thinks it's smart. Thinking of Trist and Kai in the same world is weird.

A world where both sides of my family come together is weird, and I hate that it is.

Still, I think Kai is right.

When we pull over on Scott's street and park, Kai reaches into his bag and grabs a piece of thread and a bit of thin gold wire. He picks up a strand of my hair and weaves the wire and the thread around a lock of it.

"Pretty weird you just had these in your bag," I say.

He shakes his head at me when he's done with my hair and lifts his wrist. There's a bracelet made out of the same thin gold wire and thread around it.

"Can I have it?"

Kai shakes his head no again, and then removes the bracelet and puts it around my wrist.

"It's okay to push back, Taze. It's okay to tell people they're wrong about you. It's okay to tell that dickbag, sexist coach that you got skills. It's okay to tell Merrick he needs to talk to your dad about helping you out. It's o-flipping-kay. You get me?"

"I got you."

"Yeah?"

"Yeah."

"How much?"

I take his hat off his head and pull it backwards onto mine again. "So much, Kai."

He pretends to clip my jaw with his knuckles and then pulls his hand away. "Let's go rescue those people from Dahlia."

Chapter Twenty-One

So, Scott's basement isn't a basement.

It's a furnished trailer in his backyard. I should have known it would be sus, because this is L.A. and this city wouldn't know a basement if this were *Evil Dead II*.

I don't like this feeling I get when I walk through the side gate behind Kai and into Scott Medina's backyard.

We come up to the doublewide sitting on its bricks, essentially just waiting for a good stiff wind to dance up and knock it over. But I guess none of that matters—that is, our safety from rusty nails and tetanus—since Kai lets us in through the hanging-on-by-a-thread door.

Inside is a small group of people, but it's not some circle of day-wasted alcoholic teens like I imagined it would be.

In reality, it's just Dahlia playing a game of Speed with Scott, two other guys, and one other girl, and they're . . . doing homework. The girl is easily the prettiest hippie I've ever seen. Her black hair is in two French braids that wrap around her head like a crown, and her cheekbones sit high on her face. Her dark brown skin is infused—I'm convinced—with a serum made of sunflowers and literal gold. She looks up as we enter and the first thing I notice are her dark, spiky giraffe lashes.

"Hey, Kai," she says. She doesn't say anything to me. It's fine.

"Taze, that's Victory. Victory, this is Tasia."

I lift my hand, puppet-style, and amend, "Taze. Hey." It's awkward, in case that's not clear.

The two guys are sitting across from each other, a textbook between them. Guy on the left is ginger as hell and stacked, if his shoulders and the width of his back are anything to go by, and dude on the right has a full head of thick, dark hair longer than all of ours put together. When he looks up at us entering, his smile is friendly and open, his eyes a little sharp and a lot knowing, set just so in his light brown face.

He says, "Nice job taking your time, Mr. Math Tutor." But when it comes out, the emphasis on the N is hard and prolonged. The end of his sentence is full, with more of them, the hard consonants going on for a second or two.

Okay. Tourette's. He has Tourette's.

I smile at him because he's still smiling at me and he gets up to introduce himself, whereas none of the others pay as much mind.

"I'm Sam, that ginger fucker is Cole. You any good with math, Taze?"

I nod but say, "What kind of math?"

"Trig," Sam says, followed by a series of ticks.

"She's in our class," the ginger says. Cole.

Sam shrugs and looks guilty. "I didn't see you, but that's probably because I was sleeping through most of it."

"That's not gonna help you get any better at math," I say, tucking my hands in my shallow back pockets.

Kai gives me a faux incredulous look and says, "Good point, T. Very logical. You'd think Sam might understand that and, I don't know, stop *sleeping through classes*."

My phone vibrates in my back pocket. I pull it out and see SLIM across it, but I send it to voicemail.

I can't talk to her right now. This is the first time I've been able to put Mamma and Tristan and the box and yes, even Slim, out of my mind for a while. I want to preserve that a little longer.

"You'd think," I say. And then I make room for myself next to Sam's stuff and start explaining Pythagorean identities, while Kai walks over to Dahlia and Scott. Kai exchanges a few words with Scott.

"Moving boxes isn't that hard," Kai says.

"It is when you're alone and it's hot as hell outside," Scott counters.

Victory shouts, "The average temperatures this week range from about seventy-eight degrees to eighty-one degrees. It's not that hot, Scott."

"Nobody asked you, Vic."

She mimics him. "Nobody asked you, Vic. Crybaby."

"I'll help you," Kai says. "Let's do it now."

"Now?" Scott says.

"Yeah. What else we got going on?"

Scott shrugs. It's obvious he just doesn't want to do it.

Kai's already standing, taking charge, helping *just because*. My heart does A Thing.

I'm a mess and it's all this boy's fault.

"You're not even dressed for that," Scott says. "The boxes are all the way upstairs. They're heavy. And dusty."

"So?" Kai says.

So the two of them leave the trailer and walk across the way, and with the door of the trailer wide open, I have a clear view of them lifting heavy box after heavy box and carting them into the garage. For the next thirty minutes, I watch them trek through the grass, disappearing into the house and back into the garage. I can see the sheen of sweat on them both, and it's a miracle I'm able to focus on lengths and angles of triangles at the same time.

As I'm helping Sam, Cole, and Victory with the Trig homework I already did in class, Kai and Scott walk back into the trailer. Kai doesn't speak to me. In fact, he goes out of his way to not speak to us at all, really, which I chalk up to his not wanting to disturb us. But I can't help the fact that I keep looking over at him and Dahlia, trying to gauge how close they are in proximity to each other. How covert their touches get. How they move around each other in this small space, like poetry.

For the most part, it's pretty innocent. Until Dahlia leans over and bites Kai's shoulder and he leans over and smiles at her and, I mean, if there's a way to look at someone that is "intimate" then I'd wager that is his exact look right now, and I make this weird, wounded animal croak as I turn away from them.

Victory catches my eye and announces loudly, "Tasia, can you French braid? One of mine's coming loose and I need help redoing it."

"You asking me because I'm Black?"

She's quiet and then looks at me and deadpans, "No. That's a stupid stereotype and I asked you because Dahlia doesn't even have hair to braid and you're the only other girl here, so if anything, I'm being sexist, not racist. So can you help me or not?"

I don't say anything about how my mamma has thoughts about Black people and their inability to be racist; they lack the privilege. Mamma made sure Trist and I knew that. Black people can be prejudicial, but a subjugated group can't be racist.

I honestly don't think saying any of that will gain me friends, though, so instead I nod and follow her into the trailer's bathroom. We squeeze inside, and as soon as I start to reach for her hair, she slaps my hand away and whisper-hisses, "My hair's fine. Listen, whatever little crush you've got on Kai? Lock it up, girl."

"I don't know what you're—"

"Shhh!"

"Sorry. I don't know what you're talking about," I whisper.

"Aha. But listen, you don't have to confirm or deny, but whatever he's doing or half doing with Dahlia isn't a thing you wanna deal with. It's just drama, girl. Just mind your Ps and Qs."

I smile a little. "My mamma says that all the time. Ps and Qs."

She laughs. "Mine too."

"So Kai and Dahlia?"

She shrugs. "I mean, they used to date last year. Broke up for whatever reason. There's a rumor that Kai didn't want to deal with her because she's never serious about anything and he wanted more with her."

Makes sense. "So he doesn't have a girlfriend?"

"A girlfriend? No."

"And he may or may not be hooking up with Dahlia."

"Safe bet they're doing the beast with two backs regularly."

Great. I feel sick. I want to go home. I hate that I feel this way. Jealousy is not my shit. This whole week has thrown me way off-balance, and this thing with Dahlia and Kai is just making it worse.

I wrap my arm over the top of my hair to pull it back off my face.

"I'm not saying I want to be your best friend or anything," Victory says, "but if you want to leave, I'll go with you. I got a ride with Sam, but I don't live far from here if you wanna drop me off?"

"I'll owe you."

"Solidarity and shit, you know?"

Yeah. I know.

I miss Slim.

Chapter Twenty-Two

Nobody questions us when we say we're leaving.

I drop Victory off at a one-story house in a quiet neighborhood not far from Scott's. Her house is yellow, and the paint over the garage is peeling, and the grass is all but dead. But who I presume to be her mom meets her at the door and I watch as she points back at me and smiles. Her mom high-fives her and then waves me over. I put my car in park, take the key out of the ignition, but before I can get out and head up the walkway, Victory meets me at my passenger-side window, stops me, says, "One day, Kai is gonna mess up. He's going to get caught up the way he always does and he's going to drop the ball with you. I've known Kai since seventh grade and that's just the way he is. It's going to happen."

Fumble, I think. *That's a fumble in football.*

She continues, "Because I can already see what's happening. When he does? Come find me." She pulls a pad of neon Post-Its out of her bag, writes "Victory" and then jots down ten digits, no dashes or spaces between, shoving it inside my cup holder.

And then we walk inside her house, holding hands with silence. And I don't question any part of what she just said to me, even though I want to.

"This is Tasia. She's new at school," Victory says to her mom.

Her mom is all cheekbones. All long arms and solid Tina Turner muscle and when she hugs me she squeezes me so tight, I can't breathe, can't breathe, can't breathe, please don't let go—

She does.

"Tasia is a beautiful name, sugar."

"Thank you, ma'am."

I don't know Victory's last name and her mom doesn't tell me to call her by her first name, because, honestly, no Black mom is gonna tell you to do that unless she basically raised you.

Her mom invites me inside, and even though I'm still bummed out from this thing with Kai and Dahlia and still want to go home, I accept and cross the threshold. It smells like cinnamon. I don't see much of the house except for the hallway that leads off to the kitchen, where Vic and I sit at their rickety wooden table.

Above the stove is a metal plaque with "The Du Bois Family" etched into it.

Du Bois. Victory Du Bois. It's French Creole, like Mamma.

"Tasia plays football," Victory says.

I preen a little. I am the new doll she's brought to school to show off to all who don't also have that same new doll.

"At the school?"

Hopefully.

"Not yet," Victory says. "But they can't keep her off the team, right? Is that legal?"

"I don't know, baby." Mrs. Du Bois cracks an egg in a pound of ground meat she's slopped into a bowl.

"Someone told you about that? What happened with the coach?" I clarify.

Victory nod-shrugs. "Kai" is all she says in answer. It's really all I needed to know.

"So, football, huh?" Mrs. Du Bois says. "That's a rough sport for a little girl."

It's rough for anyone. "I work hard."

"Good for you, baby. We always tried to get Tory in a sport. I played tennis all through college. I was good in my little tennis skirts, too."

I think she's talking about not-tennis.

Thirty minutes at that table and I can tell Victory's getting tired of me. I'm not trying to brown-nose to her mom, but I can't help it. I'm halfway between wanting to be best friends with Vic and asking her mom to adopt me. I don't know which one I want more. I kind of want them both.

But I get it—Black moms, they're so hypercritical. The second you bring another Black kid home who's successful in ways you aren't or don't care to be, is the second they feel perfectly validated in bringing up your shortcomings.

Mamma does it with me and all my cousins.

Oh, did I tell you your cousin Damita is graduating with

honors this year? Be nice if we could see some of that from you, Tasia.

It's hard not to hate being around your own cousins at that point.

"You didn't like tennis, Victory? I play a little with my parents. There's a bunch of courts at the country club my dad belongs to. I could teach you?"

"No."

Ooookay. "What do you like, then?"

"Tory likes TV."

"Film," Victory says. The part I hear but she doesn't voice is the missing "goddammit." *Film, goddammit.*

"Movies," Mrs. Du Bois says, stirring a pot of something that smells a little like magic.

"Okay, Mom."

Mrs. Du Bois cuts a look at Vic but doesn't say anything. I almost laugh because it's a look that is so my mamma that I don't know how to handle it. It is a look that says, "Watch your tongue in front of company—I'm still within snatching distance."

After that, Victory looks at me, chucks her head at the door. *Time for you to leave,* basically.

I do. I don't want to. I almost want to ask her why she's sending me away. What I did, how I can fix it, even though I know what's done is done.

Mrs. Du Bois walks me to the door and Victory hangs back in the entryway.

Her mom waves. Vic doesn't. I wave back, smile even though it's a lie, and then shift my Jeep into drive and head home.

By the time I make it home, it's five and Merrick is also home. His Bose stereo system is blaring some loud, classical thing, and I have to yell over it in order to get him to turn it down and eventually off.

"Oh, hey, kiddo," he says.

"This is your idea of a party?" I ask, dropping my book bag on the couch and picking up a nectarine from the fruit bowl on the table. I wash it in the sink and take a paring knife to it.

"This is how I get turned up."

"Oh my God, stop."

"What? Oh, you don't want me to say 'turned up'? I turn up so loud—"

"Merrick."

He turns up the volume on his music again to, I don't know, prove his point maybe, and then he starts to yell over it. "I turned up the volume—"

"Stop!" I rush over to his stereo and try to turn it down, but he beats me there and grabs the tiny remote.

"...so I could turn up my 'tude, T!"

I'm choking because we've reached that point where he's now *waltzing alone* around the apartment.

"All these Ts, I'm so turned up! And tuned in!"

Groaning, I fall on the couch and bury my head under one of the throw pillows. Merrick falls next to me after he realizes I'm refusing to play, music lowered now.

"How was school?" he says, and reaches for my nectarine. I bite and then hand it to him and he does the same, handing it back.

"Was good. I saw Kai. Met some of his friends after school."

He nods. "Oh, that's good. Make any friends of your own?"

I nod and shrug. Parents do not ask this question. They just don't. But, again, Merrick's new here. So I lie and I don't think he knows it. Mamma and Daddy would have sniffed it out immediately.

Merrick blows out a long, breathy sigh. "Tasia. Kiddo, have you spoken to your m—"

The door bursts open. "What's for dinner? I'm hungry as hell."

"Go home, El Khoury," Merrick deadpans.

Kai pulls the fruit from my hand, bites, and doesn't give it back. "You tell him about football yet?"

"Tasia, you made the ECR football team, kid? That's great. Knew you'd do well here."

"I didn't."

"What?"

"She ain't make the team, Merr. The coach is a sexist prick. I'm not shocked he treated her like shit."

"That's bullshit," Merrick says. I like it when he swears. You can hear a little of the Frenchman in him when he does. It makes me wonder how long he lived in France before coming here.

"You're not wrong," Kai says.

I clear my throat. "Yeah, well, I thought maybe if you talked to my dad . . . I think, if we can get legal involved, the coach will have to let me try out?"

Merrick's already shaking his head. "Screw that. I'll handle this, and we'll do it without legal threats."

Kai flexes behind Merrick's back and then points at him and shakes his head, laughing.

I shake my head back at him, listening as Merrick walks into the kitchen and starts chopping veggies for dinner with the phone to his ear.

"Have fun with Vic today?" Kai drops down next to me on the couch.

I reach for the nectarine but he holds it high above his head, daring me to reach for it. I don't give in and instead say, "Victory's cool."

He smiles knowingly. "She is," he says. "I think Dahl's a little obsessed with you, though."

"I think she's a lot obsessed with you, to be honest."

"Nah. That's just D. We been friends a long time."

"More than friends?"

"No, I told you—"

"But, before. You guys, y'know"—I raise my eyebrows—"with each other?"

He lifts a shoulder. I notice his ugly purple hat is missing. I wonder if Dahlia has it on her head. "Yeah, I guess," he says.

I guess.

"Dahlia was . . . she's like a magnet, you know? She's just as hard *not* to be around as she is to be around. If that makes any sense at all."

Too much sense.

I pick at a hangnail that's been harassing my thumb for a

week. "What did you like about her?"

He laughs with the kind of amusement you give a child you're humoring. "Dahlia just got stuff done. She wanted it, she went for it. No ifs, ands, or buts. Even if it wasn't necessarily good for her."

I hear every *beep* of Merrick's phone as he dials a number, the scent of sweet butter and garlic and paprika wafting to me from the kitchen.

"What are you doing?" I say as I get up from the couch to walk over to Merrick.

Merrick only continues to dial. "I'm calling."

"What? Who?"

"I don't know. I'm just gonna call and demand to speak with whoever's—"

"Okay, wait," I say. "Maybe . . . maybe don't call."

"Well, why not? Do you not want to play anymore?" He clicks his phone locked and turns the stove off.

I shrug. Of course I still want to play, it's just—"I don't need your help."

"You don't need *my* help or you don't need *anyone's* help?"

I roll my neck as tension settles into it slowly, like a sheet being spread over a bed. "This isn't about you," I say, walking away, crossing my arms to stretch out the muscles in my upper back. "Don't make it about you, please don't take it personally. I just. If I make this team, it's not going to be because my dad harassed someone into letting me play."

He walks away, then turns back. "Don't be out late Thursday. We're having dinner with my parents. They want to meet you."

I don't know where this leaves his feelings, but I drop it to say, "Your parents?"

He doesn't respond.

In my room, I pack my gym bag with my favorite gloves and cleats. Kai follows, sits on the floor in the corner, and watches me.

There's a new kind of anxiety swirling in my chest, the kind that sprouts up from meeting new people and also the potential for more answers about the box.

But, God, I love it when he watches me.

Chapter Twenty-Three

Mamma's unmistakable voice is coming from the living room as I'm about to leave the apartment for school. And then I hear Merrick's. It's too early in the morning for voices to be this loud.

I can remember Mamma and Daddy trying to teach me how to whisper. I wasn't that loud, as a kid. No louder than the average child. But something about whispers and children—it doesn't compute for them. So I had to be taught. Apparently, Mamma never perfected the technique either, because I can very clearly hear both her and Merrick whisper-shouting at each other.

"You can't just *show up here*, Sloane. Did you even ask T if she was okay to see you? You have to think about her and how she feels—"

"Don't you dare talk to me like I'm still just some college freshman in your classroom, Merrick. I can't 'just show up' the way you did? You showed up and stole my daughter from me—"

"*Our daughter,* Sloane. Our daughter, whom you lied to. You did everything to keep us apart, and now she's here. By her own choice. Because you and Solomon lied to her. To us both!"

"I didn't lie to you!"

"An omission is still a lie, Slo! She chose to be here. Tasia chose this for herself."

What he doesn't know is that I'm here because it was the lesser of two evils. Because I needed a fresh start. Because he had a space for me that seemed uncomplicated at the time. Because getting answers about who I am, who put that box of things together, and who sent it—all of it makes me feel too much. Both settled and uncomfortable in my skin. And yet, without answers . . . I'm starting to hate all the questions. All the unknowns. I'm starting to hate me.

"For her!" Mamma says, shouting now. "I did it for her!"

Merrick laughs an ugly laugh. "You did it to protect your own ass. You've always been about yourself. You were like that nineteen years ago and you haven't changed, Slo—"

"Stop it, stop doing that."

"Doing what."

"Using my name like that. Don't call me that. And you wouldn't have wanted her back then, so why should I allow you to have *any* part of her now? You were a selfish son of a bitch. A baby with your Black, Afrocentric, nineteen-year-old student would have been way more than you could ever handle. I did this to *spare you,* Merrick. I kept her from you for your own good *and* for hers."

"You're a bitch, Sloane. I'm handling it. I am her father, and even if you and Solomon never want to acknowledge that, Tasia knows, and she is my only priority."

Something in my chest crawls up my throat. I don't have any reason not to believe it's my heart. I wonder for the span of approximately six seconds if this moment should go on my What It Means to Be a Good Parent list.

I'm a priority. He says I'm his priority. It's not something I've heard from Mamma or Daddy since the box showed up.

They're quiet for a moment, and then Mamma whispers, "I'll make her come home. Where she belongs. With her *family*. You'll never see her again, if I have anything to—"

A slam against what I assume is Merrick's glass table, then, "You can't keep her from me!" Merrick's yelling now. The echoes of it crawl into every corner of the room. There's no way I wouldn't have heard that, so I walk into the room with my book bag and gym bag slung across my shoulders.

Merrick sees me first. "T," he says. And that's it, so I force a smile and shake my head.

"Can you drive me to school?" I ask him. I could drive myself, but I feel obligated now to get him out of here. Away from this. I hate that this feels like my responsibility. Like I need to save him from this. The need to do something rests heavy on my spine.

I mentally make the necessary adjustment to my Good Parenting list.

"Sure," he says. "Let me grab my keys." And he walks away to his bedroom.

The only thing I get to say to Mamma before Merrick comes back is "You really can't just show up here. It's not fair to me and, I suspect, it's not fair to Merrick's heart either. You can't make me come home. And you can't keep me from this anymore. You've done enough of that, and legally, I'm pretty sure it's too late to discuss parental rights. I'm eighteen and legalities don't exactly matter."

Before she leaves, she reaches into her purse and pulls out a Velcro sealed pouch. The front if it says "EPI" in big white letters.

"Didn't want you to go without this," she says, and the sound of the door shutting is gentle and final.

It might be kind of obvious, but in case it isn't, the drive to school with Merrick is mute as hell.

It's still quiet when I grab my bags out of the backseat.

He tells me to text him when I need to be picked up, then reminds me, in a faux optimistic shout, about dinner at his parents' on Thursday as I walk up to the glass doors that read El Camino Real High across them.

School sucks today. Naturally.

Except for the fact that I see Kai three times before lunch and he nods at me, specifically, each time.

I have three classes with Victory. They're the same three I happen to have with Dahlia. In Western Civ, the teacher, a bald Hispanic woman whom everyone calls Manny, tells us to partner up. The blond girl next to me asks if I want to be hers. I shake my head and say sorry because I see Victory stand and glance at me, brows raised.

Today, she has one French braid going down the strip right above her left ear. The rest of her hair is down and free, a mane around her head that I wouldn't call wild so much as natural. Her hair is so much of who she is.

Before I can nod at her, Dahlia grabs my hand.

"Let's be partners. Manny loves me. I have an A in this class for absolutely no reason that I can fathom except that maybe Manny is DTF."

"Oh, uh. Sure."

"I mean, unless you don't want to. Pretty sure I spotted Azra Sadeghi visually fondling your cleavage. You could pair up with him and not lift a finger or your shirt or anything. He'd do everything, give you all the credit, and you'd still get an A."

She's already opening her book and her notes—which are close to nonexistent—but still I say, "Nah, let's be partners." I glance back at Victory and shrug.

"Sure? I mean, I wouldn't let you partner with Vic regardless of whether or not you partner with me—swear to God, she's dyslexic. Or, like, I heard she is. Who even knows why she can't pass freshman English."

I nod. "Uh, no. I want to," I say. "I wanna be your partner."

Being friends with Dahlia is its own sort of magic. She'll make you feel loved and neglected in the same breath. Her attention just feels *that* valuable. You speak, she dedicates her entire self to listening to you. Not to mention, being friends with her makes me feel a little bit better about her and Kai, even though maybe it shouldn't. I think, maybe she just wants to be his friend and my friend, and maybe that's good. Maybe that's what it is. The three of us can just be friends even though, with Kai, I want more, and he maybe wanted more with her, and she maybe wants less than she has with him now.

Also, maybe naïveté will win me a Pulitzer.

After class, Victory packs up fast. To catch up to her, I do that embarrassing run-walk thing that all the freshmen do with their huge, too-full backpacks slapping against their spines.

"Hey," I say. "Sorry about the partner thing. We could hang after school and work together if you want."

"I'm busy after school."

"Oh. Yeah, me too," I say. "I like your hair. Can you braid mine like that at lunch?"

"No." And you know, she's gifted with legs long enough to outwalk me.

A moment after she does, Dahlia finds me again, talks nonstop about how she and Kai ditched first and second this morning to get all-you-can-eat pancakes, which ruins whatever friendship-y feelings I had about her in class five short minutes ago. And if she says "practically the world's best pancakes" again, I might hit her.

This makes me think of Tristan. I text him, *remember that time we made flourless pancakes*

I'm entirely shocked when he texts me back.
with bananas, yeah
and they were so gross
and they kept falling apart
and all we had was that gross sugar-free syrup to eat them with
and mamma got mad bc we put her nonstick pans in the
dishwasher

After that I say nothing. I wish he hadn't mentioned her. I wish I hadn't wasted this conversation on pancakes. There are so many other things I need him for right now.

Right after lunch, Kai asks me what's wrong when he spots me in the hall.

"Nothing," I say, and keep walking. The halls here are never really clear. Even during classes there's always someone in them. Right now it's pretty much chaos and Kai has to basically stiff-arm people out of his way to walk within my general radius.

"Nah, it's something."

"Okay. It's something. Drop it."

"Is it Merr?"

"No. Stop."

"Or football?"

"No, Kai. I said drop it."

"Did Victory say something to you? Is that why you're mad?"

"Seriously. Can you just fuck off and go follow Dahlia around like usual?"

He stops—quick, hard—and gives me a look that is,

quite literally, withering. Then he turns on his booted heel and walks away.

After I skip lunch to sit outside and catch up on some reading for Civ, I finally break down and text an apology to Kai, the blue bubble floating up on my screen. He opens it immediately and leaves me on *Read*.

He doesn't speak to me for the rest of the day.

My stomach bubbles with nerves as I change into practice shorts and a sports bra.

Right as I'm in the middle of taping my ankles, I get a text from Slim that is a shouty-caps *JOSIAH AND KAT BROKE UP!!! OMG!!!* And I don't know why, but that makes me angry. I'm so frustrated by it. I delete the text and turn my phone off before shoving it in one of the gym lockers.

The only way to calm the nerves is to physically wash them off, so I splash water onto the back of my neck and then walk out toward the field. No one's watching me at first. I eye the team QB and WR on the field and track their movements for a minute, studying their execution, their pace. Trying to map their routes. They're running the same play over and over. They've got corners on the field too, so I know it's a drill meant for the wide receiver, primarily. But the quarterback is getting a good arm workout from these coasting high passes he's lobbing off.

I bounce up and down on the balls of my feet, stretch my

calves, and roll my neck. It's not enough of a warm up but all I need is one shot and I'm not throwing it away. Hopefully I don't pull anything. I'll admit, their receivers are good. Real good. That is, until I take off in a hard sprint toward the field as the QB lets another ball rip toward their receiver.

This is stupid. This is so stupid. Someone could get hurt and the coach could ban me from even attending the games as a spectator, regardless of whether or not this goes off well.

But it does. I come in low and heavy, intercepting the ball and taking off down the field, dodging as I go.

I don't know why. I don't know what possesses the rest of the players on the field to fall in line with me and do their jobs, to follow this play I've basically co-opted. But they do. And this is gonna work. I feel it in my chest, it's gonna be good. And it is. I see players in my peripheral vision, coming up fast at my back. I hear the coaches screaming "Take her down!" from the sidelines, just before I get tackled hard from behind, *right* as I make it to the end zone.

And that's when everything else comes back to me. Coach Rass is yelling, two other men with clipboards are swearing, grabbing their heads and laughing in what I hope to God and Mary and whoever the hell else is amazement.

All the other players disperse after the receiver whose route I jumped elbows and winks at me. "Nice play."

"Thanks," I say. Because. I mean. *It was* a nice play.

Coach Rass blows his whistle one final time. "You."

He assesses me as I jog over to him, looking me in the eye. And then, with almost total acceptance and little reluctance, he says, "Congrats on weaseling your way in. Hope you're prepared to hurt after today's practice."

He blows his whistle and yells, "Quit horsing around, ya knuckleheads—get in here! Gather round!"

And they do. Until they spot me, and walk a little slower like they've been asked who wants to jump off the cliff first instead of who wants to greet the girl footballer.

"All right," Coach says. He directs most of his speech to me. "This is my assistant coach, Cody Jimenez. CJ, this here is . . . uh . . ."

"Taze," I say. In football, I'm never Tasia. "Taze Quirk. Cornerback."

Coach grunts at me and then yells, "Cole!" And then Cole, the tall, buff ginger I met in Scott's basement/trailer shoves his way forward. He's introduced as the "Mike" linebacker. Fricking great.

Dude nods at me, but it's different than the nods I've been getting from Kai in the halls. Before Coach can make introductions, Cole says, "I know her."

"She's here on a trial run," Coach says. He turns to me. "It's a trial. I'm not promising anything, and having a girl on my field makes me want to—"

"Yes, sir." I'm kinda done hearing how much he hates women. Best to just give him the acquiescence he wants in hopes that it'll shut him up.

"Good." Coach claps to pull us all together. "All right, let's go. Quit this lollygagging. Get this girl a got-dang helmet, for chrissake."

And then Cole, Coach Rass, and two others work with me for the rest of practice, running drills.

Cole is a middle linebacker, which makes sense. His build is great for it. Big, enough muscle to gain rushing yards if we need them, physically able to really get in there and tackle, play after play. The others are two Black guys, and one is the first-string cornerback, whose spot I'm aiming to snatch. I'm not very hopeful by the time I get introduced to him. He goes by Guy, but I don't know if that's actually his name or just a funny thing because he happens to look like Shemar Moore's kid brother. The other, with his white smile and carved-from-stone jawline, is the first-string receiver.

His name is Adrian, the "nice play" kid from moments ago, and he high-fives me and says, "Girl, I can't wait for you to take this asshole's spot."

For the most part, I kick ass. I catch every pass that's thrown to me and I even catch most of the passes that aren't. The pick-six is what I do. After catching the last one, Coach yells, "Good girl, Taze. Good hands!"

I'm *almost* as fast as Guy, what with my legs being a bit shorter than his. My ability to bust up running routes is good, and I owe a lot to Josiah because it was his call to have me spend most of my time working on breaks and keeping my angles sharp.

At the end of practice, Coach calls us all in, then he pulls me aside and says he'll talk to the necessary people who need talking to before he gives me his final decision. He also mentions that he's a little worried, not about my height, but my size. And I try to quell the anxiety over that particular comment by reminding myself that I rebound from tackles much faster than Guy does and nail my targets twice as often. So even though my shoulder is screaming as loud as the anxious voice inside my head, I walk off the field and into the girls' locker room and force a little hip sway.

I hope people are watching.

Chapter Twenty-Four

I don't bother changing in the locker room after practice, but as I walk out, most—but not all—of the guys from practice high-five me, tell me I did good, how cool it would be to have a chick on the team. Some tell me how to find them on social media—Insta or Snapchat or Twitter. And I'm so preoccupied trying to gauge how genuine they all are that I don't notice Kai, who happens to be standing just off to the left. Until I do.

I walk toward him and he takes the heavier of my two bags and slips it over his shoulder.

"Who shoved a stick up your ass today?" he says.

"Kai. Hello, friend. How was your day? Did you enjoy your hearty pancake breakfast this morning? I do hope so. Have you got much homework? Might I be of some service in helping you complete—"

"Taze."

"Is it too much to ask you to pull your punches a little, Kai?"

"Yes."

"Good God. I don't need you giving me shit like this right now. Don't you think I get enough of that from literally everyone else on the planet?"

"So?"

I reach for my gym bag but he moves away. My arm drops at my side. "Can I have my bag back?"

"I'm not going to play this game with you, Tasia. If you want to be friends with me, get honest and get used to honesty. If not, keep doing this thing you're doing. I don't have time for uncertainty in my life. I had enough of that, you know, growing up in the foster system, so you'll forgive me if I don't get hard over it now."

I say nothing.

"You don't want to talk about it? That's okay. We don't talk about it. But then it's like, don't come out the gate swinging on me because you're frustrated."

I nod.

"You nod, but do you really get it?"

I nod.

Then, because, Jesus, he has a point, and I feel like a piece of flavorless chewed-up gum on the bottom of a shoe now, I offer, "I'm sorry. I'm sorry I was a bitch. Before. This morning. My mom came to Merrick's unannounced. And she said some stuff to Merrick and Merrick said some stuff to her and . . . It's like, my parents, they don't fight. Like, ever. The most disagreeing they ever do is when Mamma's trying to get Daddy to help her choose placemats for the table at

Thanksgiving and he says, 'Now, c'mon, Sloane,' and Mamma says, 'For the love of all that is good and holy, Solomon, just point in one general direction!'

"But Merrick and my mom—Jesus. They hate each other so much. Because, my mom's my best friend, pretty much. Or, she was. And now, it's like…" I press the heels of my hands to my eyes until I see red-fire galaxies inside the blackness. "And, so my day started shitty." God. "And I get here and Vic won't say a single word to me, and Dahlia won't shut up about you and pancakes. It felt like she was rubbing it in my face, and"— before I can keep myself from saying it—"I got so stupidly jealous that you had gone without me, and I don't even know if I would have *wanted* to be there, because who even *knows* what you guys were doing. I'm just sorry, Kai. Like, seriously. Mentally, I feel like I'm falling up lately, which is so much more unnatural and uncomfortable than falling down."

Kai nods, then he hugs me. Once. Quick. And throws his arm around my shoulder.

"Merrick is a good dad," I say. I don't even know why. Not like Kai gives a shit or has any real grasp on what "good" parents are.

Kai raises an eyebrow. "Is he."

I'm a little offended on Merrick's behalf. "I mean, yeah?"

"How so?"

"Well…" And I find I can't think of a single *concrete* way that Merrick might fit into the Good Parent category. I try very hard not to weigh Merrick and Mamma on the same scale.

"Boba?" is all he says in response to my waffling.

I shake my head. "I didn't drive today. But maybe we can suck Merrick into making a pit stop."

"Gelit."

"Only you could make slang even *more* abnormal."

He chuckles.

"I'm having dinner at my grandparents' house Thursday. At your house."

"Gross."

I laugh because, yeah, I kinda get it. "Yeah. I know."

After I text and ask Merrick to come and get us, I look at Kai's clothes. This is the most normal I've ever seen him dress—grey sweatpants, a baggy, worn Hanes T-shirt with a hole in the bottom that I think might be Merrick's, hightop Nikes, an open flannel—except he's got a chain connecting one of his gauges to the ring in his cartilage.

"What are you wearing?" I whisper, laughing.

Merrick's rust bucket pulls up and Kai calls shotgun as we both climb in.

Chapter Twenty-Five

It takes Merr till the early evening on Thursday to bring up the "discussion" he had with Mamma.

He catches me right as we walk in the door. "You wanna talk about what happened? With your mom that other morning?" he says.

I shake my head. I really don't. "I get it."

"Well, why don't I talk and you can listen." Merrick exhales. "I shouldn't have lost my temper. I'm sorry. I shouldn't have sworn at your mom, and so, I'm sorry for that, too. I'm sure you know this, but … no man should ever talk to you that way. No man should ever talk to *anyone* that way. Understand?"

"Yes," I say.

"Good. And you know, if you want to leave here, if you want to go home, or spend a little time at home, then you can. That's your decision. But I want it to be solely your decision. Yes?"

"Yes."

"Okay. And I feel like I need to explain what happened before I found you."

Technically, I found him. "You really don't—"

"I do, though. Because there are consequences to my actions—good and bad. Your mom and I were together because I loved her and she loved me. But it got hard. She was with Sol—your dad—and it was long distance, so she said she would end it. But there was a morality clause in my contract that I just . . . and eventually we both realized that if we were going to be together then, waiting wouldn't hurt us. Only, waiting did hurt us. So even after we'd already been together, we split and went our separate ways with an agreement to eventually try again after she graduated, and so I quit my job and disappeared—which I'm good at—to teach music somewhere else. And then she had you without my knowledge. When I heard through some mutual friend that she and your dad got married just a year later, that she'd had a baby a few months prior to that, I assumed it was his."

Selfish. She's so selfish. The thought manifests and sticks like glue. I ask, "Would you have wanted me?"

Merrick closes his eyes, the expression on his face going tight, then loosening. It's pain, a lot of longing, some wistfulness that sits primarily in the space beneath his eyes. It's a lot.

He opens his eyes and stares at me hard before speaking again. "Then? I wish I could say yes, but the most honest answer I can give you is that I don't know. But your mom was determined to have you. I mean, clearly. Because here you are. But I think she would have had you, and I would have seen you, and I'm certain I would have been yours from the very beginning."

I want that to be true so badly, I wish for it with my whole body, while also thanking whatever blip in the universe gave me Daddy and Tristan and the Quirky Core Four, as Tammy calls us. Despite it all, I'm still *so* here for the Quirky Core Four. For eighteen years, they've been it for me. They were always it for me.

That same night, as we get ready for dinner, I tell Merrick all about how the impromptu tryout went.

From down the hall, in the bathroom, Merrick yells, "You think he'll play you?"

I shrug, knowing he can't see me, as I force a diamond stud through my lobe. "Hope so. I mean, really, I just want him to put me on the team. All I need's a shot. And I did what I could. Tried to create separation from the defenders. Tried to make sure I planted and caught what was mine and what wasn't."

"You're talking gibberish, kiddo, but that's good. I'm proud."

I roll my eyes. "You ever play any sports?"

"Nah," he says. "I was a band geek. I played the cello and stuck with AP Art. That was me. The artsy pothead. You don't smoke pot, do you?"

"Absolutely not."

He appears in my doorway suddenly and laughs. I wonder if he knows I'm lying.

I dress up for them. For Merrick's parents and Emily, who

will criticize my hair, and all the people who take one look at me, see GIRL, and just . . . expect it.

It's a little for me, but a lot for them.

I wear a lacy forest green babydoll dress that hits me right above the knees. And at first I think to pair it with low-heeled booties. Instead, I wear my Sk8-Hi high-top Vans.

Not for fashion. I don't do it for fashion.

I spend too much time thinking about this decision, picking at the cuticles on my thumb. Because I want to wear the booties. Slim likes them a lot and they make my calves look less muscle-y than they are. I choose the high-tops because people probably expect me to. Tasia might wear the booties. Cornerback Taze wears Vans, because the dress needs to be balanced out on the imaginary femininity scale that I live my life in fear of.

I am who people expect me to be.

The booties get chucked into the dark corner of my closet with more force than is necessary.

"T, let's go, baby, chop-chop! My mom hates it when people are late to her dinner table; she's French!" Merrick calls.

Meeting Merrick's parents is a thing that is not supposed to give me anxiety. But my entire life gives me anxiety lately, so the fact that this news sits in my stomach and on my neck like a brick wrapped in wet toilet paper is not unusual.

Kai will be there, and that's a win in my book.

But Emily will also be there, and that's not.

It's nice for Merrick, I'm sure, because he'll get to show his happily married parents that he is A Good Dad.

Anytime he gets to demonstrate this is a good thing. When he buys me vegetables for dinner, that one time a few days ago when he ran down to the corner store and bought me a box of tampons. The way he's been somewhat nice to Kai despite all the overt he-could-get-it looks I've been giving him.

I think Merrick thinks all of these things classify him as A Good Dad, and maybe some of them do. But Daddy never did the grocery shopping, has never talked to me about my period, and would have probably already buried Kai in a shallow grave somewhere, in stereotypical Dad fashion—and he's still a good dad too.

And this dinner, it's pretty nice for me, too, I guess because that box has been burning a hole through the floor of my closet. I wanted to bring it with me so bad, but Merrick basically chewed me out with a single look as we left the apartment.

No matter what, this is another step in the right direction. Another step toward answers. Another step toward some peace and calm and understanding of myself. Another step toward getting rid of this new anxiety that's made it impossible for me to focus on anything else.

On the drive over, Merrick hums some blues song along with the radio and asks me if I'm nervous. I laugh.

"Uhhhm…" is all I have to offer.

But Merrick takes that and accepts it as A Thing We No Longer Need To Talk About.

"Mémé" greets us at the door and is everything you want her to be. She is short and round, but curvy, and warm and blond as hell. She is rose-cheeked and has makeup game for days. She looks like a dame right out of some 1920s film, with gray eyes and hair that she must have spent hours on before "putting the roast in the oven."

But she smells like sugar-dipped grapefruit, and she cries as soon as I walk inside. I feel like we should have knocked, but Merrick didn't bat an eyelash. Mémé's accent is nonexistent. Which is to say: What the fuck? Because I have no shame in admitting that I expected her to be severely French, to use a common phrase. I expected her accent to be as thick as her hips, and only mildly impossible to understand.

It's not. What the hell was Kai even talking about?

Once we're inside, she comments on the volume of my hair, saying I get it from her side of the family, but does not touch, and I guess that, too, is a win.

I've got that "water boiling in a screaming kettle" feeling from being so overwhelmed, but then Kai walks into the room wearing a very tight white Hanes T-shirt, which I think might be mine, and a sleeveless jean jacket over it with his black jeans, socked feet.

And I exhale a little and I don't care who sees it, except Kai, who walks over to me and wraps his arms around me, pulling me in to his neck, in to himself, bringing me all the way outside of myself.

"*AHHHHHH!*" Mémé yells, and it's like hearing her voice over a sound system—she's that loud, her voice that far reaching—and I don't know what she's saying because all there is is Kai.

"What?"

Kai laughs. "She thinks I'm suffocating you."

"My only granddaughter," Mémé says. "I have one, and we need to make sure she lasts, Kai."

Kai's eyebrows meet the ceiling. "She's talkin' about your stamina," he says, and I punch him the chest.

Mémé says, "Good girl!" and then to Kai, "Set the table."

I get very caught up in the fact that everyone seems to know what to do except me. Everyone seems to be living in this weirdo episode of *The Brady Bunch* except me. I stand in the middle of the small but open living room, wondering whose way I might be impeding. Wondering if it's okay for me to take my jacket off.

Merrick's already sitting in front of a large flatscreen— probably the newest thing in this entire house—in the living room next to an older gentleman who hasn't said a word to me. No one has bothered to introduce us.

Cool.

I don't see or hear Emily, so I assume she hasn't arrived on her very own alcohol-soaked glitter cloud yet.

Merrick's mom sings loudly, but—aha!—Frenchly, as she bangs—literally, she is banging—around in the kitchen. Had I not smelled the food, I might have wondered if she was just trying to break as many dishes as possible.

Kai is seated on the floor in a corner of the kitchen, not far from Merrick's mom's constantly moving feet. Each time she passes him, her fingers find his hair for a silent stroke.

"So you enjoy football, Tasia." She pours a can of chickpeas into a brassy looking pot.

Merrick talked about me? About the things I like? About me and football?

"Yes, ma'am."

"Don't be so formal," she says, then pats the counter right above where Kai is sitting. "Sit." It's a command. I obey. "I don't watch it, but I've noticed Merrick seems to be taking a recent interest."

"He tries," I say. "I'm trying to teach him."

"Good. Men need a little instruction from their superiors."

This is when I first learn that my grandmother is like hot oil in a shallow skillet—dangerous when you get too close, but perfect with just the right amount of caution.

She stirs the pot of rice for a moment and then turns to me. "And what about college? Plans?"

"Haven't heard back from any of the places I've applied." I shrug. "Just a waiting game now."

She *tsk*s. "Waiting is hell, they say. And you'll play football in college?"

"They do say that. When I get in to Berkeley, I might take up another sport. I don't know. They don't really let women play college football." It's practically unheard of. I'm no Shelby Osborne.

"When," she says.

"What?"

"You said 'When I get in to Berkeley.' You're so sure."

I mean . . . "Well, yeah."

She laughs. "I'm not judging. It's good for women to

know we can have whatever we want."

Kai laughs. I'd almost forgotten he was down there, except not really, because now it's my hands in his hair, and every couple of minutes he turns his lips up into my palm to bite the meatiest parts of it.

"Do you speak French?" I ask. Everything's just so skewed. I'd hoped this expectation, at least, would hold.

"Not anymore," Kai says, just as she says, "Ouí."

She pours a deep glass of the bloodiest wine I've ever seen and then offers me a shorter glass, which I sip slowly. Kai drinks his like he doesn't enjoy it, in three messy gulps.

She amends, "We moved here when we married. I was very young."

"How young?"

"Nineteen." The same age as Mamma when she got pregnant with me. "The grump in the living room, he was older. Nine years my senior."

What *is it* with these age gaps?

I nod. "So you moved here. And did what?"

"Well, nothing at first. I worked to lose the accent so that I could find work."

"What kind of work?"

She hands me a cherry tomato and I pop it in my mouth to bite it in half before passing the rest to Kai.

"She was an actress," Kai says, chewing.

"No way."

She doesn't even pretend to be shy about it. In fact, her spine straightens. She maybe even preens a little. "I was great," she says. "Your grandfather worked for Les Films Corona. Very big production company up through the 1970s."

"So why did you move here, then? If he was successful there?"

"He was successful. I was successful. I had your father a few years before we moved to America and my career as a French actress had peaked. And," she cautions, "when you taste success once, you always crave more. So we moved here. He worked to make American connections; I worked at learning to lose the accent. And I did."

This story feels fantastical. Unreal in so many ways. "Were you ever in anything I might have heard of?"

She laughs. "No, mon cher. I was in one or two things before I got pregnant with Emily."

Makes sense. A lot of Merrick's mannerisms are much more Eurocentric than Emily's. His hugs are firm but less bone crushing, the volume and pitch of his voice is a bit lower.

The space around me feels thick.

Something on the stove begins to boil over, so she adjusts the heat. "Well. I can't wait to have you meet some of our friends at Mass soon. They'll love you."

"Why?"

"Why shouldn't they?" she says.

"Right. So you're Catholic?"

"We are."

Kai pinches my calf. I pull his hair.

"I didn't lose that, at least. My faith. Might be the only reason I survived this country full of blond women who judged the thickness of my words."

I hate how it sounds like she's saying she lost an integral part of who she is. Like, some French woman's diaspora. Because, to me, "French woman" isn't who she is. To me, she's just another standard white woman. I don't like that she thinks she can just . . . escape the fact that *she is a white woman.* She's not exempt from that. Every part of this feels so aggressively . . . effortful? Like, she's just trying so hard with the wine and the mention of Mass, and there's a baguette on the counter. It's just . . .

She pulls out a very large blender from someplace overhead where it probably should not have fit. "Kai, be a gentleman. Keep my Tasia entertained until dinner, yes?"

Kai laughs as he stands and helps me off the counter. She picks up his wrist and slaps the back of his hand with her potholder six times.

He laughs again and she scolds him about being a "perverted little boy." And then we make our way down the hall. And then Merrick is yelling.

"Hey, hey, hey, hey, whoa! Whoa. Where y'all going?"

Kai holds up his hands, my left still in his right. "I'm just following your mom's orders."

"Follow them in a more public space."

And then the blender shuts off and Merrick's mom marches into the living room, smacks her son with that same potholder. "I have had enough. Enough of you men. From now on—my Tasia and I, we dictate the rhythm of things."

"Like hell," the older gentleman mutters.

"Go on and show her your room, Kai."

"Like fuck!" Merrick says, and this time she hits him but does not spare the pot holder.

Emily slams the front door, announcing her arrival loud enough to crack the paint, just as Kai and I walk down the hall again, and somehow he's suckered me into giving him a piggyback ride, and we both almost die on the way there, but we're laughing too, so it's pretty much okay.

Chapter Twenty-Six

Kai's room is like a rainforest made of copper and metal bobs and bells. There's a mesh grate covering a lot of the far wall, tiny pieces of metalwork hang from the ceiling, and the most incredible art all over the place. Canvases of every size. The theme of most of them seems to be eyes, and even within those eyes there seems to be a theme—dark browns, light browns. The only variation is the hazels, which have tiny specks of green. There's a concentration of those.

"Did you paint these?"

He laughs. "Hell, no. I'm not that talented."

I nod. "No, you're definitely not." And then I'm in a headlock.

I'm about to kidney shot him but he lets me go, because I'm sure—I'm sure—he can feel the punch coming, and falls onto his bed. I crawl up next to him and position my legs across his chest. Kai runs his short, blunt nails across my calves and shins, then says, "Eww, you missed a spot," like he just fell into a patch of my leg hair.

I immediately try to pull my legs back, but his reflexes are fast and he catches my ankles. "Jesus, I'm jokes, Taze." I try to pull them back again and he says, "It's just body hair."

I want to snap at him that *I know.* But I don't. I feel a little bit chastised for reacting the way I did, about my own body, even. All of it is ridiculous.

"How come I've never been in your room before?"

He shrugs. "Good question. Probably because you've never been here before, to this place where your *grandparents* live. Couldn't exactly sneak you in for a quickie, now, could I?"

A quickie? A quick what, I wonder. Even though I know— my stomach and the chills on my neck all know. "Yeah, but Merrick's always at the garage apartment and you're there a lot."

Kai nods and drums out a beat on my leg. "Fair. But, I don't know. Merr is Merr. So it's not that serious."

"I like it in here."

"Yeah, me too."

"Will you help me make my room like this? At the apartment?"

He nods and says, "If you teach me to throw a football."

"You're charging me a fee?"

"Yeah. I am."

I like it. "Okay. But there won't be any pulling you up tight against me the way people learn to shoot pool, I hope you know."

He pauses a sec. "Damn. Fine, then I'm not wearing those little spandex shorts I know you've been dying to see me in."

That earns him a flick to the forehead as I stand and relocate to lie down on his floor. Kai follows and sits perpendicular to my hip. I spy an NYU pamphlet underneath his bed.

On the tip of my tongue, burning like a box of Red Hots, are about a dozen questions regarding his college preferences and decisions. Whether or not he even has any he feels sure about.

"Do you know if you have any siblings?" I ask instead.

"I do," he says. "I have a brother. Adam."

I jackknife and thank myself for spending time on those extra situps. "You do? Older or younger?"

"Mmm . . . older," he says. As though he had to think about it. As though, deciding right then, he could make it true.

"By a lot?"

"Why? You trying to date him?"

"Maybe!" I say, and he uses his thumb, index, and middle fingers to squeeze the ticklish pressure points on the sides of my knee.

I laugh and push his hand away. After reaching behind him for a pen, he runs a smooth line of ink across my shin. I can't tell what it is yet, but the lines are long and sweeping and swirling, like my moods lately.

Kai can make all the world's problems go away with just a minor dose of his creativity. I close my eyes and say a tiny prayer of thanks that I am the one who, I think—I hope—gets to see it most.

"He lives in New York. Goes to college up there. He's almost done. Has a girlfriend and they're super freakin' in love. It's pretty cool."

"That the reason for the NYU pamphlet?"

"I guess," he says. His voice is calm, his words steady. But his face, it gives him away. It's the sad smile.

"Did you apply?"

Kai laughs and this time it's genuine, touching the highest points on his cheeks. "Yeah. Adam made me."

"And you wanna go there? To NYU?"

He stretches, and I spy the flat plane of his stomach, the small trail of hair leading . . . "Eyes up here, Tasia."

I throw the pamphlet at him.

Kai catches it, laughing. "Full of questions tonight. To answer you: Yeah. I think I do wanna go there. If I end up going anywhere for college, I'd like it to be NYU."

I feel . . . relief? Relieved to know someone else is checking for him. "Do you see him often? Your brother?"

"Nah, not really. I snapped some photos of us the last time I did, though. You wanna see?"

I nod. "Yeah."

He gets up off the floor and rifles through his closet.

While he looks, I make a circuit around the room. On the floor, inside an Earth globe he's sawed in half, are a bunch of Polaroids. I pull one of the pictures out and the image…

The image makes me pause.

The photo is, undoubtedly, of him kissing another dude.

"Umm, hey," I say. "Are you bisexual?"

Kai whips around and looks up at me. He shrugs. "I don't know. Probably." And then he's back in the closet searching again.

I mean.

All right.

Cool.

Except the redhead boy in the picture with him is . . .

"Umm," I say again. "Is this Cole?"

"We dated for a little. So, yeah, I guess I am. I'm bisexual. Okay, I found it!"

He takes the picture of him and Cole out of my hand and is about to throw it into a copper wastebasket, but then he stops, turning back to me. "Unless you want it?"

I laugh. "Why would I want that?"

"If there were pictures of you kissing a girl, I would want those."

I shove him. "Asshole."

"Are there pictures of you—"

"No!"

"Just checking," he says. "Here." And then I'm staring at a picture of his older brother with a pretty Asian girl. He and his brother look nothing alike.

His brother is super blond and has solid brown eyes, not broken like Kai's.

I hand the picture back to him. "Can I ask you a question?"

He nods, and starts to weave some thin gold wire around a black chain. I love it when he gets distracted like this.

"Can you see okay?"

He looks at me like I just asked him if his dick is crooked.

"Yes," he says. "I see fine. It's just a birth defect."

"Would you ever lie to me?"

"No. I'm telling you—my vision's fine, Tasia."

"Don't get mad, it's just a question."

"I'm not mad."

"Okay, fine, but you just called me Tasia and you don't ever call me Tasia, so."

He puts the chain down.

He walks toward me.

We're not far apart but it feels like it takes him forever to reach me.

We're pressed close together a second later. I don't know when we got here. Not physically, but just . . . I don't know when we both agreed that we were each other's to touch as we want. I never want to go back.

My arms hang at my sides and he brings them up and around his neck, maneuvers me like a doll, and then suddenly his hands meet the back of my thighs and I'm hoisted up and against him, and then he is catching my surprised gasp in his mouth, with his tongue and his teeth and I whisper hard and fast and so desperately I want to split myself in two, begging him for "the wall, the wall, the wall, Kai." And he obliges because I am pressed hard up against the empty wall and he's pushing up against me and my dress leaves me totally exposed, and when did we stop kissing because I'm breathing in the scent of his neck—a soft scent I can't even begin to describe or put a finger on—and each hit, each push of his jean-clad hips, only adds another pulsing, radiating circle of pleasure to my entire body.

I'm starting to sweat and so is he and I don't even know who I am, because I lick a drop of perspiration right off his neck and he groans.

He's chanting, it's an incantation, it's profanity, and it's my name and somehow they're one and the same. We're both so close, I can feel it happening for him and—

"Descendre à dîner, s'il vous plaît!"

Shit.

"Dammit," Kai says. "Dinner. She says dinner is ready."

No.

And Kai laughs. I've said it out loud. Jesus.

Before I go down the hall, Kai grabs my hand, pulls me close again, kisses me soft and gentle and sweet and tender, like sunflower petals.

"Are you gonna write about our first kiss in your diary?"

I shove him away from me, mutter, "Ass," and then follow his retreat, pulling him back to me. I want to be the one to kiss him this time. It's like I'm trying to crawl inside him, trying to fuse us together. I nip his lip and then drag my lips across his cheek to his ear, whisper, "Thank you."

I'm in the living room first and Kai comes five minutes later and I want to kill him because *I know* people can tell there's some reason for his delay. He sits in his chair, directly across from me, legs sprawled and stretching into my space, as though we'd been in his room discussing politics this whole time.

I hate him and I like him. So much. Not even the universe could contain this thing we've got going.

The world's most awkward Meeting Your Long Lost Grand-daughter dinner happens in Mémé and Pépé's dining room.

"What is this?" I say. Merrick passes me a Pyrex dish full of chunky something. That's just what I'm calling it even though I assume they're mashed potatoes—"Chunky-Something."

They laugh like I just told a joke. Kai knows better.

"That's mac and cheese," Emily says.

Oh.

"And this is . . . ?"

"Tasia, honey. That's green bean casserole. Stop kidding around and eat your dinner."

There's a lot of food on this table. Some of it—mostly the traditionally French food—looks okay but most of it looks like all the color has been zapped out of it.

Kai laughs and Merrick glares at him and Pépé scoffs and Mémé tries to tell me about her bridge club in French but gets so frustrated about mixing up a few words that she switches back to English for like sixty-seven percent of the conversation.

The final straw is when Emily asks me what sort of highlight and bronzer I use.

"Melanin," I answer pointedly.

It isn't the worst family get-together I've been to, but it is the one where I feel the most like an intruder. It's the family get-together that helps me realize I don't do family get-togethers for the food. I do it for the community, the culture. I do them because, usually, the people involved are the most accepting of who I am, on every level. I attend them with open eyes and an exposed heart because at least twice a year, the Newarks and the Quirks come together and Poppa camps out in the Barcalounger and doesn't move for the entire day. I do it because usually those occasions mean Mamma will make three sweet potato pies—two for the party, one for the days to follow when we're all craving it again. I do it because after everyone's eaten and settled in the largest possible open room, I always get to nap in Daddy's study while he takes a few sneaky work calls that Mamma usually does not permit. I do it because the food is what I was raised on. The company is who I was raised with.

This whole thing with Merrick and the box, I wonder how much I might have cheated myself with impatience. This need to move and unravel the mystery.

Someone clears their throat across the table from me.

It's him. The crotchety, voiceless man at the table. Apparently, he's my grandfather.

Pépé.

He still doesn't say anything to me and whenever there is A Need to say something to me, he'll go absolutely out of his way not to do it.

Merrick's mom talks nonstop about me. Which is weird, because I'm not sure if she's talking *to me* or to everyone else.

"Tasia and her mother plant trees in the local forests, where most have been burned or cut down—did you know?" she says.

And I mean, *I knew*, but how does she?

I glance at Merrick and work so hard not to laugh hysterically. The look on his face says he didn't know either.

"Henri, darling, do you want to ask our Tasia about her football? She's played since she was a girl."

"No," he says. And shoves a bite of rice into his mouth.

Which is fine, because I don't particularly want to tell his cranky-ass about *my football* anyway.

Emily says, "Well, that's rude, Dad."

"It's fine," I say.

Merrick places a hand on top of mine. "It's not, T."

Merrick's mom continues. There's no way she's oblivious to this tension. I can't shovel chickpeas in my mouth fast enough. "She's been awarded all kinds of medals and awards, even met the mayor of Los Angeles last year after receiving one. Isn't that wonderful, Henri? She's so talented."

He harrumphs. And that's it. Nothing more. Just a grump and another shaky bite of rice.

"Dad, what's your problem?" Merrick says.

"No problem," he says. More rice.

Kai cough-speaks, "Bullshit."

And Merrick's mom swears at Kai in French. I know it's a swear because Kai taught me them.

"Dad," Merrick says. "I brought Tasia here so that we could have a nice family dinner. Maybe you should at least attempt to make a minimal amount of effort."

"I think we've had plenty of fine family dinners without—"

Merrick slams a fist down. Silverware clanks against the table, against plates, water glasses shake, Emily yelps.

"Goddammit, Dad."

"Okay," Merrick's mom says. "Okay, enough." She takes control very quickly, like she's been giving commands for years, telling Kai and me to take the food dishes into the kitchen. She instructs Emily to follow and plate up some things for Merrick and me to go.

Once in the kitchen, Emily high-fives me and says, "Good job, girl. Not much gets under Dad's skin."

"Except pushy Americans," Kai adds helpfully.

"Except them," Emily says. "And you're not that."

"Why doesn't he like me?" I ask. I use tongs to place the baked chicken and rice and chickpeas into Tupperware.

They both shrug and we're all three quiet for a second to hear whatever it is they're talking about in the dining room.

Merrick's saying, "—my kid. That girl's my blood. My first and probably my only. I can't believe you're acting like this."

"We don't know she's yours."

"Yes, we do!"

"How!"

"Because I had her DNA tested!"

"Oh, hell," Kai says as he pulls me against him. "We're getting out of here. If I can get us into Fat Freddy's downtown, you want to go?"

"Merrick drove," I say into his chest.

"We'll take the subway. You never drive to those things anyway. Parking's too pricy to valet in the city."

I nod even though I've never worried about the cost of valet.

"Wanna come, Em?"

She chugs the wine still in her glass then drags the full bottle of red off the counter before leaving the kitchen. We take that as her answer.

In the other room, Merrick's still going and I am a little bit proud to be this mistake that he has literally second-guessed at every turn, apparently.

Merrick continues, "Dad. What is this about? You didn't bat an eyelash about Kai."

"He didn't give me a choice."

Merrick laughs. "So what's this about? Because she's proof of my bad judgment? Because she's female?" He pauses. "Tell me it's not because she's Black."

Silence. Well, shit. That's kind of new. I mean, it's not, but it is. He is *supposed to* love me, as his granddaughter or something. It's strange and confusing, all at once, to know that he only sees my race. My skin. And that he sees it as inferior, as lacking. As unworthy of his love or familial connection.

Sometimes I think I would wash it off if I could.

"Don't be an idiot. This isn't about the girl at all. I am not a racist."

"You realize that from where I'm standing, it looks like . . . if this isn't prejudice, then what is it?"

Silence, then Merrick's voice, booming in a way I wasn't aware it could—a way that is different from the way he used it with Mamma that day. "Tell me what this is about, Dad!"

"Everything! So stupid, Merrick. My only son. You were a stupid boy and you've been a stupid man."

"Great. Thanks, Dad."

Merrick walks into the kitchen and Kai and I scramble to get positioned in ways that don't scream, *We listened to* all of that, *bro.*

Chapter Twenty-Seven

In the foyer, I'm shrugging into someone's coat. It's not mine, but it's bigger and would make me look a little homeless if my dress didn't cost three hundred and fifty dollars before tax.

Mémé joins Merrick and me there, and she looks sad, the smile on her face not quite bringing the corners of her mouth high enough on her face.

Merrick glances at me, and I tell him, "I'm going with Kai."

"Listen, Tasia, I—"

"You had my DNA tested?"

"No—yeah, yes, but I just—"

"I can't believe this," I whisper. "When? When the hell would you have had time to do that?"

Merrick shoves a hand into his hair. "Those few days before you moved in. I'm sorry, Tasia."

I looked it up once. Printed out the information for a sibling test and taped it to Tristan's door as a joke. Mamma was pissed. Pretty sure Daddy thought it was hilarious but didn't wanna laugh. Those results could take up to a week. An expedited paternity test could yield results in as little as twelve hours.

I'm sorry, he says. Jesus. *Sorry* is such a flimsy fucking word.

The oversize jacket scritches against itself as I wrap my arms around my middle. "Yeah, well. Sorry you didn't get the results you wanted." I say it to hurt him because I can and because I'm the only one here bleeding out on the floor.

And of course he shakes his head. Says little. And then he mumbles something to his mom that I don't hear and he takes off.

She sighs. "Someday, we will manage to do this properly. Until then, it was a pleasure to meet you, my sweet Tasia."

I nod. "Nice to meet you, too…."

"Mémé. You can say it. You may call me it. If you want."

Okay. Here is one of those moments where you apply a thing you've learned and prove you haven't just been sitting on your ass letting life teach you shit but not taking notes. I took notes.

"I don't feel comfortable calling you that." I can't. Not out loud.

She looks like I struck her.

"Not yet," I add quickly.

One time, when I was maybe eight or nine, I told Mamma I didn't like it when she had wine because it made her clothes smell funny—what I would later realize was a result of the tea cigarettes she'd smoke with her drinks—and she looked at me kind of the way Merrick's mom is now. Like I told her I didn't like her, who she was inherently.

I continue, "I just don't think I'm ready for that sort of thing yet. I want to get to know you and earn the right to call you that. I want us to be close and I want you to teach me to cook French food like you made tonight and about the side of my French history that I didn't know was there. I think I want to call you that but I can't. Right now."

She nods. "So smart, my Tasia. You can call me Vivienne. Or V. My friends called me this when I was a girl. No one does now, but maybe you could?"

I nod and I feel the smile stretch my face, push at my cheeks, and pull at my lips.

"And," I continue. "Can you tell him…" I nod toward the living room, where the television blares. "Tell him he hurt my feelings. Tell him he was rude, and he hurt me, but I forgive him."

"Okay," she says smiling. "Kai!"

He appears like magic and I know he listened in. I will give him shit later.

"Be good, you two. Not too late, Kai, huh?"

He nods.

"My sweet Tasia, next time you'll have to tell me all about running those marathon races, yes? It sounds intriguing."

We're down the sidewalk before I pause.

I'm literally stopped in my tracks. The football awards, meeting the mayor, the tree planting, the 5K. All clippings from the box.

Holy hooker.

My feet carry me back to the house faster than I'd have ever thought possible. I burst through the door and V is yelling at Henri in the most bastardized French—part English, part French, part I-don't-even-know-what.

"Tasia," she says, turning. "Everything okay?"

"No," I say. "Nothing."

"What? What is wrong?"

"The box. The box is you."

She's shaking her head. She doesn't understand. I falter a little, but then she says, "Pardon?"

And I find I have to keep going. I'm not wrong.

"You knew about me," I say. "You've known about me since the beginning. For years. You knew I was Merrick's and you didn't tell him."

"Tasia, cher—"

"No." I'm not wrong. The look on her face is enough of an admission. Her expression changes slowly, like the way it feels to try walking while waist deep in a pool of water. Her expression is synonymous with sweet bite, with soft breaking. It's the way her jaw clenches and flattens her bottom lip out even more.

V starts toward me. "Listen . . ."

"No, *you* listen. You ruined my life. You lit a match, tossed it at me, and let it all burn. Why would you do that? Why would you send me that box!"

"I—it was my box. It is. And . . . you are right. I have known."

"Vivienne," Henri says. And she shushes him, holding her hand up.

"Please," she says. "Let me just finish. I didn't tell my son because he wasn't ready to know. And clearly your mother did not want him to know. It was not my secret to tell—"

"But then you sent—"

"No, listen to me. I did not send it to you. I have kept it all these years and have seldom remembered it exists."

Ouch.

"So . . . you're saying you didn't send it to me. Had no intention to do so? At any point? Ever?"

"I am sorry, fleur."

I shake my head. Turn. Run.

Run, run, run. When Tristan was four, he fell into the pond at our neighbor's house. Mamma, Trist, Daddy, and I had been invited there for the Mamaya's annual Fourth of July barbecue. Mamma spent all morning cooking, like, five different side dishes, the house smelling like hot oil and cayenne, and once finished, she wrapped them more lovingly than any Christmas or birthday present she'd ever given us.

We were at the party for all of thirty, maybe forty, minutes when Trist ran on his wobbly toddler legs down the dock and veered too far right to course correct.

I wasn't far from him, standing on the edge of the grass, right at the dock's start. But I couldn't move. I couldn't call for help or scream. I could barely breathe.

The pond wasn't deep—not that any of us knew that. But it was, however, too deep for Tristan.

Mamma screamed when she noticed, giving chaos an actual sound. And Daddy ran in his khakis and loafers and jumped in, no reservations whatsoever, to the sound of Mamma's, "Get him, get him! The baby! Get the baby, Sol!"

And Daddy saved him.

My baby brother nearly drowned, and at six years old, I learned to hate myself for not having done more. Learned to fear myself for not being able to act. That feeling—that frozen, can't move, can't breathe, spine-numbing, hate-yourself feeling I had then—it is a mirror of everything I'm feeling now.

Tristan had nightmares for two weeks after that. He'd wake up screaming, crying, calling out for Daddy, who—in Trist's nightmare—had drowned. So Tristan slept in Mamma's bed for those two weeks, because she needed him to. Needed to know her son was safe and not at the bottom of a shallow pond.

And Daddy had slept in my room with me. Because I needed him to. Needed him to save me, too.

Now I wonder if Kai, waiting for me at the end of the block, seated on the curb, is going to be the one to save me from this. To pull me out of the pond of my inky emotions.

As we make our way down the street to the Metrolink, Kai says, "The others are already at the stop after our first. We'll link up." It's the first thing he's said since I came jogging back to him.

"You all right?"

I nod.

"Wanna talk about what happened in there?"

I shake my head.

"Well. Good job," he says. "Telling her what you wanted. And making sure everyone knows Henri is a dickhead."

"I never said—"

"Eh, whatever, close enough. You did good," he says, and reaches for my hand. I like walking down a public street holding hands with a boy. It's not like I've never done that before. I have. But with Kai, it's different. Like, maybe he's letting me keep him. Letting me keep him and his weird eyes and his hideous style and his talent and sexuality and creativity.

Confused, football-playing Black girl gets to keep something good.

It's a nice change.

But given everything tonight . . . I don't know how to enjoy it. How not to have my heart crumbling to pieces like a dry scone.

I wonder if scones are French.

Where does any of this leave me? If these are answers, why do I feel like I only have more questions? There's nothing good about any of what I feel right now.

"And my eyes," he says, like he heard me thinking about them a moment ago. "Just so you know, I don't think they're a thing that makes me special. I can see fine. They're nothing but trouble—I mean, as a kid they were just trouble. They made me a target for cliché, schoolyard bullying that never got policed. They made it hard for me to get adopted. They're not some great, special thing. But I'm okay with who I am, at the very least."

"You change your look often," I tell him. He is not okay with how he looks.

"I do." He is not okay with who he is.

"Okay."

On the train, there's standing room only. Our friends load on at our first stop. Dahlia's there and it's weird because we don't speak. Cole's there and he only speaks to Kai until I place my hand, selfishly, on the bottom of Kai's jean vest, which now sits over a gray zip-up.

Sam and Victory are there. Victory is wearing a simple black gele with orange geometric shapes on it. I love it. I wish I were that bold. I wish I felt that entitled. I wish I could and I know I can't. I want to ask her to show me how she tied it.

"Thanks for your help on the Trig bonus sheet," Sam says.

I shrug. I didn't so much help him as take pictures of my own paper and text them to him. "Sure," I say.

"You're done already?" Victory says. I don't know if she's talking to me or to Sam, but I answer anyway.

"Yeah. I could send you what I got?"

She looks at me so long that I can almost hear the thoughts in her head. She's considering it. I know she is. She hates that she's considering it. Only, maybe that doesn't matter, because she doesn't say yes or no. Eventually I stop waiting for her answer, knowing she isn't going to give me one.

My thoughts drift back to the box. Back to V and Henri and the lies I need to somehow give meaning to. I need to—

I push that away. The need. Not now. Right now I'm here. I'm with Kai, his chest pressed against my back, arms wrapped around my waist.

Soon we all fall silent and just listen to the swoosh and lull of the subway running against the tracks.

A mother holds a baby in her lap.

A homeless man sleeps with his small three-legged dog in the corner.

Kai kisses my cheek at every stop the subway makes. I have got six kisses in my pocket so far. We've got one more stop and I'm sad the predictability of his kisses will end, so I make it what I want it to be.

As we coast to a stop, I turn in his arms, push up onto my toes, and kiss him hard. Kai has to reach up high and hold on to a nearby pole to maintain both our balances. Someone takes a picture, posts it to Instagram.

But before any of that even happens—I can feel it: we are the sort of viral that exists forever.

Slim texts me as our small circle arrives at the venue.

miss you, t-dot

I text her back quickly. I know she won't appreciate it, but I don't want to spend all night catching up via text, not while I'm out. *miss you too* is all she gets.

When we arrive at the venue, Dahlia goes in because she and Sam are the only ones in our group with fakeys.

She texts Kai thirty minutes later that we should meet her around the back, and when we figure out where that is, she finally lets us inside and makes a big fuss about us owing her for it.

"Did the bouncer even card you?" Victory says. "I didn't see him look at anything but your tits."

"Which is a thing I have and none of the rest of you do," Dahlia says. She's right—we're all either A-cups or cis males.

But Victory just says, "Whatever," and shoves her way around the circle, drawing an X in black sharpie on each of our wrists to signal we're cleared to drink. There's like zero chance that it's believable because none of us, except maybe Dahlia, look twenty-one, but we make our way to the bar anyway and order drinks. I don't know what's in my cup but I drink it down quickly because it's bitter and gross. We have two more of the same size, the same drink mixture, whatever it is. Kai laughs and kisses me firm and fast after I hold my nose and finish off my third.

Cole looks hard at us.

Dahlia looks hard at us.

I kiss Kai harder to push their looks out of my mind.

This thing with me and Kai—it seems sudden to them, I know. But not for me. It wasn't sudden for me. It feels right. Real. *Fated,* if that's a word I'm even allowed to use at eighteen.

"Hey," he yells in my ear. "Just you and me." And I pull back and meet his eyes; I don't know what he's talking about, until I do. Then it's all there, laid out in front of me. I nod. I agree.

Tristan texts me too. *we owe the words "assassination" and "bump" to shakespeare. cool right??*

I text him back a thumbs-up emoji.

you ok?

out, I send back.

And he doesn't text again. He's been initiating our texts more and more lately, and I think that's basically our code for a truce.

Another band, X Ambassadors, is playing their set first and they're ridiculously good. Worth the trip alone. Bluesy and soulful and alternative with some rock undertones. They finish right as we shove our way to the front and Kai pulls my back to his front, his height and his unidentifiable cute-boy smell covering me.

Once Milky Chance comes on, we listen to a few songs before we all sort of branch off. Cole toward the exit to smoke with Sam, Kai and Victory to get us more drinks at the bar. Dahlia links arms with me right in front of the stage and sways a little.

"I gotta pee! Come with me to the bathroom," Dahl says. I glance over my shoulder. No one's come back yet and I don't want to lose them. I also don't want to mention my worries to Dahlia, so I don't, and instead I follow her.

Once we wait in line for twenty minutes and then go into a handicap stall together, Dahlia says, "Oh my God, it's so loud out there. You wanna pee first?"

"I don't have to."

"You should. Go ahead, I'll turn around."

I mumble that it's not that serious, she doesn't have to, and I squat and pee.

Dahlia babbles about nothing and also everything. How much her eyebrow pencil costs, that she's never been outside of California, how she had sex with a boy from Canoga High, a senior named Peter.

"He had tattoos," she says. "I'm a sucker for tattoos."

I flush and stand and readjust my panties.

"I think that's why I was so into Kai," she says.

I pause. Maybe I'm drunk. I haven't ever had enough to drink to make me dumb and clumsy and forgetful. But I trip a little. Not that there's far to go in the stall—there's literally only room for half an extra body in here and how this qualifies as "handicap" is beyond me.

Dahlia takes a seat. Like, right on the seat with no cover. I am a little grossed out and I focus on that for so long that I wonder if I really am drunk off those three terrible drinks I had.

"Wait," I say, shaking my head like that's supposed to clear the cobwebs. That never actually works, by the way. It makes things way, way worse. "Kai has tattoos?"

"Just one, but it's intricate, so it counts. Haven't you ever seen him barefoot?"

I nod. Have I? "I don't know. What did I drink?"

She shrugs. "It's on his foot. You haven't seen his foot?" She laughs and I'm so mad at her for laughing. I clam up, thinking that somehow this—my silence—will serve as some kind of punishment for her. I hate it—this feeling is stupid and ridiculous. "What kind of sex have you guys even been having? Fully clothed, huh? That could be hot. I guess."

I can't hold my tongue anymore. "Shit," I say, but it definitely wasn't the word I wanted to let out. I meant to think it. I want Kai. "Are you done?"

"You're so cute. We haven't even had that much to drink, Tasia."

I shake my head. Am I drunk? "Can we find Kai?"

"Jesus, you guys are attached at the hip. Always together, or always talking about each other. Here's a hint. People hate that. It is *annoying*."

I walk out and leave her in the bathroom, and she laughs as the water runs and she washes her hands and I don't look back because if I do, I'll get frustrated that I *didn't* wash my hands.

I don't go back toward the stage. I walk outside. If I can find Sam and Cole. Or just Sam, maybe. Then it'll be fine. I just need someone who's on my side.

God, I wish my mamma was here. Or not here, but around. I wish I was around her. I can't find Sam and I can't find Cole and I'm so angry. I sit down on the curb and hang my head. A strange guy, some redhead with a beer belly, gives me a bottle of water, but I can't twist the cap off.

He asks me who I came with. He smells like chocolate Axe. I know it's chocolate Axe because Tristan had a phase.

I let out one hard, forced bark of a laugh. Everything about tonight feels hard and tangible and emotionally monochromatic and *God, why wouldn't she say something if she's known about me all this time?*

Redhead Guy offers to open the water and I almost let him, even though that's against the Drunk Girl rules that Slim and I came up with.

I finally get the water open by myself and I breathe through my nose as I sip it slowly.

Redhead Guy asks people who I belong to and then asks me if I want to sit somewhere that's not the curb because "It's not safe to be so close to the street."

I agree and he helps me sit at a red-bricked planter.

Sam and Cole come walking up fast. "Oh my God, there you are!" Sam holds me close and Cole says, "Told you she was fine."

"She's not fine, Cole," Sam says, all hard, jumping consonants. Sam's whole life is hard. "Jesus. Try not to be a dick right now, just because she's with Kai."

Cole scoffs. "That has nothing to do with anything. But thanks for outing me."

"I didn't out you—you did that yourself."

Cole shakes his head and walks away. "Whatever, I'll get Kai."

I lean on Sam. God, I'm sleepy. I don't want to take the train home because it reeks and I feel like if I have to puke later it's gonna be real hard to manage.

"It's okay, T. I got you," Sam says. And then to Redhead Guy, "Thanks for taking care of my friend."

"Think she'd give me her phone number if she were sober?"

"No! You literal shit-stain on Grandmother's couch, no.

She wouldn't. Can you back off? She has a boyfriend and she'd kick your ginger ass if she were sober."

Redhead puts his hands up and backs away and a second later, Kai comes out and exhales hard. "Oh my God, thanks, Sam."

Sam releases me into Kai's arms and I slump against him.

Kai whispers, "You drank too much, little wino?" He laughs.

"Don't call me that," I mumble. I know those words don't come out right.

"I'm gonna take her home."

Sam and Victory nod. They're the only ones still outside with us.

When did Vic even get outside?

"I'll come with you," Sam says.

"Me, too." This from Victory. "Who gave her that water?" Her hand brushes up against my cheek.

Sam ticks with a series of hard Ns before he can get out, "I think that guy that was helping her."

"Toss that shit," Kai says. "Tory, can you get her another one from the bar? Or maybe, like, some ice chips?"

She nods and runs off and she's back fast. Like, so fast. So fast it makes me dizzier.

I giggle. "That stupid fucking box. She wasn't even gonna tell 'im 'bout me."

"What the hell's she talking about?" Victory says.

Sam's cologne is starting to make me sick. "No idea."

And then we're on the train platform. Kai's sitting on the

floor and I'm sitting next to him and he's running an ice cube against the back of my neck. He kisses the black X on my wrist.

A homeless man walks up and asks for spare change. Kai gives him everything in his wallet, which probably isn't more than thirty dollars, but, still, it's everything.

I think I love Kai. He's so good. But probably you're not supposed to trust feelings that big when you've had as much to drink as I have.

Then we're on another train. This one's blue and orange instead of green and gray like the first one.

And then we're in Victory's car. And then we're at V and Pépé's and I'm in bed.

Kai's bed.

It's cold and Kai helps me out of my Vans as I mumble about becoming a shut-down cornerback, out of my dress, into his shirt, out of my haze, and he stays.

I know he lives here but there is an ever-present sense of comfort I get knowing he doesn't go far from me at all. He stays.

Kai stays with me. I just breathe and apologize.

I whisper "I'm sorry" six times and wonder if maybe things aren't meant to be this hard after all.

Chapter Twenty-Eight

When your hair is brittle and your skin is tight and your palate is dry and you can feel a literal ball of puke sitting in your throat.

That is me, in all my underage drinking glory, the next morning.

Despite the fact that I have clearly been hit by a Mack truck, I still know exactly where I am. I'm in Kai's bed. Kai sleeps, curled into a tiny ball on a nest of blankets on the floor, which I know V probably made him do.

He's unmoving. Doesn't snore. Doesn't even twitch. He's a lot like that when he's awake, actually. Always in a resting state. He comes most alive when he's touching me or when he's creating things, and it's especially magical when those two things live inside one another.

I drink the glass of stagnant water on the nightstand, which wasn't there before, I know. It may or may not have been set there for me, but it's mine now. Plus, I mean, I don't wanna be tasting the alcohol twelve hours from now during the game tonight.

After finishing, I crawl shamefully toward Kai's floor-nest. I curl up and shove my way under him. He rolls, his long legs stretching, pushing into my space, his lanky, Slenderman arms pulling me toward him. He murmurs, "What time is it?"

"Six fifteen," I say, which means I don't have long to linger here, since I have to be present and accounted for during the school day in order to be eligible to play tonight.

He groans, "Fuuuuuck . . ." but pulls me closer.

Pause here. I don't know what to do with the very obvious morning wood pressed against me. If I'm obligated to do something about it or if it's like a wandering pigeon, something that just is, a thing you ignore until it goes away.

Eww.

When I think about sex, I think about it being beautiful and vocal and ripe and, like, maybe a good workout or pastime or whatever. I don't think about it being obligatory or coincidental all because morning wood is an unavoidable biological response.

Still, I reach for Kai's boxer brief-clad hips, rub my hand against him. He flinches away and shakes his head. "Shhh…"

It's his version of "you don't have to, it's fine." Okay. So, basically I was right about the bird. Ignore it and it will go away.

But now that he's telling me I don't have to, I've suddenly decided I want to. I need to. I'm starting to throb and it's a good feeling. I want to prolong it.

I kiss his neck, pull his hand toward me, between my legs,

and he doesn't hesitate, even though his eyes are still closed, even though he's still at least sixty percent not-awake.

I lift my shirt—Kai's shirt that I am wearing—higher.

He pushes my panties aside.

I panic about the state of *me* for literally only the moment it takes him to say, "You're okay. Let me? Please?"

When I don't say anything he says, "Do you want me to? Or not want me to?"

I don't even know the difference.

"You can say no."

I nod and breathe, "I'm scared."

He pulls back fast. He is officially eighty percent awake. "Are you a virgin?"

"No," I say. "Not—" technically. "No."

He gets it. I see it in his cracked, mismatched eyes. Slow. He knows this means go slow.

He rubs me again. Staring into my eyes to be sure that it's okay to pull my panties aside once more. And when I do it for him, he smiles a little.

Insistent, fast pressing and then the slick slide of one knuckle into me.

Kai doesn't kiss me. I don't kiss him. But he holds my stare like he can break my eyes up into the same colors as his.

I want him to.

I want him to.

I want him to.

I come apart. I nod to him and I come apart.

Later, I tiptoe into the bathroom, doing my damnedest to avoid V. I wash my face, pat my neck down with water, and swirl toothpaste around my mouth. Tie my mountain of hair into a bun on top of my head and find Kai down the hall, in the living room.

Normally we'd catch a single bus and be back at Merrick's but it seems we're both incredibly languid and made of water, and also needing to punch a metaphorical clock to get to school, so we Uber to Merrick's and get there in fifteen minutes, and Kai piggybacks me up the stairs to the garage apartment.

We almost die twice and it's great.

I don't think about the box once.

Chapter Twenty-Nine

For a lot of high school football players, Friday Night Lights is more than a TV show starring perfect human specimen Kyle Chandler. It's the time we're basically made into kings, revered for what we can do with our bodies, our time, our dedication.

I die a little inside when our team walks onto the field to start warming up. It's not that I haven't seen the field before. I have. It's just that it's a different thing entirely at seven o'clock at night, lights blazing from high above, a crowd full of people watching, their chatter barely a hum from where I stand. I'm no one right now. Aside from those scant few who do know me, everyone else will have to wait and figure me out as the night goes on.

It's been a pretty brutal ass-kicking, trying to get Coach to start me. Two-a-days are required. I add on one more, a solo, to really push myself. To put my skills on a figurative display shelf.

Plus, Taze Quirk lives for the opportunity to prove people wrong on the field.

Though, as much as I breathe for this, the inside of my mouth goes numb with anxiety. I can barely feel my mouth-piece. My pulse beats heavy in my wrists and the bottoms of my feet.

It's not comfortable, no. But it's also the happiest I've been in a long time. Slim has always been right to call me a pain slut. Not many people could do what I do on this field and enjoy it. Talk about it like it's precious metal.

I go through our warm-up drills feeling like I've got wings. That is, until the anthem. The teams line up on their respective sides and the announcer welcomes the friends and families to tonight's game, then requests all to rise for our national anthem.

All around the bleachers, people stand and hands come up to meet chests. The faces blur together. A girl from our school named Endira is introduced to sing.

I'm kneeling with both hands crossed on one of my knees.

I hear somebody swear behind me. It's probably Coach. A few guys from the team laugh or mutter things like, "She's mad fucking disrespectful. My dad's a Marine."

Teeth gritted, I say nothing, continue to kneel, eyes forward.

To my left, Adrian and Guy both kneel as well and it's then and only then that I can breathe a little easier, that I settle into who I am as an athlete, a woman, a Black girl. Only then, when two other Black kids join me. This is the first time

I've knelt, although police brutality against Black people has been a longstanding tradition in America. I think maybe I've just started a new pre-game tradition of my own.

After the last note's been sung, I stand and pull my helmet over my braids, and Adrian pulls me into a hug, smashing his helmet against mine in solidarity.

"Black girl magic," he says.

"Black boy joy," I volley back.

And then, smiling too hard at each other, we get ready for the coin toss.

We've played an entire half and it's not going too hot. On both D and offense, we're all dicking up every single play. I'm having trouble getting to the ball in time and Cole isn't reading their QB, who's young and probably inexperienced, because he's basically just firing off these whack-job shots like his receivers are Speedy frickin' Gonzalez. This should've been *easy* for us!

I watch Cole screw up his billionth play and then amble off to the sidelines, where I pull my own helmet off and march up to him.

"Cole, are you shitting me, use your fricking brain—why aren't you plugging these gaps and driving this RB into the dirt?" I shove him.

He shoves me back. "Piss off, Tasia."

"Maybe I would if you could just pull your head out of your ass. I don't care if you're mad at me because my boyfriend used to be yours. You're pissing all over this game for me—"

"Screw you, Tasia! This isn't about him. But maybe if you pulled your head out of your cunt for a second—"

I shove him again and, ohh, it's a good one. But he shoves me back even harder and I'm about to Hadouken *the shit* out of him when Coach Rass lifts me up by the waist and practically throws me across the field.

"What in the actual fuss bucket, daggonit! What is this shit on my field?" Coach can never decide whether he wants to be a man that swears or not.

"She started it," Cole says. His helmet's off now. I didn't even notice that'd happened.

"He's the one running around the field like he's Stevie Wonder out here."

Cole yells, "Work your own position!"

I ignore him. "This is why y'all aren't winning games. And I swear to God, if I have to play on this team when y'all lose one more—"

"Oh, screw you, Tasia. Seriously. Don't worry. Kai doesn't care whether we win or lose. As long as you suck his—"

"HEY!" Coach yells.

Half our team erupts in laughter. The opposing players on the field, too. I can't find it in me to worry about how they've all just witnessed me losing it.

Especially since, after Cole's comment, I'm going off like a Tasmanian Devil and it'd almost be funny if it were anyone but me all, *Hold me back! Hold me back! Somebody HOLD. ME. BACK.*

"BACK OFF. BOTH OF YOU. NOW. AND YOU'RE BOTH BENCHED FOR THE SECOND HALF." The veins in Coach's neck stand at attention, all the way up to his very red face. The red's pretty odd for him, considering he spends so much time in the sun, soaking himself to a toasty bronze. "Maybe we can win without either of you knuckle-heads convoluting up my team's plays."

No. No, no, no, please, no. "Coach!"

"Coach. I got scouts here! Please," Cole says.

Coach lifts an eyebrow. "Maybe y'all should've thought before you popped off at the mouth? I'm not just training you to use your body; use your head, too. Now get your asses on that bench and rest your feet. Monday's practice, you got death waiting on you in the form of suicides."

I'm silent because I know this is mostly my fault. And because if Cole really does have scouts here, I might have just upended his entire future.

I don't even have the option of playing college football because no team is letting a girl play. I don't have any illusions of grandeur about that. But I feel exactly like a hot pile of sludge that my temper messed this up for Cole.

Jesus, what is wrong with me?

No. I know what's wrong with me. I just don't know who I am anymore. I'm not this person who completely . . . loses it like I just did.

There's no winning here. Not on this field with Cole and not in last night's messy situation with V and the box and whoever frickin' sent it. I can't breathe.

I make the mistake of glancing up into the stands. Merrick's eyes meet mine.

If the answers to this riddle aren't what I needed to feel better, then what is? How do I end this disquiet with who I am? How am I supposed to feel better about myself?

Still no answers. A thousand and one more questions.

Chapter Thirty

Two not stellar things happen on Saturday morning.

A woman leaves the apartment wearing nothing but Merrick's T-shirt and her own combat boots, a pair of white jeans folded over her arm.

I'm so grossed out, I drop the spoonful of Frosted Flakes that's halfway to my mouth. It clatters harshly in the room, but I do this on purpose. I want this I-don't-give-a-shit girl *and* Merrick to know how much I don't approve.

As I push my bowl away, Merrick follows shortly after and his hair is a mess of waves and curls that, again, tell you just how EU he really is. He yawns and scratches his T-shirt–clad stomach like he does every morning. He is predictable, and this is the thing I'm telling myself when I want to beg him to grow up and stop doing this "romance" dance.

I leave the apartment with an almost negative amount of words to Merrick. When I text Kai and ask him if we can just walk around the pier, I get a picture text back. It is a really extreme, very intense close-up of Dahlia's growling face. In the background, I can see Kai with a spray paint can. The text just says, *beat you to it*. Like we're in a competition for his time. And maybe we are. Most especially when he's creating something.

He's so lost in whatever he's drawing now. I can tell that, even from a single picture on a grainy screen. The air and the space around him, when he's like that, is so stagnant and impenetrable. I don't even blame him for that.

I feel a quick pang that they're hanging out without me. That Kai is somewhere using up his creativity with Dahlia as a witness.

It almost felt like his creativity belonged to me, for a second. Which is a really selfish way to look at things. I'm not that narcissistic. But this is the second stupid thing that happens and my throat suddenly hurts.

While I'm walking circles around the parking lot, I get several messages back to back to back, my text alert assaulting me. It's Tristan.

tasia

Then, *hi*

Then, *good morning*

did you know there are no clocks in vegas casinos???

why would I know that tristan, then, *why do YOU know that?*

lol, then, *kinda miss you*

That hurts me so much. I haven't avoided his messages so much as forgotten that it's our primary line of contact.

miss you so much, then, *is mamma there*

no

I'm coming to get you, let's go to sprinkles

I'm not eating sugar, but yeah let's go

Square. My brother is a square.

Then, a more final realization. My *half-brother* is a square, but I shake that thought away like leaves in my hair.

Traffic is horrendous. It's that nagging relative we all deal with out of obligation. It takes me seventy-eight minutes to make a nineteen-mile drive to get Tristan. Once we're there, I park my Jeep and text him two seconds before he slides into my passenger seat.

We spend a few minutes idling, trying to Yelp other places we might go, where I can get sugar and Tristan can get, I don't know, a bran muffin or a fiber waffle or something.

"Why are you so quiet?" I say, swiping across my phone like all the secrets of the universe can be found in a Yelp review. Spoiler: they can't.

He only shrugs.

To give myself something to do, I toss my phone into the center console and just drive, even though we haven't picked a location.

"Come on, Tristan. What's the point of us being here if you're just going to—"

"I kind of hated you when you left."

My Jeep's tires coast over the hot highway pavement, the only sound the soft swoosh of cars passing. It seems too soft, too calm, for what Trist just said to me.

"You hate me?" I merge onto a new freeway and, as usual, it's packed.

"Yes," he says, skipping through song after song on my iPhone. "No," he amends. "I did. Or I thought I did. I was so angry that you thought you could just go off and leave me behind like I don't matter."

"Trist, it wasn't about you—"

"I know that! I know, I'm just telling you how it felt. Like you thought that by leaving them, it was okay to leave me too. And you left me there without even thinking about the fact that I would have to pick up the pieces of your exit. I told you nothing needed to change and . . ."

I went and changed everything. Not just for me. For him, too. "I'm sorry."

"Are you?"

Yes, because this has all proven to be a mistake, for the most part—V's box and meeting this new white family that also doesn't get me. The only part I don't regret about leaving is getting away from Mamma and meeting Kai. Kai, my one good thing. But I don't know how to say that out loud to Tristan.

We end up at Urth Caffé, and that's as L.A. as things get, pretty much.

"You're going to have to talk to Mamma sometime."

Tristan doesn't pull punches. We've never gone easy on each other. I think that's why we're so close. "I know."

"When are you gonna?"

"I don't know that." I don't know why I need to talk to her, other than *forgiveness heals people,* which is a thing our Poppa says. *Forgiveness heals people, and grudges are toxic.*

Tristan starts, "Grudges are—"

"I know, Trist. I just don't want to forgive her, because if I do, it's like saying what she did was okay. That I'm okay with it. Like, with enough time and space, I'll just make peace with the fact that she's a liar."

He takes a sip of his matcha. "That's not what forgiveness is, Teez."

"Okay, Tristan." I roll my eyes and cut into my football-size vegan cinnamon roll.

"I'm serious. Jesus." He pulls his phone out, taps around for a second. So I pull mine out, too, and browse Instagram. The first thing to pop up in my feed is a picture posted ten minutes ago. It's Josiah's picture.

The caption reads: *josiahQB1: #aboutlastnight #thisgirl #mygirl*

Slim comments with the heart-eyes emoji and four of the red lip emojis, because apparently one just wasn't enough.

Someone else comments: *#Slimsiah5Ever*

And in the picture, Slim is on his lap and their lips are

locked and she's smiling into his kiss and I am green and a nasty, bruising deep purple. I am yellowing and decaying inside, worse than any football bruise I've ever had.

I hate them for two seconds before Tristan speaks again.

"Okay. 'Forgiveness, noun. To exonerate'—damn. No. We need to list. This definition is the exact opposite of—"

He pulls out a small notebook from his back pocket. It's worn and crumpled like my personality these days.

A pen appears from, I assume, another pocket. I am only barely paying attention to him. Which is not that much different from usual.

"Number one?" he says after scribbling *WHAT FORGIVENESS IS AND ISN'T* at the top. "Number one: Forgiveness isn't a pardon or excuse for the person's actions."

I nod. But I don't think that's true. I tell him that.

He says forgiveness, on this list, is whatever we logically want it to be.

"That's not—"

"Yes, it is," he says.

Chai drips over the lip of my fat mug as I lift it to take a sip, then decide Urth Caffé is cancelled because I end up doubling down on brown sugar.

"What's number two?"

I shrug. "I don't know. I don't know what you're asking me."

"Number two: Forgiveness doesn't excuse the fact that there is future work or reparation to be done."

My brows raise. Okay, I kind of like that.

Trist can tell. He uses his index finger to draw an imaginary checkmark in the air. A sort of "got you" signal.

I give him number three. "Forgiveness doesn't mandate that I verbalize the words 'I forgive you.'"

Tristan smiles big and we high-five and it feels good. My insides regenerate a little.

"Number four," he says.

I finish, "Forgive and forget is bullshit. Remembering is key."

"Good," he says, and writes it down as fast as he can. "Forgiveness doesn't mean you can't still develop more feelings regarding the person or the situation."

And that stops me. I don't want more feelings added to the ones I've already got. I feel like I'm overloaded. Stacked like too much cotton in a glass jar.

Right now it's like that one's a trigger going off inside me. Because I immediately start to get nervous, and that's a new sensation with regard to this situation. I'm nervous about talking to Mamma, nervous that none of our rituals will be the same, nervous that we'll never be as close as we once were. Nervous that she will expect me to forgive her in ways that are not on my list.

Tristan knows. He says quietly, "Let's get going." But as we walk to my car, he stops me and hugs me and says, "Forgiveness is not something you do for the other person. Let your life be about you."

That night, I get a text from Dahlia. She wants me to help her choose a dress for the homecoming dance. A thing that could not be further from my mind.

Before I agree, I wonder, *Why me?* And text her exactly that.

She responds fast. *I don't know. Because I like your style. You know what looks good.*

That makes me feel ridiculously cool. Extraordinarily feminine.

And then immediately after saying yes to Dahlia, I switch text threads and iMessage Slim about helping me find something for myself.

She agrees after telling me I don't love her enough to respond unless I need a favor. I tell her I am a literal shithead and she agrees—*that's right, your head is made entirely of shit*—and says she'll come by.

I have weird feelings about spending time with Dahlia. I both want her to be my friend and I don't. I know nothing about her. But what I do know is that her attention is nice. It makes me feel so fricking wanted, and every time she asks me about a brand of lip stain or some dress she sees me wearing, I grow a little more attached to that—her attention.

Dahlia picks me up the next morning in her aunt's new car. When I slide into the passenger seat, I ask her if she's allowed to be driving it. She laughs, says I'm "so cute" for wanting to get permission for her.

But, still, she doesn't answer whether or not her aunt knows we're drinking vanilla milkshakes at ten in the morning in her brand-new convertible.

We've spent the entire drive not speaking to each other, but instead singing along to the songs coming up via the Bluetooth. When we get to the outdoor mall about forty minutes from the Valley, Dahlia finally asks, "Where'd you stay that night? After Fat Freddy's?"

"At Kai's." I'm not ashamed or worried about that. Kai is my one good thing. I've been saying it like a mantra. My entire drive and reason for wanting to know this other side of my family was because of the box and now that's empty. Kai is the most secure, most musical thing in my life, and I never doubt that until I'm around Dahlia.

She grunts. "I guess it's fine for you guys to do things like that since you're basically related."

"Okay, well, except you're being gross and we are so not related."

She only laughs, gestures at some trinket shop up ahead. "You wanna go in here? They have good stuff we can totally make into better stuff."

I grunt.

In the store, when Dahlia finally notices I'm more quiet and introspective than contributing, she pauses like I've offended her. She's angry, like I'm the one kicking dirt all over the vibes.

I guess I am. I don't even know why I'm here.

"Look," she says. "I'm just gonna say this. Take it however you want. You know I was kidding, right? About you and Kai?"

Grunt.

"Oh, my God," she says. "Can you not? I was joking. Like, me and Kai were so whatever. He hooked up with anyone who asked. And I know you two aren't, like, actual family or whatever. But Kai has always been free with his—"

"Okay, stop," I say, running my hands over a rack of thigh-length silky dresses.

"More than just me and Co—"

"Dahlia. I get it. You think my boyfriend is a whore." I'm overlooking the fact that that is a ridiculously shitty thing to presume about a bisexual person.

She laughs. "But is he your boyfriend? It was all about who was there at the time. Flavor of the month."

I exhale. She's under my skin and I don't have the scalpel to pick her out. And I understand on the weirdest level that she isn't even trying to be cruel.

"Dahlia, where does this even get you? Like, Jesus. Why? You want Kai back? Fine. Tell him that, if he's so easy, so quick to stray. So anti-commitment. Don't tell me. I don't even care."

She stops trying on the rings on display. "You don't care? Okay," she scoffs. That time she is a little cruel. I don't think she can help it.

Shit, shit, shit. I hate this feeling. I hate being this angry at people, where everything they say is offensive, even when it's not.

I used to know what kind of person I wanted to be. What kind of adult I wanted to grow into. I thought I was sort of on my way there, but it's suddenly very in my face that I, apparently, am not.

I knew what kind of thoughts and opinions I wanted to have without having to try very hard for them. But now my entire existence is wrapped up in parental angst and familial angst and racial angst and friendship angst and is-he-my-boyfriend angst and I live minute to minute, in a state of teenage anger that's been slowly trying to swallow me whole.

"Tell him you want him, then. Tell him I don't care. If that will get you off my back about it, Dahlia. If that will end this competition crap, then yes, tell him, for the love of God. Are you in love with him or something?"

Dahlia's quiet. The girls who work in the store have also gone quiet. I grab a scarf sitting on the table to my left and march up to the counter to buy it. I don't even know why. It's hideous. But I feel like I owe the store something after my outburst.

I buy the scarf and six gold bangles. Dahlia doesn't say anything. They are my apology accessories.

Chapter Thirty-One

As soon as we get back to Merrick's, Dahlia lets me out without a single word. Her big sunglasses sit perched on her face and they look great and quirky against her olive skin, with her shaved head.

I spent the entire drive back thinking about how I should just burn that stupid box that's sitting in my closet, still waiting for *Who sent me?* answers.

Hate to tell you, box. No answers coming anytime soon.

When I get inside, I have a text from Slim that she'll be on her way in an hour. I suddenly don't want to do anything but eat cookie dough from the tub and binge old episodes of *The OC*.

I wait long enough that she should have arrived already. When she isn't here, and I'm getting impatient, I call. "Hey," I say, once she picks up the phone. "I kind of just want to stay in. Bring some of your dresses and I can pick one of yours."

"Yeah, I figured, so I'm strapped with all the options. What's wrong, Taze?"

"Nothing," I say. I text Kai while I've got Slim on speaker-phone.

I miss you

"I can hear it in your voice. It sucks that you think you have to lie to me."

I nod. "I know. I'll tell you when you get here. Can you just get here?"

The door slams.

Murmurs of people whose voices I try to parse out.

I'm right here, Kai texts back.

Mm. The voices. It's Merrick and Merrick's latest midlife crisis in female form.

All the best things happen at once—

Kai texts me a picture of us. In it, he's crossed his eyes and is nearly licking my face. In it, I am smiling big and toothy and uncoordinated. I hate it and I love it. Slim comes into my room and gathers me up into her arms and, God, hugs are just the best things: cathartic and re-centering. I know whatever burst of feelings I'm having right now is mostly for her. She's my best friend, but we don't do this feels-gasm stuff much unless we have a reason to. The last time either of us got this raw with each other was in eighth grade when Slim had sex for the first time with an ironically named eleventh-grader, Junior Justice.

And she came to me the next day and said she thought something was wrong because she was experiencing so much pain. We were both so scared, all I could do was sit with her in the bathroom while she soaked in a tub of warm water and cried while swearing that she wasn't.

I have a text from Tristan.

a non-colorblind person can distinguish between like 500 shades of grey. probably horrifying for those colorblind people who loved that 50 shades book.

Then he texts again. *remember mamma's great uncle Xen? isn't he colorblind? can you ask him*

Then again, *wonder if he read that 50 sexes book. ask him that too*

Slim reads all the texts to me and then laughs. I smile but don't laugh. Leave it to Trist.

"Tell me," Slim says, cradling me like I am a toddler.

And I do. I tell her everything. I give her all the dirty details about meeting my "grandparents," about the box and how empty I've felt since figuring out that the box is V's, that it belonged to her, that she cared about herself enough to put it together but didn't care enough about me to send it. I tell Slim about the concert and the drinks and Cole and I tell her every. Single. Detail. About me and Kai. I tell her, descriptively, about every touch and every look and sexual thing we've ever done together, and she doesn't flinch or tell me I'm gross because that's the kind of best friendship we have. I tell her about Dahlia and Victory. And after a moment, I'm silent. Because I know—I know—she's wanted to tell me about her and Josiah. I know it.

"You can tell me about him, too," I say.

She shakes her head. "You don't want to know. He's like your brother."

"Nah, not really."

"But close."

I shrug. I think she thinks football makes us much closer than we really are. If I was a dude, that'd probably be the truth, but. "Yeah," I say, "but I want to know."

She pulls back. "Do you, Teez? Do you really want to know? Because every time I've posted a pic or something, or Tweeted about it, you never like or respond to it. And I hate to be that person who's all, 'You don't like my photos and I notice you not liking them,' but I super notice! And it seems like you hate me sometimes. And, like, Siah can tell that you feel that way too. It sucks, Tasia."

Oh, God. "I don't. I don't hate you guys. I was just so mad that you guys got so happy so fast, and that it was while I was dealing with so much. While I'm falling apart and losing people and getting nowhere, you guys were coming together and gaining each other, and *I don't even know* what kind of stupid jealousy monster I've become, but I can't help feeling like that. I still feel like that now, a little."

I reposition us so that Slim is right next to me and we're on our backs and keeping conversational tempo by tapping our palms together.

Slim's lips blow a raspberry into the air. "I get it now. I'm sorry I didn't before. But you're saying it, and it makes total sense and, like, I made him a priority. And I should have made you my priority."

"No, shut up. I just—"

"Teez. You are my best fricking friend. I love you beyond all reason. When you're a bitch to me, when you talk football and nothing else, when you don't text me back. I love you because you're funny and fun. I love you because you always tag me in the best stuff on Instagram. I love you because you bake two cookies and two cookies only, but then give one of them to me." She pauses. Asks, "Wouldn't you have made me a priority?"

"I would try to. If I knew what I know now about us, I would try to. I can't say how successful I'd be, but I would do my best."

She nods. "I'll do my best," she whispers. "Lets bake cookies. You have stuff?"

I nod. I've got stuff.

Slim and I bake six cookies. Two for each of us, one for Kai, one for Josiah. We are those girls. It's perfect. We snap selfies of us baking and caption them accordingly.

@dontTazemebro: KITCHEN MAGICIANS w.
@SlimJimSandwich

@SlimJimSandwich: Damn we're good w. @dontTazemebro

Later, after I've chosen a homecoming dress from Slim's closet and Slim has chosen one for herself via mine—a white one that makes her look like a beautiful, naïve young bride—we sit in the living room and watch bad reality TV.

Slim says, "I think you need to talk to your mom."

"I guess."

"No." She sits up and looks at me. Looks down. "She's, like, not doing well, Teez."

I jackknife up. "What do you mean? Like, she's sick? Like, a cold? Or like a—"

"No. Just, like, I don't know. You should see her. Or talk to Tristan."

"He hasn't said anything."

"Why would he? There's nothing he or you can do."

"Then why should I go see her?"

"It would be good for you to do that. That's why."

I lean back, slouch deep into the couch. "I'm probably gonna have to see her soon enough, for whatever reason. We'll talk then."

Slim exhales. "God, you're so difficult."

"Okay, Slim. Whatever."

"I'm gonna get going. I need to do a little homework, and I will seriously punch you in the shin if you keep being a douche."

I press my hands into my eyes. "Okay. Okay okay okay. Sorry, I love you. Text me when you get home. What's the homework?"

"AP Chem."

"FaceTime me if you need help?"

She nods.

I nod. "I will talk to her. Or, like, if I'm too much of a pride monster, I'll talk to Trist."

And that seems to be good enough. At least for her, it's good enough.

But then, that's how it is when Slim Lim is your best friend.

Chapter Thirty-Two

We lose our game Friday night. I don't know why I expected anything different. Cole comes down with mono earlier in the week and he still tries to play. I don't think he's actively trying to play well. I think he's just trying not to die on the field, and he's managed that, at least. A nasty rumor has been going around school all week that Cole has the kissing curse and that he got it from Kai, but I know that's not true because I've had my mouth all over Kai's and all over him all week and I feel like I could dead lift an ox.

Still, I play like shit. I very seriously screw up three attempts at a forced fumble, I'm flagged for pass interference, can't bust up any running routes on time, and I'm pretty sure I'm walking away from this game with a concussion right now.

So we amble into the away team locker room, heads hanging, only to get reamed through the ass by Coach. I'm not in the mood for it today, and it's got nothing to do with how I played the shittiest I ever have.

I'm mad that Mamma was there to witness the game. I've resolved that I do want to see her, but I feel like this should get to be on my terms.

Ordinarily, after a rough game, Mamma would cart me home, unbraid my hair, and we'd stop at the sporting goods store and buy me a new pair of gloves, or a new pair of practice cleats or running shorts or a set of really cute sports bras. Because we were sure—*we were sure*—that it was the reason for my shitty game; bad gear.

That doesn't happen now. Instead, now, I leave the locker room and get in Merrick's back seat with Kai in lieu of taking the school's bus with the rest of the team. As Merrick drives home, he talks on the phone to some girl—woman—girl, named Stephanie. He calls her "Stephy."

I mumble from the back seat, "I swear to God." I can't believe I'm going to be stuck listening to this for the duration of the drive home.

"Hang on, Stephy," he says into the phone. "What's that, kiddo?"

"Nothing," Kai says for me.

I laugh. Because screw that. "I said 'I swear to God'—as in, 'I swear to God, if you invite some girl-child over tonight—'"

"Let me call you back, Stephanie."

I scoff. "Oh, now she's Stephanie."

Kai faces me, shakes his head. *Be smart,* the look says. *Shut up now,* it says.

But I'm not and I don't.

"What is your problem right now, Tasia Lynn? I'm sorry you're having a bad night because of the game. You can't win every one—"

Kai clears his throat. "I can catch the bus the rest of the way home."

"How about, for once, Merrick, you don't assume you've got everything right—"

"You wanna let me out the car right here?"

"What's that supposed to mean?" Merrick says.

"It means, you don't need to stick your dick in a different chick every night, *Dad*."

He doesn't say anything.

Kai says, "Fuck." And he's not quiet about it.

Merrick doesn't hit the brakes or pull over or anything like that. He just keeps driving. And the roads are relatively clear. And the radio isn't on because Merrick had *Stephy* on the phone and I had Kai.

When Merrick pulls into his driveway, he turns the car off, gets out, and shuts the door. Not a slam. He doesn't storm up the stairs to the apartment or anything.

And I burst into tears in the back seat. The most physically painful tears I've ever experienced, and I hunch forward to protect myself from them, hands over my eyes. The inside of the car is dark, and in a moment Kai has his arms around me and his body shielding my back, and at first I think he's rocking us, but really it's me rocking back and forth and him holding on to me tight as he can.

Kai seems distraught, his mouth opening and then closing without a single word. Like he doesn't know what to do with me or how to help. He begs me like a broken record to tell him what to do, how to make it better, and I have a weak moment, crying, "Please, please make it stop, please," because every tear that comes feels like it's being wrenched out of me.

"What do you need?" he says.

"I need my mom."

Kai and I get in my Jeep and he drives us to the westside. I'm North again for the first time in a while, and I'm more content about it than I figured I would be.

She's already made it back. I see Mamma's car in the driveway and Kai parks my Jeep right next to it, cutting the engine. Propping his feet on the dash, he pulls a tiny, wrinkled notebook out of his back pocket and begins to write in it, ignoring me as I work up whatever nerve needs to settle in.

Nine times out of ten, Mamma is in her home office, so I head there first when I finally get out of the car.

The house is quiet aside from Tammy clanging around in the kitchen. Probably getting prepared for dinner. It's late, so I'm surprised no one else is home. This feels illicit. Like I shouldn't be here.

Mamma is not in her office. The space is a mess. There are floor plans and contracts everywhere, a pair of Jimmy Choos in every corner, an untouched cup of tea on her desk. It's been there a while.

I walk into the kitchen to find Tammy.

"Hey, Tam?"

"It's that my little duck?"

I smile. Tammy's known me since before I could walk. When I first learned to, I waddled, as she tells it. I've been "duck" ever since.

"It's me." I squeeze her. She smells like flour and I inhale deeper.

"What are you doing home? I'm happy you're here—don't get me wrong. But . . . well, we didn't expect you."

"I know. Where's my mamma?"

"Oh, honey. She's upstairs. In bed. Went straight there after your game."

I nod.

"Sorry about the rough loss, duckie."

"Thanks. So . . . bed, huh?"

I glance at the clock above the oven. Tammy catches me do it. "Want me to go up there with you?"

"It's fine," and I make my way up the stairs toward Mamma. I wonder if she's worse than Slim made her seem. I wonder if I'm supposed to be affected by it. I wonder if I'm capable of a downward spiral like that too. The kind that sticks in your chest like old gum, with no real remedy.

As I push open her door, I notice how the hinge no longer squeaks the way it did. It smells like penicillin. No more rose water hanging heavy in the air. More contracts in here, all on Mamma's side of the bed. Her side of the room is ordered chaos. Because, even at the end of her rope, I think Mamma would still have a handle on things better than most people.

I don't say anything. Because I'm not here to apologize, I'm not here to condemn her or fix her or question what this is.

I just crawl into bed with her.

She's not asleep. But she doesn't open her eyes. I put my hands in her silk-wrapped dreadlocks. A smile crawls up her face. "I prayed for you," she whispers. "I prayed that God would give me a baby that looked just like you."

My back to her front, I doze and doze until I hear voices, muted, but carrying, through the house downstairs. This house is like that. I've always thought it was a sign that it's too big and too new for our family.

Mamma sleeps still, but I pull out of her arms and kiss her cheek before I escape downstairs like I've stolen something precious—and I have: her time—only to be caught by Daddy and Tammy. Tammy smiles. Daddy doesn't. I shake my head and then I'm sliding into the passenger seat in my car. Kai has moved from his position in the front seat to the back seat, but as I buckle in, he maneuvers again to his driver's seat post, cranks the engine, and pulls out of the circular drive.

"Ready?"

"Yeah," I say, like it's a surprise.

"Tristan gave me this," Kai says. He holds out a folded piece of paper.

It's a list. Of course it is. Across the top it reads, *6 WAYS TO REACH FORGIVENESS! T-DOT VERSION.*

1. Have an honest conversation with Mamma. Ask her how she's doing. Expect her to tell you the truth—no matter what that means.
2. Tell Mamma one way you've changed since you moved out.
3. Think of her as "just another adult." Not "my adult parent." Trust me—this works.
4. Swear at her. Tell her how angry you are and use as much colorful vocabulary as you can. There's a huge chance she will kill you after this—but if she doesn't, it'll probably be effective.
5. Ask Mamma what she loved about Merrick.
6. Talk to Mamma about Kai.

"You read this?" I hold up the note.

His eyes don't leave the road. "Nope."

"Really?" I say.

"Nope."

I flick his shoulder. "So what do you think?"

"I think Tristan is kind of brilliant."

Well, yeah. I almost say, *Of course Trist is brilliant. He's my blood.* But Trist is only half my blood. Maybe that's why he's so smart. Or maybe it just has nothing to do with me and everything to do with Tristan just being who he is.

I nod. "You trying to start a bromance with my brother?"

"I don't know. You guys don't look much alike, but he's kind of—"

"OH MY GOD, DON'T TALK ABOUT TRISTAN LIKE THAT, STOP."

"Why? You forgot about that whole bisexual thing? It doesn't go away, Taze. Ever. Even when my lips are *all* over yours and I'm *all up inside your*—"

"Kai!"

"Heart! Your *heart,* you sick little twist."

Jesus, he's something else. "No, I didn't forget about the bisexuality thing. I mean, are you nuts? My only goal in life is to watch you make out with Jason Momoa someday. I'm trying to see if Merrick can use one of his celebrity connections."

I really couldn't forget about Kai being bisexual even if I wanted to. And I don't. It's a piece of Kai as much as his eyes, as much as his style, as much as the way he laughs that silent chuckle of his. All of Kai's pieces matter to me. Together and separate.

"I think Tristan and I could be good friends, though. He has a good point." Kai merges and switches freeways. He looks so comfortable here in my driver's seat. His right foot on the accelerator, his left leg bent at the knee, both limbs spread wide and long. He rubs his left hand at his mouth as he talks.

"You want some honesty?"

"From you?" I take his hand. "Always. I want all of you."

I watch his lips spread, the corners kicking up, his teeth glinting as he continues to drive. The lights along the shoulder of the freeway whoosh by us.

"I'm jealous of you," he says quietly.

"Jealous? Of what part?" I hope he's not talking about

the house. The McMansion is gross and extravagant but I've never lived any other way, not before Merrick.

I think for a second about how I now live in an entirely different tax bracket. At ElCo, a lot of the Black kids are from families that are working middle class. And I think that's where Merrick might be too. I wonder, had I grown up with Merrick, had I lived with him, had he and Mamma never split, maybe I'd feel differently about the McMansion and Mamma's charity events and Daddy's weekly country club breakfasts.

Kai says, "Of the fact that you're getting so in-depth with your family. You're getting raw with them and thinking about how much or how little to include them in your life, and you have that option."

I nod. "I am your family."

"You are." And we don't even make that joke about him being my "uncle."

"But I wonder about my brother, you know? And my birth parents, and even a few of my foster families."

"That's fair. And maybe we should do something about that?"

Kai shakes his head, slows down a little to take a long curve. "Not everything needs a solution. Not everyone needs a whole family just because it's mildly available." He lets go of my head to shift gears.

I don't know what else to say. I'm eighteen. My family problems are overwhelming enough.

Kai laughs and reads my mind. "You don't need people around who are this complicated."

When he smiles like that, I suspect I could sleep in it all day. Kai is a little bit irresistible when he's like this. When he's trying to save me from hardship. But Kai is no hardship. "You're you."

"Brilliant observation, Tasia, bravo."

"No, I just mean, it's you. You're complicated with or without parental issues, and I love you anyway."

"You love me anyway?"

"I love you anyway."

"I love *you* anyway."

"I know," I say.

I pick up Kai's right hand from the gear shift and kiss the back of it six times, and he gets that attractive-guy partial smile going on.

Chapter Thirty-Three

October comes unexpectedly, though it's not like it's changed its place in the calendar. It's the first Thursday of that month when another unexpected thing appears. This is the year that grandparents have learned to text, and I receive the world's shakiest, grammatically incorrect message from V with an invite.

U want 2 ,, come to hOuse for
Tea ,?

And I agree, hesitantly at first, sure. I ask Kai to be there for some kind of weird support. But he more or less goes out of his way to *not* be there.

I take my Jeep on Thursday after practice, arriving sweaty and smelly and dirty, much to V's dismay. And she feeds me tarte Tatin and some chamomile tea that tastes like dry leaves when it hits the back of my throat. I don't like it, but as soon as I get up and she notices my cup is full, she makes me down it.

Most of this happens without a single word from me. I'm here for reasons I don't quite understand, having agreed to come without thinking all of it through, and so I do my best to ease, gracefully, into each of the amber evening's moments.

V and I go out into her garden, illuminated by bell-shaped hanging lamps. There isn't a single difference between autumn in Los Angeles and any other season. The running joke is a) Angelenos don't know what seasons are and b) those two days during the year when we get some pretty heavy rain obligate us all to jump on the 405 southbound freeway. Both of those things are painfully accurate.

Still, V's garden is immaculate, a small piece of wilted, golden-hued poetry set in her suburban home's backyard. She talks for a few awkward moments about her garden needing to be a festival of colors, pointing out the fat, mustard-colored squash, wine-red roses, and the wet emerald vines that cling desperately to their gate.

We work there in silence until she pulls a plant out of the ground and, holding it out, asks me what I smell.

"Fire," I say. Which technically is the right answer because a brush fire's sprung up off the 210. It's been going for nearly a week.

V mutters something about my inability to appreciate the smell of raw rosemary, then, quietly, "Tell me about my Kai."

A smile pushes its way onto my face. "Tell me about my box."

She smiles tightly in return. "What do you want to know?"

Wish I could say I hadn't been holding on to these

questions. I have. But I haven't been thinking I'd get to ask them. I'm, like, I don't know, 97 percent certain that it isn't why I agreed to come here. Okay, ninety-four percent. "Why wouldn't you tell Merrick?"

She exhales. She had to know that one was coming. "He was . . . not ready. Your father, he's never been the most responsible man. He was not a responsible boy growing up, either. It was the kind of thing we hoped he would grow out of. He did not."

This is my shocked face.

"He didn't hide his affair with your mother. Not well. There wasn't much reason to hide it from us. We didn't pry, though perhaps we should have. So when things ended and we noticed him making many changes, to attend school elsewhere and quitting his position there at the university, I—well, it wasn't hard to ask around, you know . . ." She hesitates.

"To spy."

"Well, yes. So, I spy. And I find your mother. And I keep track of her, because it's what I do. Your father is my firstborn, and I've been protecting him in ways I never had to protect Emiline. And so, your mother, not long after all this, she is pregnant."

"With me."

"With you, cher. Yes. Later she marries your papa. And that is when I start keeping my box. Your box," she amends.

God, I'm a jackass. It was never my box. Never intended to be mine. It is a box of me, to be sure. But it's not *my* box— it's hers.

Suddenly, I know with 100 percent certainty why I agreed to come. I came to meet my grandmother, this uninhibited version of her, different from the woman I met at dinner. The one that speaks with a soft emphasis on even the heaviest things, her voice going nasally before evening out. "You can have it back, if you want," I say.

She waves it away. "Why do I need a box like that if I have the milk for free?"

"I mean, that's not—Okay."

"I thought many times about sending the box. Wrapped it for sending and had gone so far as to write your name and address on it."

"And in the end?"

"In the end, I did what I thought was best."

"For Merrick."

"*For you*, cherie. You seemed happy. Well loved and lacking for nothing. I didn't think you needed anything or anyone else, even if we needed you."

God, if only this could be simple enough that I could take it all at face value. Right now her reasoning feels flimsy. She's said it herself, she's been protecting—babying—Merrick his entire life and continues to do so.

Just . . . I don't know. It doesn't feel like enough yet. This particular wound, it hasn't quite scabbed over. Though I get the feeling, just by the way she's looking at me now, all eyes and pride and heart, that it could start healing pretty soon.

In a rare moment of clarity Tristan might be proud of, I realize V was maybe a little desperate. For her family. For her son. For the granddaughter she thought she'd never know well enough to ask about the way her boyfriend treats her. There isn't a malicious bone in her body and I don't know how I ever imagined there was.

"What do you want to know about Kai?" The soil feels good between my fingers. It's cold, because the weather is just cold AF now. At least, for Los Angeles it is.

"He's kind to you?"

A secret smile that belongs to Kai and Kai alone spreads across my lips. "Kai is, like, the nicest person I've ever met. Let alone the nicest boy."

"You date a lot of boys."

Is she asking, or . . . ? "No. I've dated a few. I'm eighteen. These things happen."

Then she laughs. "True. I was a tart at your age."

"V!" I think my grandmother just called herself a slut.

"It was France. It was the 1960s." She pauses. Looks up from the echinacea she's planting. "Honestly, that whole period is a little of a hazy."

"A blur," I correct.

She grunts. "But I was young once."

"You're still young."

"Vous êtes un menteur."

I shrug.

"Lies. You're a cute little liar, my Tasia."

I am. It's just one of those things . . .

She reaches over and puts her cold, powder-soft hands on top of mine. "You have to pack this soil tight, for the

Erica heath. Otherwise they'll come right apart in the windy months."

I nod. And we plant in silence. And I glance over at her like I can't drink her profile in fast enough. She's gorgeous, and maybe she's more than either of us know. Maybe she is more than just a white woman, a French woman, who's chosen to give up her French connection. Maybe she's a reservoir of power and potential. My grandmother is beautiful. Her hard gray eyes are the diamond of her person, a sophisticated contrast to the soft curve of her high, pillowy cheeks. It strikes me as so, so impossible that we are related on any level. That part of me is her. Part of me is delicate and part of me is a gale-force wind. Just like her.

Maybe part of me is protective, too, the way she is. The longer I think about it, with cold soil between my fingers, the more I understand how and why she would work so hard to protect her son at any cost to me or herself. It's what she does. It's who she is. Strip her bare, and family is all she has. I've felt that way before—like the time we flew to Cannes a few years ago and every passenger in our first-class section eyed us like we might send the plane into a nosedive at any moment.

After, V and I go inside to wash up. V brings me fancy, pretty-smelling honey soap and a matching lotion, and she washes my hands and forearms for me.

I spot Pépé in the living room, reclined, doing the *Los Angeles Times* crossword puzzle.

V nods at me. *Go. Make him yours,* her eyes say.

I walk over, hands pressed to my hips, and I glance down.

His pen hovers over five across. "Athletic supporter." Three letters. "Fan," I say.

He shakes his head. "The letters don't match up."

I think again. The last two letters would have to be Es. "Tee," I say.

He writes it in, but says, "What is this? 'Tee'?"

I pull out my phone and Google a picture. "It's, like, in golf . . . ?"

He nods. "Sit down. Aidez moi."

So I sit, and Pépé and I do the daily crossword. I stay until Merrick texts me that I need to be home by 10:00 p.m.

As I gather my things to leave and head back to the garage apartment, I think about rituals. About promise and potential and staying power. I think about the way Mamma would undo my football braids after every game and about the way Kai puts them in now, how these two things started as basic practices, breezed past ritual, and now sit inside tradition.

I think I maybe want that. To drink awful tea and plant in the garden with V and do the crossword with Pépé. I think I'd like to call that tradition someday.

Chapter Thirty-Four

As Kai's hair grows out, he tells me its texture has grown differently. It's changed, he says. The weather changes, and with it, Kai's look. Merrick brings home another girl and the only thing that stays the same is that I am still, somehow, angry at Mamma—though with time, maybe that means something different now.

Another thing that doesn't change is that I still hang out with Dahlia like she has the answers to all of life.

We end up at the mall one Saturday and run into the drama teacher. His name is Joseph Goddard, and most of the students just call him plain old Goddard, even though he always tells us to call him Joe.

Dahlia's talking about a strapless bra she just got when I see him.

"Oh, hey. It's Goddard."

For this moment, he is her prey and she literally drags me toward him. "Joseph Goddard. In the mall. In the wild," she says.

"Dahlia," he says, pleased. I can tell he's pleased. His face says, *I am pleased at this.* "Taze," he continues. He calls me Taze, and I have to say, I like it. I know once we've walked away and Dahlia and I gush about seeing him *in the wild*— that's the phrase she and I will use when we tell people at school—I'm going to talk about how Joe Goddard called me by my very personal nickname.

"What are you girls up to?"

D shrugs. "Just browsing. I needed a new strapless." She shrugs again like this is the kind of thing you can totally talk to your male teacher about. If she shrugs any more or any harder, she's going to dislocate something.

"A new strapless, huh? A strapless what?" But he knows what. Obviously he knows what.

"A bra," she whispers. They are having verbal sex in the middle of this very crowded, family-friendly establishment.

"I don't know," he says. "I've always been a fan of that whole visible-bra-strap look."

"Yeah?"

"Yeah." And he tilts his head toward me like an adorable puppy. He body checks me—full on scans my body from head to toe—then does this boyish smirk that is, I have to say, very appealing.

But he is pathetic, I remind myself. And I am grossed out and appalled, but only because I think I'm supposed to be.

After Dahlia makes up some excuse for why we have to leave, she laces her fingers with mine and we walk away like we're too important to care about whether or not he wanted to continue to talk.

I think about that encounter for the rest of our mall trip. What made the situation weird wasn't that he's our teacher, or that he's thirty-eight and we're eighteen. It was that he has been married for as long as we have been alive, and the most I know about commitment is that some of my friends have just recently given their first blowjobs to boys who would never speak to any of us again.

I wonder if Mamma had thoughts like this about Merrick.

I know immediately that it's something I want to talk to her about, which is great because I happen to have Tristan's list in the back pocket of my shorts.

GAME 6 – EL CAMINO REAL VS. BIRMINGHAM PATRIOTS

Homecoming is a week after my mall trip with Dahlia.

Friday's game is comical.

Like, ECR isn't known for its football prowess. We're not over here breeding future NFL players. Right out the gate— the other team fumbles.

They pull their running back and swap him with another. Poor guy. We spend the entire half cracking jokes at his expense. It should've been an incredibly sweet gain. Instead, it puts their offense in a huge hole.

The second half isn't much better. They opt for an onside kick, which, if you ask me and the scoreboard, is a mistake, given the Birmingham Patriots still have plenty of time to get a stop and get the ball back—probably with a better field position. Every time we pass the Birmingham bench, I hear a few curses from their coaches. I revel in it, knowing how much the desperation to win this thing has started to bleed into their play calling.

At the final whistle, I walk into the locker room after one last glance at the scoreboard.

Final: 38–8, El Camino Real.

For all the games for her to miss—I wish my Mamma could've been there.

Saturday, my mood's on a figurative upper. I expect Kai to show up to Merrick's dressed outrageously. He doesn't. When I asked him if he wanted to know what color my dress is, he laughed and said no.

Which makes sense, since he showed up wearing all black. Black slacks—fitted. Black button down—also fitted. Black tie, black wingtips. The one thing that he does deviate on is the thin gold chain hanging from the hoop in his nose to the diamond in his right ear.

Merrick does not hassle us for photos the way Mamma would have. But Emily is here and she does. Slim, too. She does her job as my best friend and takes "candid" photos of Kai and me being cute together.

Him kissing my cheek, me staring into the camera.

A photo of us from behind as we hold hands.

Couples show up slowly. Dahlia and Scott first. Then Victory and Sam, who can't keep their hands off each other, which excites me on some pretty ridiculous levels. Cole and a boy whose name I don't know. I don't stress about it, because before I get a chance, Kai looks me in the eye, smiles, and shakes his head, a reprimand that says, *You and me, remember? Drop it.* So I do.

Guy from football is there with his date Kayla, who tells us, vehemently, not to call her Kayla, but KK instead, so we do.

Adrian bear-hugs me and then introduces me to his date, Lyssa, a tiny Japanese enby with silvery hair styled like Rufio's from *Peter Pan.*

Chasia is the cheer captain who I've asked several times to redo up my French braids during football. They're the only one going solo since they broke up with their partner two weeks ago: "I'm not talking about it, but singlehood looks best on me, is all I'm saying."

So we take them at their word and then all pile into the Hummer limo, which we all say is trashy—because it is—but the funny thing is that we're all a little bit excited about it, too.

The night is good.

The music is good because the DJ is good. The decorations are cool, even though we'll never admit it, because our theme is Steampunk—suggested by one of our nerd teachers or the nerd dean or the nerd-something. The punch is, much to the chagrin of many, not spiked. But we all take shots out of Adrian's flask before we go inside a broom closet that smells like Cheetos. And Sam, Dahlia, Lyssa, Guy, and Kai and I all take turns pulling hits off the pipe that Dahlia pulls out of her black clutch.

The only stain on the night is that toward the end of it, our group makes its way to the bathrooms to check makeup and help each other carefully out of our dresses and tights to pee.

Shortly after, all the football players are called onto the stage to be lauded for our Homecoming game efforts. When they call Cole's name first, he's nowhere to be found.

This whole charade is ridiculous. I mean, we won because the Patriots kinda sucked, so although the win feels pretty stellar, the celebration around it feels a little forced. It's all hilarious because most of us are either tipsy or high as hell, or some mixture of the two in a cross-fade cocktail.

As we're all coming off the stage, I halt. Cole and Kai are talking. Though, it looks like more than just a casual discussion. It looks like they're disagreeing. It looks like they're having an intimate argument.

Kai leans against the wall, arms crossed over his chest, and Cole leans into Kai's personal space from right in front of him.

Kai uses small gestures to discount or reduce whatever Cole is saying to something insignificant. That's Kai. He's a total Scorpio if ever I've seen one.

Cole grips his red hair repeatedly and then throws his arms out wide. At one point, he grabs Kai's shoulder and I watch his mouth slowly form the word *please.*

"They used to have these little spats so often," Dahlia says from behind me. "Like, before you. It didn't matter who Kai was with. You can't keep them—"

"*Why* are you doing this?" I spin on her, feeling the fabric of my dress kiss the top of my knees as it moves with me.

Dahlia holds her hands up. "I'm just saying. Look, don't be mad, okay? I'm really trying to just give you a heads-up. I step back whenever they get like this, because Kai can't say no to him. So if I ever wanted to keep him on any level, I had to let him figure out what he wanted. And since we never labeled our thing—"

"You never told him you wanted exclusivity," I say.

She nods, shrugs.

"But you did want it."

She doesn't speak.

Kai's chin lifts and his gaze touches mine. Cole still stands beside him, but he's facing away, toward the wall, arms around himself.

I nod toward the exit and Kai follows me outside, leaving Cole. The feeling I get, seeing Cole alone . . . it makes my teeth itch.

When I feel Kai approaching, I turn, swallow, and try to focus.

But it's impossible to focus with love in your throat.

My arms come around his neck and I don't give him a chance to say anything before I whisper, "You're my boyfriend."

His hands find my hips. "Taze. Listen. In there—"

I shake my head. "You're my boyfriend. And I'm your

girlfriend." My one good thing. I promise to be honest with him the way he's been so honest with me. I can do that, at the very least.

I drag my lips back and forth across his cheek and Kai pulls me flush against him.

"I'm your boyfriend," he says.

Chapter Thirty-Five

We spend the night, all of us, at KK's house. Her parents' bedroom is downstairs, so we have the entire upper level to ourselves and I don't even know what kind of parents would let their teenage daughter have a coed sleepover after a late-night dance, but here I am wondering how best to slip them a copy of *Holistic Parenting* magazine.

We hurry through the upstairs portion of the house in pairs, trying to find some private space. Kai and I end up in a guest bedroom that's been turned into an office. It's smaller than a kidney bean in here. Half the size of my room at Merrick's. A quarter size of my bedroom back home. The rest of them who don't find bedrooms end up in walk-in closets and guest bathrooms.

Still, Kai and I have a pallet of five blankets and as many pillows, all of which smell like somebody's grandma's oatmeal cookies.

"Are you sure?" he says. "You've been drinking. You smoked part of that bowl."

"Are you asking me if I'm sure I want to have sex with you, or if I want to do it in here?"

"Both."

"I want to have sex with you, even if it's in this straitjacket of a room. You're not sober either. Do you want to?"

"Y-yes. Yeah—I-I'm mostly sober. Yes, I want to."

"Okay. So do the sex." I shrug. *Jesus Christ, Tasia. What?*

"Merrick would kill me."

"Oh my God, Kai, don't talk about my dad when—"

"When we're about to do the sex?"

I collapse facefirst into the oatmeal pillows, but not before I manage to throw an embroidered one at Kai.

It takes us longer than it probably should to decide if I would be the one to remove my clothing or if he should. After we each present our defense on it, with counterpoints, he helps me take my dress off and it is easily one of the most awkward moments of my life. I'm pretty sure he's just broken my zipper. We do his together which, again, awkward.

The last thing I remove from him is the chain connecting his piercings, slowly.

"That didn't have to take you twenty minutes," Kai laughs.

"Shut up, asshole! Neither did you breaking my dress zipper." I punch him good, right in the arm, and he laughs at me again, cringing like I actually hurt him.

"That hurt."

"No, it didn't."

"It did," he insists. "Kiss it better."

With a smirk, I do. I kiss up his elbow, to the space I

punched, around the rounded apple of his shoulder, and then I press a straight line of kisses to his neck.

And then we are kissing each other. We're kissing so much and so long, my mouth hurts. But it feels good and I never want to stop, but we do so that Kai can grab his Sweet Mint eos to press first against my fuller lips, then a swipe across his.

I smile.

He smiles.

He removes my bra, my panties, his briefs, and then he guides my hand, slow, slow, slowly, to his dick.

I don't look. I can't. I'm not that bold yet.

He laughs and hisses when I squeeze too tight, so he helps me readjust my grip and I stroke him slow, and—after a moment—I stroke him surely.

Slow seems to be the name of our game.

He is fumbling, but sweet and dedicated, as he presses his hand between my legs and then pushes a finger into me.

We are familiar in this. We have done this. More than once. We know this and that's why, when he adds another finger, I don't flinch or give it much thought at all.

The pressure is a lot and it doesn't feel good at all.

"Yeah?" Kai asks. I say yes, but I'm starting to tense up a lot and Kai is about to pull his hand back when I stop him.

"No, no, please. I want to, please. Just go slow."

"I've never been with a virgin before. You're not a virgin."

I shake my head. I don't know if this is a question. I don't think it is, but I've told him about it. "Not really. I've done it before, once. Last year. For like a second."

Kai exhales. "Oh, yeah. Right, right. Okay." He places his fingers against his mouth and then presses them back into me. The feeling is better, and when I press a hand to my clit, things finally click together like a bolt sliding into its lock.

Kai slips on a condom. He's very sure about that.

And when he pushes into me, he does it slowly. Too slowly. I ask him repeatedly to "just go fast." And after asking gets me nowhere, I *tell* him. But he won't.

We're laughing so much that my abs start to hurt. We're laughing so much that I barely even notice that he's all the way in until he flexes his hips and I mewl and he says, softly, sweetly, "Sorry, sorry, sorry." And he kisses my cheek. "I'm sorry."

I nod, and I cry because it hurts and I ask Kai not to stop because it makes something in me feel good, emotionally.

And we learn each other that way.

We learn each other steadily, clumsily, lovingly.

As though we are each the other's syllabus, a detailed course guide.

And I wouldn't have it any other way, this boy and his sweet mouth. Sun in his throat, honeyed tongue. I don't come. But I know—in the second that he comes apart above me—that he's been singing panties off of hips since his voice dropped, that hip logic was his first lesson in geometry, that boys like him don't even have to try, that not just girls—but anyone—would be helpless against him.

Kai El Khoury is the kind of dizzying that makes wind twist in the blood.

In the morning we Uber home, bags under our eyes, blisters on our feet, lazy, unsure smiles on our faces, all of us having grown up just a little more overnight, all of us bonding on a wave of unspoken words, as though we've just survived a week lost in the wilderness. Kai and I catch one together because apparently doing the sex has made us inseparable. *More* inseparable, that is.

We arrive at Merrick's as though we've drifted here on a cloud, Kai leaning against the seat, me—back to his chest—draped languidly.

Before I get out, we don't kiss. I think the Uber driver is sick of us doing that, so we refrain.

"You love me," I say.

"I love you," he confirms.

Inside, after the Uber takes Kai away, after a long bath, after a few hours of homework and watching game tape and reading some school email about receiving college acceptance letters, I text Slim.

hey hey heyyyy
sup fat albert, how was it??
omg slim. stacy lim. I have to tell you ALL ... who's fat albert?
lol. FT?

So I FaceTime her.

She picks up fast. "You guys had sexxxxxxx!"

I can feel the blood ripping through my cheeks. "Shut up, oh my God, you're so loud."

"Sorry, sorry. But, okay. So? It was?"

"It was good. I don't know. There were bad parts, but the good parts were really good and all I'm thinking about is doing it again and again."

She laughs. "You sore?"

I nod. "I took the longest bath ever. Merrick's pissed because my bath ball left glitter in the tub."

"Ha. So, like, you're definitely seeing your gyno tomorrow, right?"

I . . . am not sure. "My gyno?"

"Oh my God, Teez. You need to see your OB after sex."

"I thought that was only for the first time!"

"It's been over a year. You need to see them yearly."

My God, I didn't know that. Mamma never told me that! Nobody ever told me that!

Okay. Chill, chill, chill, Tasia.

I search everywhere for my doctor's information, which I thought fate might have left in my email inbox somewhere.

I don't find it, but I do find several places on Google that might see me. If I can get my health insurance information to them.

American healthcare is bullshit.

I learn this with 100 percent certainty when I call six different doctor's offices and they say they can't book me unless they have my insurance provider. So I find Merrick in the living room polishing off a bag of Lays. Watching—of all things—football. I'd be proud if we weren't still weird about each other. But we are, and I'm about to make it worse.

I stand in front of the TV.

"Your father's not a glass maker, kiddo. I can't see."

What? "I need something."

"Can it wait until the game's over?"

This. This right here is what sets me off. I hate him for a second and I decide to make him my prisoner simply because I can.

"I need you to call my OB/GYN and give them my health insurance information so I can make an appointment. It needs to be now, before *the game* is over. I had sex last night and I need to be checked out."

And then I walk into the kitchen to make a sandwich, which I eat standing right there at the bar. Then go to my room to worry for the rest of the day.

Just a quick twenty minutes later, Merrick walks into my room and hands me a small piece of paper with a date and time written down for my appointment.

"I'm sorry," he says. "I made the appointment. Thank you for coming to me. And . . . I'm sorry."

Chapter Thirty-Six

I'm at practice guzzling a twenty-two of water when Coach tells me I'm starting in Friday's game, which is tomorrow.

It's taken so much longer to get it across to these guys that I'm good. That I'm fricking great. Longer than it would have taken if I was, y'know, male and had a penis. Longer than it would've taken if I was a white girl, too.

"Quirk!" he yells. So I trot out to him across the field in my practice jersey, practice pads, and cleats.

"Yeah, Coach?"

"How you feeling?"

"Feel okay."

"I'm not asking if you're PMSing, Quirk. I'm asking you how good you feel about the plays, your defense. How you're gettin' on with Cole."

Cole has been incredibly standoffish with me and when he's not being standoffish, he's being hostile or outright mean. I have wondered, in the part of my mind that holds petty dismissals and half-assed goodbyes, if it's because of my skin. But then I see him with Victory and he is kind and gentle. He is funny and playful.

But that thought is always there. Sometimes, even unconsciously, prejudice creeps in for people who can barely even spell the word *racism*.

It's hard to attribute his moods to Kai when Dahlia's been with him, too, and there's essentially zero angst there.

"I feel real good about the plays, Coach."

"Yeah?"

I nod, sure. "Confident. I feel focused."

"Good. I gotta say, I'm pleasantly surprised. I'm not wrong a lot, and when I am, I don't admit it. I'm admitting it now. You're making good breaks on the ball, keeping your hips open, and your tackling has gotten more sure, which we worried about with you at first. You're not stepping in the bucket, and you're visualizing the picks—I can tell. You're doing excellent things for the defensive game and I have not seen that from other corners in a long time."

Oh my God.

Coach's hands go to his hips, his clipboard held under one of his arms. "You see holes in the offenses' positioning and that's not a skill a lot of high school corners have. I'm being honest." His voice gets quiet. "If you were male, I'd work to get you a scholarship, placed on a good college team. But the chances of that—"

"Nonexistent. I know. I just want to play ball here, now, Coach." Anyway, the team at Cal hasn't had a good season since about the fifties.

"Good enough. You're starting tomorrow. Eat good tonight, rest up. Come ready to play."

On the inside, I am screaming like I just hit the jackpot playing the penny slots. On the outside, I am cool as a cucumber. I offer Coach a simple bro nod and say, "You got it, Coach."

I turn to walk away when Coach calls me back. "Quirk!"

"Yeah, Coach?"

He switches his clipboard from arm to arm before speaking again. "I, uhh, I had a meeting with the school counselor."

My head cocks to the side. What's that got to do with me? "Okay . . . "

"Yeah," he says, slowly. Coach Rass doesn't do *anything* slow. Except this, apparently. "I'm gonna need you to make some time to see her."

"What?"

"Check in," he says. His voice gets loud. That's when you know he's done with the conversation. "Go see her. I don't wanna hear that you took this in one ear and let it leak out the other. You know where that office is at?"

No. Never had any real reason to know. "Yes."

"Good. Get in there at some point."

"Uh . . . okay, Coach."

"Yeah?" he says, louder still.

"Okay. Yeah. Yes. I will, Coach."

He grumbles something I barely hear, breaks eye contact—which I only had about thirty-eight percent of to begin with—and walks away.

It is the strangest conversation I have ever had with any coach, ever. But the wild, blooming sensation of *hell, yes!* nips at my heels and settles in heavy. I'm a starter now.

I practice harder and better than I ever have. Guy gives me horrible looks, but before I make it into the locker room, he pulls me aside and tells me he respects my hustle.

After practice, sweaty in that gross way and grinning hard, I throw myself into Kai's arms. It's the best I've felt in a long time. Until I see an email from Mamma with details about her company dinner party.

Until Kai drops me at my car and takes my keys from me. "Home, mulatta?"

"Yeah, I guess. But . . . you should probably not keep calling me that."

Kai stops, and it is the most serious he has ever been. One of the best things about Kai is that you don't *need* eye contact from him in order to understand or gauge his moods. But in this instance, he gives it to me. It's steady and reminds me, curiously, of my Poppa.

He squares out his jaw. "Does it offend you? Honestly."

"I don't know. I just think you shouldn't use it. There are certain words you shouldn't say. That is one I don't exactly understand. I mean . . . I've only ever identified as Black because I thought I was only Black. And now that I'm not,

I don't know what being anything else means. I haven't done the research or talked to enough people who are also biracial, I guess."

Kai places a kiss high on my cheek. "I won't use it. I'm sorry for saying it. For not thinking and for using it as a punch line. I was wrong to do that."

My arms come around him.

"Forgive me?"

I nod.

Kai crowds me against the door of my car. "Forgive me," he says again.

"I forgive you," I whisper. And I don't think, for very long, about what amount of time it might take me to forgive Mamma and V, the two strongest women in my family. The two women who have lied to me for so long.

That night, after Kai catches the Orange home from the apartment, I finally pull my phone out and text Tristan.

sorry for going MIA again
you're not MIA if you're still using instagram regularly
fair, then, *so mamma's dinner??*
you gotta be there

Oof. Mamma's gala. It's not just any dinner. It's an important one.

Still, I text, *lol no I don't*
you do tho, then, *I need you there*
Then, *ok trist, I'll be there*, I promise.

For him, I can be there.

On Monday, during Speech class, Mrs. Wu sets a note, facedown, on top of my desk.

The note is a summons to the in-school therapist's office. Coach's request that I make time for this sings in the back of my mind. I've never been before, have never had a reason to see her in the time I've been a student here. And I don't really know anyone else who has, either. But maybe that's the point.

Last year at Westview, one of the freshmen was exposed for some eating disorder. I don't know. They're pretty common, but apparently this case made school officials sit up and take notice. So they added an in-school psychotherapist. I'm a little surprised to find ECR's got one as well.

Now we're all supposed to be writing down our speeches from memory. I stop to raise my hand. "Right now? Do I have to go see her right now?"

"Yes," she says. "Pack your things. You'll miss the rest of class."

I am not one to look a gift horse in the mouth, but I do experience .0006 seconds of terror that I might be getting called in because of a grades-related football thing. It makes absolutely no sense, but I've learned that anxiety has a tendency to be irrational.

And, like, two juniors have been benched this week alone for GPA drops. I worry that this is my fate too, but the truth is, it's not likely. Because Merrick might be half-assing this parenting thing, but the part he's not half-assing, he seems to be excelling at. Trig kicks my ass, but Merrick stays on top of me and my homework and my grades as best he can. This could have everything to do with the fact that he was a teacher.

I push into the counselor's office after a quick series of three knocks at her closed door. She calls, "Come in," and I find myself in front of Dr. Meshell Lloyd who is easily the most confusing "counselor" I've ever seen. She's got long blond hair, green eyes, and a green apple in hand that she's going to town on.

"You caught me in the middle of lunch," she says. "Have a seat, Tasia."

Her office smells like lemons. But it's warm. There are shelves of books covering every flat surface, and I feel like the whole display is a farce, because there's no way she's using any of these books on a daily basis.

The chair I take a seat in is way too comfortable. "You know who I am?"

"I read your file. All student files have photos."

"Okay."

"And, TBH, I've seen you play football. You're amazing. I totally want to be you when I grow up."

"You're making me uncomfortable."

"Is it the slang?" she whispers. "That displaces a lot of people when they meet me. Or maybe it's that I look like a Barbie?"

"All my Barbies were Black, actually. It's really more that you keep licking the apple juice that's sliding down your hand."

"Oh!" she laughs. "I like you, Tasia. This is going to be fun."

I sit back in my brown leather chair. "Yeah, okay. Um.

You felt the need to read my file. So why am I here, again?"

"Typically, my service is called into play in two situations. A, the student reaches out to me and requests my aid; or B, an authority figure, the student's parent or teacher or legal guardian, will recommend I step in. In your case, obviously, it was an authority figure."

"Who stepped in?"

"Your father."

"Which one? The one that doesn't want me or the one that's only known me a few months." I say this purposely to unsettle her, but it doesn't work.

She smiles and wipes her hands with a baby wipe. "So I see we do have things to discuss. This is good, since your seeing me has been highly recommended."

"Highly."

"Yes."

Wait. "Holy hooker. So, then. What—someone suddenly thinks I'm troubled youth or something? I'm not. I'm just pissed off in general, and unlike most teens my age, I have the right to be."

"Everyone has the right to be upset, Tasia."

I shrug. "I'm just saying, my frustration isn't because of some spike in hormones." She says nothing, so I continue. "I've been living with Merrick for almost two months, and this is only now coming up?"

"Both your mother and Merrick feel this would be good for you. But, more important, how do you feel about them making this a necessity?"

I throw my hands up, roll my eyes for good measure. "My mom's involved in this?"

She nods. "Would you rather she wasn't?"

"I'd rather they talked to me about this first."

"If they had spoken to you about this first, what would it have changed about this? Would you be more cooperative?"

"Probably."

"Probably. But they didn't, and now we're here. So, what do you want to do?"

What's she saying? I mean, is there anything that needs doing? This isn't the kind of thing that you just gloss over, I know. And I also know that the adults in my life doin't necessarily owe me anything.

I don't know what I want to do. I don't know any of that right now, and I guess . . . I guess I've made some kinda weird peace with that. There's so much that I'm unsure about when it comes to what action needs to happen next, but maybe there is one thing I do know.

With an exhale, I offer, "I want the adults in my life to know what the hell they're doing."

She nods. "Understandable. But there's a good chance that even you, when you're an adult, won't know what you're doing all the time."

"I'm eighteen. I am an adult. And there's also a chance that I won't screw up half as bad as the three of them have."

I remind myself that they're all working on it. Even Merrick. They're all learning how to deal with this now and they're doing it for me. They're starting to get it. It doesn't exactly negate the screwups, but it's a step I'm really grateful they're taking.

"True," she says, and then scribbles something down. "You can leave if you want, but in the interest of honesty, no football is the consequence for not meeting with me twice weekly."

Being told what to do . . . essentially held under thumb, by a white woman, of all people. It rankles. "I'll be kicked off the team? You can't mandate that I see you."

"No, but your coach can bench you for the duration of the season."

I throw my hands up again. Probably overdoing it with this gesture, but I'm getting a frustration-induced headache. "Great. Coach Rass would never voluntarily get involved in this," I say, suspicious.

"I may have approached him with the idea, with permission from your parents, of course."

Why the hell didn't my parents *talk to me about this?*

"Great," I say again.

She stacks the papers on her desk, settles in, leaning on the left arm of her chair, overly comfortable. "Let's get started, then. I like to start out all my sessions this way: Are you angry?"

"With who?"

"Me, your teachers, your football coach, your teammates, your friends, your boyfriend, your parents, your new family, anyone? You have a right to be upset with any of them. With all of them."

"Not Kai."

"Kai is your boyfriend."

"Kai is my boyfriend."

"You're upset with everyone but him?"

I shrug. "You're all right."

"Dope," she says. "I made the cut. Why are he and I exempt?"

"Well, I don't know you."

"Fair. And Kai?"

He's Kai. He touches me with magic and patience. Talks honey-soft about hard things and takes a hundred terrible pictures of me, but says he loves every. Single. One. Kai El Khoury is, like, my healing. My key to unlearning panic. It's easy with him. But also not. And when it's not he whispers that he won't leave me, won't replace me with someone else, and then begs me to trust him. There's so much I could be saying about Kai to Dr. Lloyd, but it all amounts to "He's the only one who knows what he's doing right now."

"Maybe. For you. He knows what he's supposed to be doing for you. That's what you're saying?"

"That's all I'm asking for."

There's that voice again, whispering that Mamma is actively *trying* to get it. And so far, she's succeeding.

Dr. Lloyd nods. Scribbles. Turns another page in her Steno notebook. "Let's make a list."

I mutter, "Okay, Chick-Tristan."

"What's that?"

"Nothing. Let's list the shit out of some stuff."

"Good. Now, at the top, I'm writing your mom's name

and your dad's name—Merrick's name. What are some specific things you want from each of them? Not things you wanted that are no longer relevant—honesty from your mother regarding your birth father, for example. But in the future, what do you want?"

It's not a bad question. It's a question I haven't been asked or thought of, and I hate that I didn't consider it sooner.

"Honesty. I just want general honesty moving forward. In all things. From them all." Because I can't help but wonder . . . I mean, honesty would obviously have prevented all of this.

"And are you getting any of that from them now?"

I don't even need to think about it. "Mostly. Yes. Yeah, I think I am."

"Is that enough to help you consider exoneration?"

That one I can't answer. Because the answer isn't one I'm ready for. Pride is partially to blame, but also, I'm not ready to open up yet. I like being closed. Protected.

But still, I settle in for the next hour and Dr. Lloyd and I list a few things.

When I leave Dr. Lloyd's office, I spot Victory hurrying down the hall, her large jacket clutched close to her body. She looks panicked as she pushes her way into the bathroom, and I don't know what would possess me to follow her in, but I do.

I practically fall into the bathroom just as she's dropping a pink rectangular box into the round metal garbage bin.

My stomach drops.

I pause just inside the doorway.

Her head cuts right toward me. "It's not mine."

"What's not?"

Victory rolls her eyes and turns the sink knob to wash her hands.

I don't even know how to talk about what I just saw, but Jesus, all I've ever wanted to do is be her friend. "If you need to talk—"

She laughs. "Can you stop pretending you're better than me for like five minutes, please? Goddammit, Tasia. Five freaking minutes."

Hands up, like I'm being held at gunpoint, I say, "I don't have any idea what you're—"

"Oh, you don't?"

I shake my head.

"Okay. Go fuck yourself," she says.

And I make the mistake of muttering, "Are these pregnancy hormones?" I mean it as a joke, but . . .

"I'm not pregnant, you asshole! But good thing, though, right? Just another Black girl statistic? Sorry to disappoint you. Sorry I couldn't be your punch line."

"I wouldn't use you as . . . You're not my punch line, Victory. I just got awkward for a second. I'm sorry. But . . . I mean, I saw the box and I know what a pregnancy test kit looks like—"

"Yeah? Then you also know what a false alarm is. You also probably know that it's possible to take a pregnancy test and not be pregnant. Jesus."

Even I'm relieved, to tell you the truth. "I don't think I'm better than you."

"Well, good, because you're *not* better than me."

"Okay," I say, like a dismissal. Like I'm humoring little old her. Like I'm looking down on her, just the way she accused me of doing.

"God," she mutters. "You don't even get it."

I get chills hearing her say exactly the thing I've been saying to and about my family for months.

Victory shakes her head. "Everything with you is 'North this' and 'Beverly Hills that' and 'My BFF is better than your BFF' and everyone on the entire planet is inclined to think you're so great *on principle,* just because you're this light-skinned Black girl with blond hair who plays football, like you're some kind of eighth wonder. News flash, Tasia. You're not. Your family's fucked up too. You came here and tried to be *just another Black girl,* but you're not. You're white, too, Tasia."

I flinch. But she doesn't notice. She's still got blows to throw. "And you know what else? Literally eighty percent of the school knows your boyfriend better than you do, and you're so busy chasing Dahlia around trying to be her friend that you don't even realize when *real* friendship, like, actual solidarity, is staring you right in the face. Like, I got over your BS fast, and now I'm just waiting for everyone else to see that you've lost your shiny new-girl appeal."

Seismic energy rumbles underneath my glass house. "'Real' friendship? You mean you? Because, Vic, I gotta say, it doesn't seem like you've tried to be real with me on any level. I've been trying so hard to be your friend and to get you to just like me, so much that it's practically killing me. And you've been kicking the shit out of me while I'm down this whole time. And you know what? If Dahlia had dated *your boyfriend,* you'd be trying to keep her close, too! You just have this awesome way of making me feel like shit, and I'm so tired of brushing that off."

"You're saying I hurt your feelings. Often."

"Yeah. Yeah, I kind of am. I feel like you're constantly calling me out and reading me—"

"Not bad for a dyslexic, huh?" Her sad smile is like cold honey dripping off a spoon back in on a pile of itself.

And I am a vase that's shattered against the marble.

As Victory pushes her way out of the door, I realize this is what it's like to be left for dead.

Chapter Thirty-Seven

GAME 7 – EL CAMINO REAL VS. RESEDA REGENTS

The night of our last game is epic. It's a satisfying 42–20 win over the Reseda Regents. I'm not saying we snatch up a spot in the playoffs because of me, but that is exactly what I'm saying.

I play at full speed all night and I feel like I'm the one guy our defense can look up to every time. Cole and I do excellent on field together. I somehow finish with just two pass breakups. But I manage to stay consistently physical and in the face of Reseda's receivers, affecting receptions even without actually nailing down the ball. By the second half, it's obvious just how much of me is in the other team's heads.

That weekend it's a brisk, just-chilly-enough-to-inconvenience-Angelenos sort of cold. Tristan and I walk around an outdoor mall to Christmas shop, which is dumb, because Halloween barely had time to squeeze it's ass out the door before Santa shimmied his own down every retailer's chimney.

But Tristan likes to get a head start because he's predictable and enjoys beating his own schedule into submission. I agree to tag along because I'm still reliving yesterday's game, and that basically puts all Trist's planning and lists in technicolor.

Every year he pretends he didn't get me anything and last year was the first where I finally stopped believing him. This year he doesn't pretend, but he does go out of his way to hide my present from me.

"You've had enough lies for the year, I think," he says.

It's true. I've had enough for a lifetime.

The mall we're at is large, as are all SoCal malls, but this one happens to be an outdoor sort of monstrosity.

Both Trist and I have been seeing people we know from school all afternoon, so I don't know why I'm shocked when we come up on Dahlia and a woman who looks nothing like her. The woman is average height. Square-bodied, of some obviously European decent.

And she's awful. Shrill in voice and demeanor, which I would have known even had I not heard her just insult Dahlia for her "comical attempts at originality."

Her hair. She's talking about D's hair. Or the fact that she doesn't have any.

"I don't have any control over that—"

The woman spares only the briefest moment to give Dahlia a withering look of exasperation. "Lupus would not have robbed you blind and left you with no hair, no eyebrows, no nothing,

Dahlia. You didn't have to remove it all. I'm not going to keep having this argument with you—you did this to yourself."

Tristan wanders into the Apple store and all I can do is stand and stare. I've always been taught not to stare, but somehow all my "lessons" about how rude that is have made themselves scarce.

"Dahlia," I say. I say it like I didn't just stand here and watch this woman insult her on her looks alone for five straight minutes.

"Tasia," she says. "Hey."

I glance at the woman. I expect her to judge me but she doesn't. Not that I can tell. She also doesn't look like she's going to ask me for my autograph, but I can probably live my life without that.

"Zia, this is my friend Tasia. She's Kai's girlfriend. Tasia, this is my zia, Celine. My aunt."

We shake hands and the woman laughs. "At least you've got something in common."

The woman, with her inky, wispy hair, wasn't hideous until right this second. She's like tea that's sat and steeped too long, or a stagnant glass of water with hair in it. You only know it if you're that close.

The woman walks away and I wait all of six and a half milliseconds before I stage-whisper, "Oh my God, why is she awful?"

Dahlia laughs, "My mom used to say that God doesn't—"

"Give with both hands. My mamma says that too."

"Maybe we do have something in common."

I shrug. "Your mom here too?"

She shakes her head. "My mom, she . . . no. Celine raised me. It's just her and me, as usual."

"I'm here with my brother." I gesture over my shoulder. "If you want to come hang out with us."

Dahlia peers behind me and then lifts both brows. "Nah. It's okay. Your brother's ridiculously good-looking and I don't want you to hate me for making him fall in love with me."

I shove her. "Oh my God, you're disgusting. You and Slim."

We're quiet. The crowd of shoppers isn't as heavy as it will be in another week or so, but it's bad enough.

"About your hair, though—"

She waves me off. "Stop. I don't care about Celine or her opinion. Every night, 1999 tries to sext her and ask for its style back, and the bitch won't answer. Seriously, don't worry about it. And, like, it's not a big secret or anything. The lupus. I can get falsies and pencil in my brows when I have a flare-up, and I keep my head shaved so that you'd never know baldness wasn't my first choice. Guys still think I'm pretty, and you're the only straight girl I haven't gotten to kiss me, so I think I'm doing okay. But, like, all the same, if you could just not—"

"Your secret's safe with me, bitch. But hold on. Rewind. Pause. Replay. You've made out with Victory?"

"It is literally my greatest achievement in life. But, like, Scott bet me a hundred dollars last year that I couldn't get her to kiss me for seven seconds, so I told Victory about the bet and we went halfsies on it when we won."

"Best fifty bones ever."

"Ever," she says, holding on to the "r" long.

As Tristan arrives at my side, he holds up a slip of paper and says, "The Apple watch is literally the dumbest invention. I made a list of reasons why."

"Oh my God, Trist. No one cares about this list or the Apple watch."

"I care," Dahlia says.

Tristan smiles with half of his mouth—his stare-at-my-perfect-teeth smile—and I punch him in the stomach because I hate this smile on account of all the girls who love it that aren't me, including Mamma and Tammy.

"We're leaving," I say, and grab Tristan's hand. "Bye, D!"

Just quietly enough that I can only kind of hear it, she says, "See you later, T-Dot."

It's then that I realize I'm seeing a different side of Dahlia. It scares me a little.

Kai, my soft, sweet boy, isn't the only person who is a patiently scrambled Rubik's cube. Kai has sides that only I get, sides that only Merrick or V get. Slim and Josiah have sides that belong only to each other. Mamma has a side that is her own secret thing—or, rather, she did. That side that belonged to Merrick, and he, her.

But I think this is a good thing, that people have sides and I'm really not entitled to know any of them unless they say so. Their lives have felt very solid to me, and I'm realizing now they are anything but.

I leave that mall feeling like I learned something big and important.

Chapter Thirty-Eight

PLAYOFF GAME – EL CAMINO REAL VS. NOTRE DAME
KNIGHTS

We win our first playoff game against the Notre Dame Knights. Their team's coach called it "a hell of a win." And, God, I have to agree with him. Notre Dame had a nineteen-point lead at the end of the first quarter and I thought for sure they were on their way to a blowout.

The entire game my coverage assignment can't gain more than a few steps on me, and I feel like it sets the tone for how I play the rest of the night. We take it 27–19.

Afterward, a bunch of people from ECR have decided to head up to the Third Street Promenade to celebrate.

Kai decrees, with all the power in his bones, that we gotta go to Santa Monica Pier instead. No group Third Street hangout for us—which, let's be honest, I'm okay with. Even when Kai tells me his plan. He wants to "beautify trash" and

I tell him not to talk about Emily like that.

Still, he tells me we have to swing by his place to grab supplies—literally any paint, glitter, wire, or twine we can find in his room.

"Are you going to just starfish on my bed or are you actually going to help me look for shit? This is all for you, you know."

I do know. All the bottles and broken shells and junk we "beautify" are getting hung somewhere in my room at Merrick's. That's Kai's plan, anyway.

He pulls chalkboard paint out of his closet and I sit up, bouncing on the bed. I'm like a kid in a fricking candy store. I love chalkboard paint.

"Oh, she rises."

The yawn and stretch that moves through me is long. Hurts a little, because although postgame soreness feels ridiculously good after a win, it also kinda burns to do basic things, like stretch or walk or help Kai dig around his room.

"Fine, Warden," I say. "What do you want me to do?"

He shrugs, reaching up to the top of his closet for who knows what. He keeps finding things and throwing them into the box of junk we're taking with us to the pier. "You could check in my file cabinet. Sometimes I keep candles in there. We can do some stuff with the wax."

My head turns sharply in his direction, but he still isn't looking at me. Just chuckles while he reaches up higher on the shelf.

In the file cabinet, I find a few very good things. I kneel

down to the sound of my knee popping and pull out a ton of tiny pastel candles, marbles that've been cracked in half, Pogs, a half-inch binder full of pressed flowers. I take all of it, seeing the way Kai's mind moves when it comes to art. He sees potential in everything.

"I'll be back," Kai says.

"Wait! Where are you going?"

"To the garage. I have some stuff in there that'd look stellar on your ceiling."

His footsteps grow softer as he makes his way down the hall, and I'm so exhausted in the best way, I'm tempted to just lie on his bed again and wait for him to come back and do all the rest of the work. I'm too impatient for art.

I'm wondering if I can convince Kai to stay here with me and forget going out in favor of making out, but it hits me that he is doing this all for me. He is creating for me. So I get to my hands and knees and start searching under his bed.

I don't find any dirty mags or peen rings. I don't even find any dirty socks or boxers. Kai is one of the cleanest people I know.

The notebook I pull out isn't your standard college-ruled school thing. It's a hard-backed journal, basically, with *kai el khoury* embossed in gold letters on it. I undo the leather binding around it before I even question whether or not I should.

A photo of me falls out.

A ripped photo of me.

A ripped photo of me that is clearly part of a larger group photo.

I don't need to turn it over to confirm what I already know. To know that there are words across the back. But I do turn it over.

It's the missing tear-out from the box. In Kai's journal.

My heart beats hard in my chest, but it's not anxiety or anger or sadness this time. This time, it's just telling me it's working in overtime. Telling me it's too tired to feel anything. Too tired to deal with being lied to again.

I can't believe I'm here again. That I let this happen.

I flip idly through the rest of the notebook, but there are no other photos of me, nothing else he'd taken from the box.

There's been this constant feeling I've had since all this began. A slow and steady ease spreading across my chest. A symptom of unlearning panic.

But all of that . . . now all of that unravels. All the growing I've done turns again to aching, and all I can do is sit here on his floor, my heart ripped open like a pomegranate in Kai's hands.

"Are you doing nothing again?" he says as he walks back into the room, his arms full of knickknacks and bobbles, filtered light bulbs and plastic planet shapes.

"Tasia?"

I look up. Then, "You lied to me?" It's a plea. I am begging him to tell me I'm wrong. That he would never.

He can't. He sees the photo in my hands. He doesn't say a word, instead coming to kneel in front of me, placing a hand on my knee.

With Kai El Khoury is where I learn to love physical contact. With him is where I learn why people need it. To press in close, so that every part of me is touching every part of him. To curl up inside of him, hunched and nestled in deep. It's those moments where he's just breathing inside my personal space, dragging his cheek against mine repeatedly, touching his nose to mine, as though the act is simply another means of communication, and yet still another, whenever his lips press hard on my chin, just under my bottom lip.

I know when I'm older—not by much, but just slightly more mature and sure of myself—I'll look back on my experience with Kai and know what kind of things he gave me.

I'll remember him as the young, humble king that he is. Meant to inherit millions, who'd have worked twice as hard to give it away. I'll remember he was on the receiving end of a bum deal.

The fact that I hold Kai in such high esteem isn't lost on me. I worship him. And I thought I knew, with every bone in my body, that he felt the same. That he looks at me and sees a conqueror, that he's too young to look at me and see something that ought to be exalted—and yet. Yet, he's shown he feels that way about me, constantly.

Still, I know that although Kai is my rock, my most solid thing, I am not his.

If I were, he wouldn't have lied to me.

I push his hand off my knee. "You sent the box."

Chapter Thirty-Nine

I drive myself home that night and I don't even know how. I've got no memory of pulling in behind Merrick's Benz or walking up the stairs to the apartment, or shuffling into my room, of shutting out the lights and everything else.

But apparently I did.

He didn't even try to stop me. Oh, God. Why didn't he try to stop me from leaving?

All of it, every single moment with him, without him, with Merrick and V and Mamma and the box, it all just comes in like wildfire. I walk into the bathroom at Merrick's and sit down inside the tub, try desperately to hold myself still, to just be the brush embracing the burn. I can't be inside my room right now. I know immediately that its empty, undecorated walls will whisper to me as soft as the flick of a lighter, and I just don't think I can stomach that right now.

Why wouldn't he tell me? Why would he lie? Why didn't I see it coming a million miles away, when I was learning to trust him or falling headlong into this petal-soft, incinerating kiss.

Mamma always says healing is kinda like the ocean running its fingertips over the shoreline, like the snake as it sheds its skin. She says it's the process of feeling pain, aching, then growing from it, over and over again. She says that end part is the crux of it.

Maybe that's why I'm here, in this pit of repetitive licks of pain. Maybe that's why I've had to have the important people in my life lie to me.

Maybe each of their lies was my over-and-over-again.

I don't want whatever this end product is. The pain doesn't feel worth it. Doesn't feel like healing. I haven't come out on the other side intact. Now, instead, I'm wearing lies and the weight of this new world of mine on my back.

Mamma was wrong, I think slowly. It occurs to me that Mamma's gala is tomorrow. I don't even care if she's been wrong about healing or the box or Merrick or any of it.

I need her, I need her, I need her.

On days like today, when heartache and homesick are synonymous, I wish I could just disappear. I do my best to get there inside a tiny, porcelain bathtub. Just until I can get home tomorrow.

Chapter Forty

Mamma's gala is tonight and I don't know if I'm ready. I need her, though. Or maybe I just need something normal. Maybe I just need to pretend for a while.

Six steps across the room bring me to my closet, where a gown hangs. I pull it out, lay it across the bed. Exhale.

The Newark Group, so named for the powerful women in Mamma's family who chose to keep their maiden name—this does not include Mamma, who hyphenated to Newark-Quirk—hosts a celebration of its newest acquisition.

The moment Tristan and I walk into the Newark Group's event, I'm tackled with a sense of awe. Mamma enters a room, takes control, commands attention, and directs with a steady voice and a sure hand. Men of any race, size, color, and creed follow her with no questions asked. And the ones who do second-guess her are curbed very quickly. I've seen her in action before, once, when one of her board members questioned a decision she'd pretty much declared as law. She set him straight with a pretty smile, a few blinks of her heavily mascaraed lashes, and eight hard words: "You can call the shots when you're president."

Now the building we're in is all glass walls and titanium borders and fixtures. Soft lights and clean angles. Men and women in black buttondowns walk through the space with trays of finger foods I've eaten at a hundred of these events, and Mamma's business partners—whom I've known since I was old enough to walk—smile and greet both Tristan and me.

Raul and Natalie Cabrera are my parents' best friends. They stop, ask Trist and me a few questions about school. It's obvious they don't know about what's happening in our family, but they understand that something definitely *is* going on. Tristan and I smile, nod a bit, answer the same questions they all ask us, in the same tone and with the same inflections. We play the sibling game because that's what we do at these events. What we've always done.

Mamma finds me standing at one of the fruit tables just before dinner is about to be served. She knows me so well, well enough to understand that I will bypass dinner in favor of several plates of fruit plus dessert pastries.

"I did this for you," she says. She means the fruit table. It's the most elaborate food table. There's fricking cubes of dragon fruit and roasted jicama—with a sprinkling of sugar, the way Poppa taught us to love it.

I smile, say quietly, "I know."

The list Tristan and I made burns a hole in my dress pocket. When I slipped the list in there, I couldn't even take a second to appreciate that the dress does indeed *have* pockets.

The list has been long since memorized, so I don't know why I've taken to carrying it around everywhere. It's like a paperweight, holding me down, centering me and reminding me about the existence of gravity.

1. Have an honest conversation with Mamma. Ask her how she's doing. Expect her to tell you the truth—no matter what that means.

"How are you?" Now is not the time to have this conversation. I should have chosen another number on the list.

She smiles. Nods, though I don't know at what. But after a second, I know she's actually going to be honest with me. I don't know how I know, but maybe it's the way her shoulders square out or the way her collarbone suddenly juts forward. Honesty sits in her body language.

I am both ready and not ready for it.

"I'm not okay," she whispers. The steadiness in her voice is false. "But I'm here, and that's more progress than I've made in . . . too long."

"Not okay," I say.

Mamma smiles. "No," she says, soft.

"Trist says you haven't been getting out of bed some days."

She's human; she glances around the space to make sure no one is within earshot, then says, "Textbook depression. It's a bitch."

I laugh—a totally heathen *bark* of approval—because Mamma does not use words like that. She'll say "hell" and "damn," maybe, if it slips. But never the hard words that can only be said with rough-sounding consonants.

"It's my faul—"

"Not even if you cut off all your hair and eloped with a Republican in Vegas," she says. "This couldn't ever be your fault."

"Okay. I mean, yeah. I . . . okay. But when I—"

"This, me with depression and not handling life well, I've dealt with it forever. Since I was maybe fifteen or so. It's part of the reason I got so close to—Anyway, I've been dealing with this sort of thing for a very long time."

I nod. That feels true too. Honest. And it helps me see her as a little more human. For a moment, I wonder why parents don't tell their kids these things. What if I have it too?

3. Think of her as "just another adult." Not "my adult parent." Trust me—this works.

The dimples in Mamma's cheeks make an appearance as she says, "I really should go up there and give this speech."

"Did you write it yourself this time?" The last speech she had to give was written by someone else. And you could tell it wasn't what Mamma had in mind. Halfway through she stopped and said, right into the mike, "Who the hell wrote this? Jesus, this is boring. Okay, listen." And then she proceeded to give the speech of her life.

Now, she laughs. "I did. You remember that other one?"

I nod, smiling. "And Raul was like, 'Sloane, it was one speech!'"

"'One damn speech, Sloane, and you couldn't just read it and exit stage left?'"

And then we've both been set off, and we're laughing together and then Mamma sobers and says, "How are you? How's Rick?"

It occurs to me that Merrick is her Rick, but I ask anyway. "Rick?"

"Merrick was Rick. And I was always Slo."

She was his Slo. For one awful, terrible, horrifying moment, I wish they were together. I wish my actual parents were still together and in love and happy with each other. But they never will be.

I think about Daddy and I know, without a doubt, that Mamma will always love him. No matter what. And he, her. That much is obvious, if my existence is anything to go by. Solomon Quirk will stand by his wife through anything. And the same is true for Mamma—come hell or high water, she's in his corner.

"Merrick's good," I say. But that's a lie. It's the kind of lie that you don't even realize is false because the response is so common.

Someone says, "You okay?" You say, "I'm just tired."

Someone says, "What's wrong?" You say, "Nothing."

Someone says, "How are you?" You say, "Very well, thank you."

Mamma's hand comes to her chest, as though she just *has* *to* feel the deep inhale and exhale she's taking. "That's great. I'm glad you guys are getting along—"

"Actually. I mean, it's just . . . There's a learning curve, I guess? And Merrick is, like, not the most awesome student?"

She laughs. "But you're okay? Not emaciated or sleeping in a closet or anything?"

I shake my head. "No, I'm eating well. Sleeping in a bed of my own."

She nods, and I feel her about to walk away, and I don't know how to stop it or freeze this moment, and it's making me nervous. And would grabbing her by the arm be unwelcome or look suspicious, or would that be me admitting defeat? I don't know, but she saves me instead, for just a moment longer, when she asks, "And Kai . . . ?"

I swear my heart must be a bone. It cracks and splinters just a little more. Shaking my head, a very gentle smile on my lips, I say, "How'd you know?"

"I can read your sadness like my own," she says, and maybe it's just me, but my heart, that bone, I feel it warm a little, I feel it mending.

"And," Mamma continues, "I think Kai and Tristan are friends on the video game. Your brother didn't say much, but he said enough for me to wonder."

Jesus. They're all much more entangled than I thought. The ache is back. It's a big, soiled, green thing, like moss that's been stepped on one time too many.

"You still like him?" she says. She wants to know. I think she's probably imagined herself present for most of this situation in my life.

I nod.

"A lot?"

I nod.

"You love him."

I shrug and nod again, and I smile *because I can't help it.*
When I think about Kai I really can't help it, but so much of
last night is ash. It's just soot and debris now.

"What do you love about him? This dress is pretty," she
says as an afterthought.

This is what Mamma does. It's not calculated or planned.
It's just Mamma, loving on me the best way she can. In exactly
the ways I need, pulling my new, bright green roots out of
the ground with her bare hands—even through all the rubble
that's burned.

My heart takes off, full speed to the space it knows is
home. "He's weird. He says what he's thinking and seems very
sure about a lot of his opinions and a lot of his knowledge.
But he's actually not sure about a good bit of who he is. Not
his style or his looks or his friends or even where he comes
from. Not his family or his nationality. And he's giving. Very
giving. And . . . and he's a good kisser?"

She laughs, her mouth long and open and wide, her face
full of scandal and excitement. She grabs my forearm.

And it's so us. It's so classic us, and I'm so incandescently
happy for the briefest moment in time that I almost forget
what he did. How he lied. How he let me glorify love with
him, sing its praises, call it godlike.

A tear slips down my cheek. There's no reason to fight it.
Poppa used to tell me never to fight tears, since they're just

your own confusion and frustration made tangible. "He sent the box. He lied to me about sending the box."

Mamma doesn't look shocked, but I can tell she's hurting with me. I watch it move through her.

She grabs my wrist and pulls me outside onto the patio. Heads turn our way as we leave. I know she's gotta go and give that speech, but all I care about is that my mamma is here and she's got me and that's just enough for me right now.

"Do you trust him?" she says.

I don't know. "I thought I could. I thought I did."

"Your answer right now, the one you just gave me—it's not a no."

She's right. It isn't a no. Kai has done exactly the thing the rest of my family did to me. "So what's that got to do with the lie?"

"Did you know I'm getting help? I'm delegating more of my work so that I can see that therapist I told you about. I'm also making time to see an emotional counselor. Which is basically just a therapist who makes more money for less work."

I smile and shake my head, still not seeing the connection. "What, is Kai your money-hungry emo counselor? Did he lie to me about that, too?"

She rolls her eyes at me. Her favorite thing to do when my dramatics are busy working. "No, angel. What I'm saying is this: I'm getting help. I'm working on me so that I can be deserving of your trust again. I'm working on me so that I can be a better mamma to you and Trist."

I nod, connecting the dots she's setting in front of me.

"I lied to you too. I had a reason for it—admittedly," she says, holding her hand up before I can take off with that, "not a good reason. But I'm becoming a better person because of my mistakes. I hate that it was at your expense, though. I do. I wish that part didn't have to happen. I wish I could have spared your heart that. But it did happen. And you taught me something. And I'm growing into someone new. Someone who makes mistakes and handles them properly."

"I see."

"My question to you is this: Do you trust Kai enough to give him the same grace? Doesn't he deserve a second chance too?"

He does. That's not even the question. The question is whether or not I am someone capable of forgiving the people who've hurt me when they're the same people who are supposed to love me best.

I shouldn't ask her this next question while we're here. I should maybe save it for another time. But I can't, so I say, "What did you love about Merrick?"

"A lot," she says. The jump in subject doesn't seem to surprise her at all, like she'd always planned to answer this for me, like she was just waiting for the wind to blow a certain way, for things to come together the way they maybe are now. "I liked his music, and that he laughed a lot, and once I saw him with some friends in the park, tossing a Frisbee, and when he ran to catch it, his T-shirt rode up, and I think I liked that about him a lot, too."

I'm a little grossed out but I still smile, nose scrunched up, head shaking. "Okay."

Mamma glances at the watch on her wrist. "I have to go give this speech now, but . . . if you need to talk this through some more . . ." She leaves that open ended. And I get it.

"Good luck," I say. "On your speech."

She doesn't say anything back or smile at me. Just squeezes my arm again, nods, and walks away.

And after she's already up on stage and well into her speech, I do the same. Nod and walk away.

As I'm walking out the door, I pass Daddy. He says my name, grabs my hand as I pass, and squeezes it gently twice. I squeeze back once before we both let go.

In the car, I pull out the list as tears cascade down my nose and onto my dark blue dress.

I cross off numbers 1, 3, and 5.

Chapter Forty-One

It hits me as I sit in my driver's seat, keys cold in my lap, that I have nowhere to go.

Until.

Until that ugly neon Post-it note looks back at me. The soft pencil scratches on it have faded a little, the paper is damp in places, but it's still intact, if a little wrinkled. I text Victory two words: *he fumbled*

And she texts back about two minutes later. *You remember how to get here?*

yes, I type.

Victory answers her door in a big T-shirt and a pair of men's dress socks.

"Smells good in here," I tell her as I walk inside, my long dress dragging on the ground. Her house is like a tiny piece of comfort made tangible. The walls are a dark, blood-red burgundy, and it's so unconventional that I find myself staring at them for longer than I should. This is my second time being here and I'm still a little enamored with it.

Palm-size figurines decorate the house's bookshelves and mantels—mischievous Black boys posed for a run, pretty little doe-eyed Black girls with innocence heavy on their shoulders and in their rounded hips, fat-cheeked Madeas with smiling faces and wooden spoons in hand. On the walls, there is art. Each wall holds an ode to a New Orleans that doesn't exist anymore, when jazz was played in the streets for no reason at all, when women's skirts were as loose and flowy as their morals, and a storm hadn't caused a statewide devastation.

The entire house is an ode to her Blackness, and maybe mine, too.

"My mom did up the roux for tomorrow," Victory says, snapping me out of my haze.

I laugh because my mamma probably cooked her roux today too for tomorrow's Olympic-size pot of gumbo. I like that Victory doesn't feel the need to explain this to me.

This is a thing we have in common. Our Blackness, it seems, is connected after all.

We go into the den. There's a flatscreen, and Victory unpauses her movie. She's watching *Eloise at Christmastime*, which is one of Tristan's favorite Christmas movies, though he'll deny it forever and ever.

"Are your parents home?"

"They're asleep."

"Okay."

"So what's up?" she says. "It's kinda late. What'd he do? And what are you wearing?"

I shrug, but then I remember the healing. That everything grows back, and poison can be sucked out. I imagine taking a rough tackle, pretend the pain is the same. I always get up from those, too. "Sometimes," I tell Vic, "I feel like my Blackness is in competition with yours, and I've never felt like that with anyone else."

She laughs. "I feel like that all the time, but that's internalized racism for you. That's classism at work, too. And it sucks, right?"

"Oh my God, so much," I whisper.

"Yeah."

"I never felt like that before I found out about my dad."

"About your dad?"

"My bio-dad is white."

"Oh. Yeah," she says again. "I know I probably don't think hard enough about the fact that light-skinned Black girls have it just as hard as us dark-skinned girls do. I mean, you're strong. You know? You're not a Black girl that needs help. And, listen, what I said before—in the bathroom—you're Black. Okay? You know that, right? Don't you ever let another person tell you you're not. If I've learned anything from my parents, it's that all it takes is the smallest percentage and the will to stare the rest of America right in the face. You're Black."

She's quiet, then: "You know, the assholes I come into contact with are usually very overt in their hatred of me, or in their fetishization of me. But I imagine being like you, pretty and light-skinned. Coming into contact with some racist piece of shit and not knowing they hate who you are inherently.

Because they'll never say it. Because they've accepted the tiny part of you that isn't Black. It's like . . . who can you even trust, you know?"

I do know.

"I'm sorry," she says. "We, like, really have to stick together."

I flick her knee, watch the way her lashes press softly against her cheek when she blinks. "You're pretty."

"What?" She laughs.

"You said you imagine being like me, 'pretty and light-skinned.' But you *are* pretty. My mamma's as dark as you. Darker, probably. And she's the most gorgeous woman I've ever seen. Her skin is smooth and she walks into a room or out of a room and eyes follow her. She breaks necks. But I think she had to learn that, you know? She had to learn that her beauty was hers, especially after being told so many times, right to her face, that she wasn't pretty at all. That her skin was a problem."

Victory is visibly crying now.

I smile at her and think about how many tears people in my life have cried this week alone. "Can I hug you?"

And she nods and then we are scrambling over couches toward each other. And we are holding on and we are fighting without moving, without speaking. We are promising our allegiance to each other and we make a nonverbal pact then and there to love ourselves and to love each other in the way that only we can.

When we pull apart, we're both crying a little and we don't pretend we're not, using our thumbs to wipe each other's tears away.

Vic laughs. "Did we just coat our friendship in cocoa butter?"

I high-five her. It's a seal on our magic. "Basically."

I like the way we've just opened up this dialogue between the strongest pieces of who we are, when I never imagined we would.

It's two mornings later when I pack up a few things from my room at Merrick's. It's a small gym bag, plus one of the four pillows Merrick bought for my bed. I walk out into the living room and find him on the floor in front of a wooden box. It's got a vinyl on top.

"What's that called again?" I ask.

He shakes his head. Laughs. "I can't," he says. "It's called an eight-track player."

"Oh. Yeah. I knew," I say, and then amend, "I forgot."

As I walk toward the door with my things, Merrick calls, "Baby, you going somewhere I should know about?"

I clear my throat, turn, thumbs in my jeans pockets. "I'm gonna take this stuff to Mamma's."

He opens his mouth once, then closes it before giving it another go. "Okay. You moving home, then?"

I shake my head. Walk back toward him and set my stuff down. "It's not about Kai. I just want to take this stuff over there. I like these pillows you bought. And Pépé bought me a sweater like the one he has, and I wanna have it in my closet over there. Just a few things. You know, so I can maybe go between houses sometimes."

I let that dangle and Merrick picks it up. "I know I should say that's good. As the adult here and as your dad, I should say it's good you're making headway with your mom. The human in me, though—that part is wondering how badly I've messed up, knowing a large part of what happened with Kai is my fault."

"You didn't. You didn't mess up," I say.

"I used poor judgment there. I still don't know if I should have kept you both apart, should have intervened more."

"You didn't mess up," I say again. "Not too much."

Merrick laughs and pulls me to him. I sit in the circle of his arms as he talks against my temple. "I love you. Okay, kid? I love you. I want nothing but good things for you. I want you to love my family and your mom's family. I want you to understand your heart and your mind and both parts of your culture. You make me want to put my shit in order."

I pull back and look him in the eyes, and I ask him for what I need. "No more girls, Merrick. Please, please," I whisper. "I'm not saying never, just, in and out the way they have been, like a merry-go-round. It's hard . . . for me."

He nods, but the look in his eyes is basically just *Oh my God, I'm that clueless.* "I can work with that. I can work *on* that. Tasia, I'm learning here. I'm slow on the uptake. And I'm not saying the speed at which I'm learning or applying myself is acceptable. What I am saying is this—if I fuck up, feel free to let me know. 'Merrick, you're fucking up.'"

I parrot him. "Merrick, you're fucking up."

He laughs and I'm back against his chest. He sniffs. "Don't tell your mom I let you swear, yeah? We're French: it's who we are."

"Dad?"

He is corpse-stiff when he grunts.

"I'm going to call you Dad from now on," I say.

He nods and nods and nods. We sit there for a few more minutes and he rocks us back and forth and he just nods.

Chapter Forty-Two

"So tell me about your weekend, Tasia." Today Dr. Lloyd is wearing an exact replica of the R sweater from Harry Potter. I'm torn between asking her where she got it and pretending that I don't understand its reference.

"What part of it?"

"The part that's heaviest is usually not the place many people start, but that's up to you."

I nod, itch my chin where I'm having the world's shittiest breakout. "I broke up with Kai."

"That's heavy."

"It was a heavy couple of weeks, to be honest."

"And how do you feel about that?"

I love when she asks the clichés. "I hate it. I hate everything about it."

"Was it mutual?"

"It was my decision." This chair I'm in is getting less and less comfortable. My back hurts. At my feet is a stack of books, the top one is called *The Pollination Process of Bees.* Why does she have a book about bee sex?

She nods. Writes a thing down. "How does he feel about it?"

I shrug. "I haven't talked to him. Haven't seen him. He hasn't been around at my dad's or at my grandparents' place. Which is weird, because he fricking lives there."

She nods. Writes down another thing. I don't like all this nodding she's doing. All the shrugging it's inducing in me.

"But, like, okay." I readjust in the chair. "I think I expected us to be a little . . . seamless? Like, incandescent, almost." Jesus, it's getting hard to breathe, and an uncomfortable sense of urgency hits me.

"Breathe," Dr. Lloyd says. "Take your time. There is no rush. Everything you're doing right now, all that you're saying—it's okay. It's coming out just as it should. You have no place to be but here."

Her words are like an IV of Valium.

"Tell me about this expectation. You have issues with that."

"With expectation?"

She nods.

"That's fair." I look down at my hands, twist my fingers around one another, and when that starts to hurt and feel repetitive, I switch to twisting my thumb ring.

"I didn't know Kai and I were going to have to work at being together because every part of that relationship was easy. The way we fell into it from being annoyed at each other to being entirely consumed with each other."

"Easy in comparison to all the others."

"You lost me."

She puts her pen down, pushes her sleeves up. "You've been playing Tetris with all your relationships. With your mom, with your dad, with Merrick, with your best friend, with your new friends, and your grandparents. Even with your sport."

I . . . nod? I nod. "Yeah. Yeah, I guess I have been."

"So it makes sense that this one relationship would feel easy, because all the others suddenly got so hard. Do you want to tell me about the reason for your breakup?"

No. "He lied to me."

"And that was a deal-breaker for you?"

I shrug and mumble but they're not words.

"What about? What did he lie about?"

That's not a part I'm okay to talk about. Not with her. "My problem is that he lied at all, when I've only ever been honest with him. I've been the most honest with him out of everyone in my life, and he didn't treat me the same. I hate being the last to know."

"Like you were the last to know about your biological father."

"Yeah."

"Do you plan to talk to him?" She steeples her fingers over her flat stomach.

"Yes. But I think that talk isn't going to bring us back to where we were. I think Kai was meant to be a lesson. I'm real grateful for that, but I think it's okay to learn a lesson, accept it, and then move on."

She nods.

I nod.
She says, "That's fair."
The bell rings.

Chapter Forty-Three

I don't speak to Kai. I see him here and there in the classes we share and I see him walking the halls sometimes when I know neither of us can help it.

I see him walking with Dahlia, I see him walking with Cole, I see him most often walking with Sam, who always says hello to me as he passes.

And I know Kai sees me, too.

He passes me now in the hall, Cole at his side, and doesn't even glance at me. He doesn't look at me at all. Victory laces our fingers and squeezes tight. So tight. Too tight. It's perfect and grounding.

What a metaphor. He sees me.

During practice, I get rocked. Three times. Each and every time, I line up against the receiver that seems to have the most to prove. I'm so tired of it, but still I keep pushing. By the end of it, they jam me at the line so hard, I hit the ground in a plank, like someone jumper-cabled my ass to a Chevy.

My helmet flies off as I go down.

The ball pops out of my hand and Coach's whistle blows, shrill. "Quirk! Where the hell's your head at, girl!"

I shake it off as one of my receivers, Nathan, helps me stand. "Sorry, Teez."

"No sweat, nice hit," I grunt. Which is funny, because I'm covered in it. My shoulder is screaming, and when I flex my back, I feel it pop. Hurts good. I need that wake-up.

After Coach reams me out for a solid three minutes, he calls us into huddle, tells us to be at the weight room by seven a.m. tomorrow, and dismisses us, telling us to carb up and get to bed early tonight. You'd think we were playing in the Super Bowl and not just a high school state championship game.

Cole walks by me as he wipes a short towel across his forehead.

"You did work on those running backs today, Cole." I don't know why I say it. I do, on some level, but I think usually I'm good for a little more finesse than that.

He nods. "You need to talk to me."

The amount of laughter that I beat into submission is ridiculous.

"Uh, yeah. For just, like, a second, though."

At the bleachers, he sits, towel on the back of his neck, sports bottle in his hand. His hair seems redder, if that's possible, and I can definitely understand what Kai sees in him, looks-wise. The sharp edge of his jaw, the hollows of his cheeks, the Anglican nose. All of it culminates into a not-unsatisfying package.

"So talk," he says.

He's not going to beat around the bush and—what do you know?—apparently, neither am I. "Are you guys back together?"

"Are you serious, Tasia?"

This is the first time he's ever used my first name. Usually it's just "Quirk!" coming at me in the form of a reprimand or a heads-up on the field.

"Yeah, I guess." I start to take my braids down. They're shitty because Merrick has been trying to learn to do them. "I just want to know. And, like, I guess I technically could have asked him, but . . . I don't know. I think you know what it's like to want him and not have him."

Cole flinches.

"I'm sorry," I say. "I'm honestly not trying to be a bitch, if you can even imagine that."

"You're not a being a bitch. I get it. I get you and I get this question and it's like, Jesus Christ, the only thing I don't get is Kai."

Yep, because honestly, he isn't alone.

"I don't think that's meant to happen. I don't think we're supposed to understand him entirely," I say.

"That doesn't seem fair." No, it doesn't. Cole pats the metal next to him and I sit.

He turns me around so my back is to him and he helps me to take my braids out.

"We're not together."

I probably knew that, if I was thinking logically. I know Kai, at least on that level.

"Know what's funny?"

"What?" I shiver when his fingers ghost over the middle part on my scalp.

"He's asking a lot of questions. Like, about himself."

"How's that funny?"

"Mm, just in that he's asking them about himself. About you. He's asking like I'm supposed to be an authority on him or you, or you guys together."

The self-concerned part of me is thrilled Kai's been thinking about me. About us. Even if in a roundabout way. But the other part of me hurts for him, hurts with him. I've wished more than once that there could be a way to make this chaos mean something.

"What kind of questions?"

"Like, 'Do you think you know me?' and 'How permanent did Tasia and I seem?' and 'Does my life look perfect to you?'"

Kai's life has never looked perfect to me. But to someone who maybe doesn't know him, I think it probably does. Probably my life seems that way to a lot of people, too.

Cole pretty much confirms that with his responses. "Know what I said to him? I said, 'Kai. I don't know you anymore. I knew you once and then I didn't anymore because you didn't let me.' He didn't like that. But I told him it wasn't an attack. It was just . . . facts, you know? And I told him that I thought you guys were pretty freaking permanent. That that's why I hated you, I think. Like, you could have been anybody, but it was just the fact that you came along and suddenly Kai wasn't everyone's anymore. He was just Tasia's."

He moves on to the second braid after running his fingers through my loose hair for a moment.

"And I told him his life does seem perfect. That he'd gotten adopted by some really cool people and that the rest of his family—your dad, I guess—seemed pretty dope too. I told him that people love him and he doesn't really have to try in school and he seemed to be functioning pretty well in terms of life stress and, like, he's the only person I've ever met who hasn't had an issue with coming out to people."

I don't even have words for that. Kai's sexuality isn't a thing we discuss. It's just another way I don't know him. I don't know if Mémé and Pépé and Merrick know he's bisexual, and I don't know if he has so much "come out" as he's just doing whatever the hell he wants with whomever the hell he wants, no questions asked or answered.

After my last braid is out I say, "Thanks."

Cole nods. "I can't tell you what to do with him, Tasia. And even if I knew, I probably wouldn't, because if it comes down to you or me, I still want it to be me. I guess that makes me selfish, but . . . ."

I don't say anything else. I don't thank him for his honesty or smile or offer a truce or anything. I just get up and walk away, certain that—now—I definitely am a bitch.

Chapter Forty-Four

CHAMPIONSHIP GAME - EL CAMINO REAL VS.
CLEVELAND CAVALIERS

The day of the championship game isn't as heavy as I've always imagined it would be. As a senior who's played varsity football since ninth grade, I thought I might have invested more in this game than I actually do.

And, in probably the strangest turn of events, I'm pretty okay with that. I'm okay with it because I get it now. Football is part of who I am. Always has been. But there's room for more. I'm just getting started, and the next new part of me is in a box somewhere waiting to be mailed.

Still, the weather is heavy and warm and dry, and the Santa Anas sing both through the leaves that've fallen off the branches and the ones still clinging to their trees.

A little shiver of excitement tickles along my scalp and then comes to a rest in the palms of my hands. I look around at the college stadium we're at as the crowd trickles in like ants. And it's enough for me, to know I get to play here at least once. To dance up and down this field like it's mine, as the sun sets and the stadium lights hit their marks.

It's louder than I imagined it would be. I've been to college games with Mamma plenty of times, but I've never been on this level, on the turf, feeling like gravity is working overtime on all my vital organs. When Beyoncé's "Formation" comes on over the speakers, I know for sure tonight's gonna be the peak of my healing. Not an end, but a crescendo.

I'm stretching my hamstrings and running through some footwork when I hear, "Choowwwww! Get it, Teez! You look super hot in your pads, girl, worrrrrrk!"

My head snaps in her direction and my eyes zero in on Slim. She's wearing my heart-shaped sunnies and my away game jersey, and her big-ass head full of curls is free and dancing in the wind.

I pull my helmet off and walk in that direction, and everything opens up.

They're all here. Slim, Josiah, Israel. Next to Is, I see Trist, Daddy, Mamma, Merrick, Mémé, Pépé. Even Emily.

Things dim a little when I notice who's missing. Until he isn't.

Kai makes his way up to the bleachers on Slim's side. Victory, Sam, and Dahlia trail him and take their seats. I watch as Mamma leans over and waves at Kai.

They're here. All my people, they're here. For me.

I shouldn't be shocked. This shouldn't shock me, to know that these people who are supposed to love me really and honestly do.

After shaking my head, I put my helmet back on and then run back onto the field to finish warming up. I'm immediately anxious about the game. But it's a good kind of anxious. The kind that means pressure and fire and movement.

I'm more than familiar with it.

We're down by twelve with three minutes and a handful of seconds left in the game. Half the team has already decided they wanna just take a knee, but I think Adrian, Cole, and I are having too much fun watching my family be dorks in the crowd. Tristan's got this huge-ass sign with my name and jersey number on it, followed by a list of five reasons I'm awesome. Number one is *RELATED TO TRISTAN QUIRK* and the rest pretty much follow that line of thought. Slim's up there calling out random sports terms that have nothing to do with football. And Mamma, well, she's just loud, like every Black mom at her baby's football game.

Cleveland's receiver is scrappy, and even though I've been on him like white on rice, he keeps shaking me. True to form, our offense runs through Adrian, our running back; he's the one to score most of our touchdowns. I've notched five tackles and two pass breakups, but as soon as I step back on the field after that, their offense sniffs me out.

Their QB lets off a pass and it's beautiful. Arcing. And as soon as I see it line up and reach their receiver's hands—not at all where I thought it was going—I position myself and head full force directly at the ball carrier.

My training kicks in. All I can hear is my own breathing. Coach's voice carries, but only barely. "Like you know, Tasia! We been here!" he's screaming.

I do know. I shorten my long stride and widen my base to come in for the tackle. The ball goes flying, wild, and I take off fast to recover it and pick it up ten yards before I'm taken down.

Sound comes back in like blood spreading on concrete—slow and thick.

Coach is screaming and Adrian peels me up off the turf and then grips me by the mask to bash his helmet into mine.

"YEAH, BABY! YEAH! THAT'S RIGHT!"

My brain is fuzzy. Holy hooker, the adrenaline.

The offense takes over, and I watch from the sidelines as our QB takes the snap. Adrian sheds his block, fakes like he's running a vertical route, and then fakes back inside. That's where our quarterback finds him. Wide-ass open like a cloud-free sun. Streaking across the middle of the field. With a quick juke move, he dodges a would-be tackler, and then he's off. Making for the end zone like a bat out of hell. He's across the goal line so fast, he has no choice but to literally catapult his body, so he does—reckless and stupid—falling on his back and then hopping up on his feet.

I run up toward him, jump in the air and meet him in a full-body chest bump before we both come back down.

And that's game. And we *lose!* And it's still so beautiful. And my entire body hurts, and I don't realize I've said it out loud until Adrian shouts, "Shit! Mine too, girl!" with a grin.

It's such a personal victory to feel the way I do right now. I'm awake and I am alive and I feel so light. I'm the sun that dances between the leaves. The wind that kisses the skin of all those people—God, there are so many people—in the stands, watching me dance.

Once, I felt so heavy. So recently. Some days I still do. Sometimes I'm all sink and seep and don't swim. Sometimes I'm like the darkest piece of the ocean. Sometimes I'm heavy rain.

But today, right now—I am flicker.

I am flight.

I am free.

And, Christ, I'm so grateful for this little place of love. I wish I could stay in it forever. Maybe, in some ways, I can. With the right people around.

They surround me—all those right people. I'm trying to differentiate hugs and who says what and who promises to kick my ass later for not winning the game—pretty sure it's just Josiah and Is.

But it's not until I grab Slim around the neck, thanking her, and squeezing the life out of her that she whispers, "Kai. It was all Kai. He got us all together. Made sure we were all here. It was all him."

I kiss her cheek, let go of her, and scan for him in the crowd. I open myself up completely to the fluid lifeline that is him, to the heavy sadness, to the sunflower boy that I've come to know. To the turbulence and the opulence and, in that moment, I feel like I cross an ocean trying to get to him, though he's not far. I don't waste time or words. I don't even give hesitation a chance.

My arms are around him and I don't ever think I can let go again.

Chapter Forty-Five

I do let go. Eventually we all end up North again, back at the McMansion.

Mamma has some elaborate foods catered and Tammy puts together all my favorite nutless things, which I love her for, because an allergy flare-up right now would seriously kill my vibe. Kai, drink in hand, eyes me from across the living room, which has been rearranged and opened up. The chandeliers—only ever used for holidays—are blazing. I guess now we use them for the prodigal daughter's return, too. I jerk my head in the direction of the front door and hold his gaze only long enough to steady my nerves.

I walk, and he follows, closing the front door with a small click. That small click sends a blip of anxiety running through my chest, up into my throat.

"You did great today," he says, so softly. Like he knows I need the equivalent of an emotional Alka-Seltzer.

"Yeah, not really my best, but . . . ."

"Okay. Yeah, if you say so."

I sit on the porch steps and he sits next to me and my heart goes wild, a fan in the stands. "You didn't really know any of what was going on during that game, did you?"

"No, not a frickin' lick." He chuckles. I love his laugh, how it comes out like a surprise to him. "You know, when I sent that box, I didn't know who you were. I wasn't, like, in on this thing or trying to be malicious or anything. I sent it because it sorta sucks to be in the dark about your family. I mean, I've had a good bit of that myself, so, knowing there was some girl out there who maybe didn't know about the truth of who she was . . . it hit me a little hard. So I sent the box and didn't think twice."

"Yeah," I say. I guess I knew that.

"Yeah, so. I mean, once I found out, though—like, really found out what I had caused—I kinda thought it was . . . I don't know. Bringing it up felt weird, and I thought I could just help you move through it and help you where it really mattered. I should have told you. And I could have. But I didn't. And I'm sorry I didn't."

It makes sense. It does. I remember the Forgiveness list I made with Tristan. How he said forgiveness could be whatever I wanted or needed it to be. Right now, I think I need it to just be . . . love, the verb. And healing. A cocktail of the two, plus Kai. I feel good about this remixed definition.

"Thank you for being honest." I reach for his hand, but he pulls it away.

"Hold up. I'm not done."

Oh.

Maybe this is it. Maybe he doesn't want to be with me. Maybe he's just being a good person and trying to help me like he said he'd intended to and maybe I screwed myself out of this perfect thing we had by jumping without really looking at things, by reacting without first pausing to assess the situation. I did it with Mamma and the box, I did it with V, even with Merrick.

"I was jealous. A little. I mean, your truth was just sitting there. In a box. A perfect little box. And there are these two sets of families who care so much about you. I kinda had to fall into a caring family by way of the government, and that shit sucks."

"Kai, you know we can try to find your family if you want to. I just want you to have—"

"I know. You're right. And I honestly don't want to. Or need to. I have Adam and I have Merrick and I have you and Mémé and Pépé, and that's enough for me. I swear it is. Family is such a sore fucking wound for me and, you're right—I'm not entirely comfortable with who I am, because I don't know all of who I am. And I never will because I'm not willing to deal with all the emotional trash fire of finding out and connecting myself to people who don't want me."

"I want you."

His head turns my direction, finally looking at me. God, I love the way he looks at me. Like I am everything. Like I created the sun and he is Icarus.

"You just want me for my body."

"True," I say.

I pat my lap. "C'mere." And he lays his head softly there, his honey-wheat blond undercut sharp and angular, the longer strands falling over my thighs.

"Can I tell you something?" I say.

"Is it sexual?"

I smack him right in the stomach. "No! You asshole. It is kinda corny, though."

"Tell me."

"I want to know you, Kai. Not just the quiet, joking, boy-of-few-words version of you. I want to know who you are and how you feel. I want to know you better than anyone you've ever loved before. And, like, maybe that's kind of selfish, but I want to be special and set apart from everyone else you love. My mamma used to say that the people we owe the most love to are those who not only put up with our shit, but those who go out of their way to tell us our shit isn't, in fact, shit. Your shit is not shit to me, Kai."

"She has a good point. Your shit's not shit to me, either."

"Okay."

"All right." He nuzzles into my lap.

"Good."

I press my lips high on his cheekbones. I kiss him six times in the same spot and whisper, "I'll always want you," between every one.

Kai turns his head until he's looking up at me, reaches his hand up, presses his callused palms into the back of my neck, pulls me down until our lips meet. This kiss—oh, this kiss—it's a hot, blue swirl, a nebulae swallowing us up.

"You moving home?" he asks once we break.

"I don't know. Probably not just yet. I'll want you either way, though. Home. Away. I'll want this with you for as long as you'll let me have it."

"You love me."

"You're all right, I guess."

He chuckles. I *really* love his laugh.

"You should come back down here and kiss me again. It's been at least a minute since," he says.

"Make me."

And he does.

Sometimes I wonder if I just sped through the important stuff. Sometimes, when I've got Kai's lips on mine or when Victory and Slim fall asleep at my house, I think maybe I made up the whole big struggle.

But then, on a wave of remembering, on a wave of Mémé's watered-down Frenchness, on a wave of unraveled football braids, on a wave of stop-and-go traffic on the 405, I know that I worked for who I am, chopped at it like an ax on wood. That it was infinitely harder because I didn't think I'd survive it.

I know with a cold sort of certainty common to the drop in temperature from an L.A. summer to its shakiest fall, that progress—healing—comes as slow as, if not slower than, a change in the seasons. I still have a lot to learn, still don't know what my opinions are on politics or carbon emissions or even what I want for breakfast tomorrow. And I still walk around with Trist's Forgiveness list in my pocket, just to help me remember.

But I do know that it's okay to define what forgiveness means to you, to only make it halfway through the things you put on that list. I know that I'm loved unconditionally, widely. I know how to love that way, too. And I know what Kai's kisses taste like after he's cried, after he's flossed, after he's said "I love you" six times. Kai El Khoury still kisses me like every word in the world fits inside his mouth.

And I feel like I just scored a game-winning touchdown on fourth down.

Acknowledgments

ak-NOL-ij-muh nt

—*noun*

• recognition of the existence or truth of something: the acknowledgment of a sovereign power.

• an expression of appreciation.

Here's to all the sovereign powers in my life—

To the most sovereign, Jenn Laughran. Thank you, lady bug, for kicking my ass in the right direction constantly. They say making a book is a labor of love. Well, whoever "they" are was right. From day one of our working relationship, it's been a literary love affair.

To my editor, Ashley Hearn. Girl, thank you for believing in #TEAMTAZE, thank you for getting it. Thank you for welcoming me to #TeamPageStreet with enthusiasm, love, dedication, Darth Vader GIFs, and football wisdom. I approached publishing with my heart half caged, half winged, concerned that my girl Taze wouldn't get the eye or the attention we deserve. Smash, with you, I never had to worry.

I'm striving to learn to live my life in joyous, grateful service of writing stories that need to be told. That's been possible for me to continue because of my Page Street

Publishing/Macmillan family of hardworking sovereigns. Thank you from the bottom of my creme-filled heart to Will Kiester, my publisher, who may not remember—BUT I DO! —the very Merrick-esque Dad Joke he told the first time we spoke over the phone. I'm not saying that solidified things for me, but I'm not NOT saying that either.

To Marissa Giambelluca, Meg Baskis, Laura Gallant, Meg Palmer, Lauren Wohl, and Deb Shapiro—you little buncha sunflowers, thank you a million and six times over.

To Tashana McPherson, thank you for creating the illustration on my beautiful cover. Seeing it for the first time was the only time I've openly wept during this entire process. My chest cracked open upon seeing a Black girl with her wild hair and even wilder spirit displayed so fiercely.

To my person, my platonic life partner, my soul sister, my one good thing, Tehlor Kay Mejia. I love you, okay? This book is better because of you and my heart is more whole because I've got you in it.

To my team of cheerleaders in leather skirts/the mothers of my East Coast Godchildren. Emery Lord and Dahlia Adler, you two queens of my life have been the glue holding me together for what feels like eons. Here's to a few more.

To Lauren Billings, Christina Hobbs, Karuna Riazi, Ellie Woofinden, Aisha Saeed, Jay Elliot Flynn, Katie Locke, Eric Smith, Chasia Lloyd, Ryan La Sala, Nic Stone, Alyssa Furukawa, Sarah Spicer, and E.V. Jacob—thank you. Name the price and I'll pay it to know how you babies got so frickin' amazing.

In the words of Cady Heron: *double air kisses* "Love ya!" This, to my gorgeously talented #ChicasMalas, Anna-Marie McLemore (Karen) and Lily Anderson (Regina). Chicas 2K16 is where I first dared to hope this could be real. I have you both to thank.

To my beautiful mamma, Lynette, thank you for letting me spend so much time locked in my very dark, not-very-clean room, reading. Thank you for raising me up the way you did. You did it all on your own and my success is very much also yours. I love you.

To my siblings, Donnis, Trisha, Jewnya, and Stephen—thanks for putting up with me, in general, while I angsted through this entire growing up/doing life thing.

And, lastly, to Brandy Colbert—thank you for lighting the spark on my #BlackGirlMagic.

About the Author

Candice Montgomery is an L.A. transplant now residing in Seattle. By night, she writes YA lit about Black teens across all their inter- sections. By day, she teaches dance and works in the land of early childhood Deaf education. It is the goal of her stories to integrate the spaces of race, love, the body, gender, and sexuality, all while being a witness of life.